A Taste of Death

Her shoe got bogged down in some mud, and she had to yank to pull her foot out, losing her shoe in the greenish muck. "Damn!" Her foot covered in mud, her arms scratched up, and mosquito bites rising along her neck, she was foolishly looking for some phantom juvenile delinquent who got his *cojones* off spying on unsuspecting women. Could it get any worse? It would definitely be worse if Derek found her like this.

But even worse than that was when her bare foot brushed against something that didn't feel like a prickly bush. It tickled, but not in the way a bush should. She looked down and saw a hand. She screamed as her eyes followed the hand deeper into the bushes. There was the body of a man with thick grape vines pulled tautly around his neck, his brown eyes bulging out of his purplish face. His dark, longish hair covered in mud. He wore a green shirt, and across the right side of his chest on the shirt was his name—Gabriel Asanti. With a flash of recognition, Nikki knew she just met the winemaker . . .

Dedication

*In memory of my loving Grandmother Clara,
the kindest person I've ever known,
who always believed in me.*

Acknowledgements

There are so many people who have helped me in this process of not only creating *Murder Uncorked*, but also the Wine Lover's Mystery series. I'm certain that I will miss someone here and I apologize. I could go on for pages to acknowledge everyone who has helped me in writing this book and subsequently the series. I generously thank Quelene Slattery for all her expertise on wine, Terry Beswick for showing me around wine country, Bob from Grape Connections, Bob Hurley, Sergeant Davis, Holly Jacobs, Don McQuinn, Glenda Burgess, Elizabeth Lyon, and Karen at the Glen Ellen Inn. I also have to express the utmost gratitude to Emily Cotler and the team at Wax, Theresa Meyers at Blue Moon and to the *best* writing coach in the world—Mike Sirota and the gang, Paul, Mark, Ed, and Angela. This series would not be possible without the constant support from my first reader and red-liner, my wonderful mother-in-law Sue Vosseller. To Jessica Faust— agent extraordinaire, who patiently waited for the manuscript, and my gracious editor Samantha Mandor. I am grateful to have you both. Last of all I want to acknowledge my family— my children Alex, Anthony, and Kaitlin who left me alone to write (most of the time); also my husband John who used to throw away rejection letters so that I wouldn't get discouraged. I want to acknowledge the two people in my life who taught me tenacity, patience, and how to go after my dreams without ever giving up—my parents Dal and Nina Scott, who have supported me and my dreams in every way possible. I love you both. Thank you.

Murder Uncorked

MICHELE SCOTT

BERKLEY PRIME CRIME, NEW YORK

THE BERKLEY PUBLISHING GROUP
Published by the Penguin Group
Penguin Group (USA) Inc.
375 Hudson Street, New York, New York 10014, USA
Penguin Group (Canada), 90 Eglinton Avenue East, Suite 700, Toronto, Ontario M4P 2Y3, Canada
(a division of Pearson Penguin Canada Inc.)
Penguin Books Ltd., 80 Strand, London WC2R 0RL, England
Penguin Group Ireland, 25 St. Stephen's Green, Dublin 2, Ireland (a division of Penguin Books Ltd.)
Penguin Group (Australia), 250 Camberwell Road, Camberwell, Victoria 3124, Australia
(a division of Pearson Australia Group Pty. Ltd.)
Penguin Books India Pvt. Ltd., 11 Community Centre, Panchsheel Park, New Delhi—110 017, India
Penguin Group (NZ), Cnr. Airborne and Rosedale Roads, Albany, Auckland 1310, New Zealand
(a division of Pearson New Zealand Ltd.)
Penguin Books (South Africa) (Pty.) Ltd., 24 Sturdee Avenue, Rosebank, Johannesburg 2196,
South Africa

Penguin Books Ltd., Registered Offices: 80 Strand, London WC2R 0RL, England

MURDER UNCORKED

A Berkley Prime Crime Book / published by arrangement with the author

PRINTING HISTORY
Berkley Prime Crime mass-market edition / October 2005

Copyright © 2005 by Michele Scott.
Cover art by Cathy Gendron.
Cover design by Rita Frangie.
Interior text design by Stacy Irwin.

ISBN: 0-425-20684-X

BERKLEY® PRIME CRIME
Berkley Prime Crime Books are published by The Berkley Publishing Group,
a division of Penguin Group (USA) Inc.,
375 Hudson Street, New York, New York 10014.
The name BERKLEY PRIME CRIME and the BERKLEY PRIME CRIME design
are trademarks belonging to Penguin Group (USA) Inc.

PRINTED IN THE UNITED STATES OF AMERICA

10   9   8   7   6

Chapter 1

Nikki Sands hated her job almost as much as she hated her past. She straightened her crisp white blouse and put on her best smile. She approached the couple at the table she was serving, and couldn't help but notice the woman watching her with that unmistakable glint of self-importance that judged Nikki to be nothing but the peon who was waiting on them. The woman had a glamour-girl theme about her, but that hair needed a good hairdresser. Hadn't she heard that frizzy platinum blonde was passé? Not to mention the Pat Benatar smoldering-eye-makeup look.

"Tell me about your wine list. What do you recommend as a good red?" the man asked her. His look, compared to his date's, was all-the-way chic. Dark blond hair with exactly the right amount of wave to it, mesmerizing ocean-blue eyes, high cheekbones, a golden tan, and a few fine lines gave him the right amount of that rugged-man look. Nikki couldn't help thinking that Casanova was luscious.

"I'm partial to this nice Medoc-Grand Cru Classe. It's an excellent choice," she said, pointing to one of the more expensive wines on the list. "The Bordeaux blend is

smooth, and there's a hint of fruit to it, so it's not too dry."
If she'd had the money, the stylish Bordeaux would've
been her first choice. The Medoc wines dated all the way
back to Napoleon, and since that time had remained as
some of the best out there. "But if you prefer something
lighter, a good Red Zinfandel would be nice. We have a
small production wine from Napa from the Downing Vineyards. It's right here." Nikki's finger moved to the red zin.
Glancing down at the man, her stomach lurched. He smiled
up at her. "The Fly by Night Zinfandel," she said.

"I think we'll go with the Medoc," the man replied with
an approving smile.

Nikki walked back to the bar to order the drinks from
her pal and bartender, Maurice. She winced when an in-
strumental version of "Stormy Weather" started playing
over the stereo system.

"What is it, doll?" Maurice asked. "You don't like the
oldies but goodies?"

"Are you kidding? I love them. What I can't stand is that
this place is supposed to be so upscale, yet we have to pipe
in music on a system. I think management should really go
all out and get a pianist in here."

"They're too cheap," Maurice replied.

They both laughed, knowing that was the reality. Nikki
glanced around to make sure their manager, Steve, wasn't
lurking. Nikki loved music of all kinds. She compartmen-
talized areas of her life by listening to music and songs.
Stressful times, happy times, the handful of boyfriends,
life in Los Angeles, and life in Tennessee, even her
mother—all of them were associated with their own song,
and each of them conjured up memories when she listened.

Nikki noticed that the woman from the table she was
waiting got up to go to the powder room, Manolo Blahnik
pumps click-clacking as she sauntered across the hardwood floor. She caught up with Nikki at the bar.

"Do us right, hon. I'd like tonight to be special, because
I don't want this one getting away." She lowered her voice
and leaned into Nikki, who got a whiff of her strong

gardenia-scented perfume. "Tone down the wine expertise for me, okay?" The overblown blonde winked at Nikki, then proceeded into the rest room, coming back out after a few moments with her collagen-plumped lips painted raspberry-pink.

Something was wrong with this picture, but it wasn't up to Nikki to make a judgment call. Lately, she'd been attempting to try something very anti-L.A. The concept of not judging others—something she found *exceedingly* difficult to do, especially in this case.

However, after that out-of-place comment and the trip to the bathroom to do the lacquer thing on those lips, Nikki shamefully threw her new practice out the window and made her first—okay, maybe third—judgment call of the evening. She dubbed the woman "The Bimbo." What was that asking her to tone down the wine advice about anyway? She was supposed to make suggestions about wines. It was part of her job.

The Bimbo wore something that resembled a Band-Aid across her chest, with a skirt so tight and short that her date looked to be guaranteed to get a return on his dinner investment in the next few hours.

Nikki's stomach knotted, noticing the way The Bimbo stared at her, as if she were so much better than Nikki, just because she could snag some rich guy. Although her night job was far from glamorous, Nikki *was* an aspiring actress, after all—a *profession*, which seemed to garner notice from some men. But, at that moment the thought of being an aspiring actress-cum-waitress made her feel slightly queasy. She'd checked the mirror before coming to work, and there were signs of age that wise women referred to as "the signs of a life well lived." Nikki called them what they were: crow's feet. And crow's feet were the death of *every* aspiring actress.

The pesky wrinkles aside, Nikki felt pretty good about her looks. She still maintained her natural blonde hair, which she wore just past her shoulders, and she thought her eyes were her best feature. They were kind of a mix between green, gray, and blue, depending on what she was wearing. The handful of boyfriends Nikki had in the past always told her that she was beautiful, even sexy. She was comfortable with her looks, but she didn't think of herself as a sexpot by any means. Besides, all those compliments had come from men who were hopeful to get a little booty and shake as paybacks to their endearments and attention. Most of the men she'd dated had turned out to be no good . . . But this was no time to think about rotten men. There was wine to be poured.

Nikki filled Casanova's glass with a tasting of the velvety red potion. He swirled, smelled, sipped, swished, and swallowed. "Excellent," he said. "It's got a different flavor to it. I can taste the berry, but . . ." He looked up at her.

Nikki glanced at The Bimbo, who at that moment looked like a cat about to pounce on her prey. Nikki smiled sweetly. The hell with it. "You're right, the berry is a currant, but it also has a very smoky blend, with tobacco and fatty flavors," she replied, while filling both of their glasses.

"It does."

"Fatty?" The Bimbo asked.

"She's talking about a bacon-type fat. It's not put into the wines, but it has to do with the fermentation process, as well as the age of the wood in which the wine gets barreled."

"Fascinating." The Bimbo looked up at Nikki. She was vibing some serious daggers. "I see you don't serve foie gras?"

"Actually, we do," Nikki replied. "But it's not always available. May I suggest the escargot? It's excellent. The chef does it in a puff pastry shell with a white wine and garlic sauce. It would also complement your wine."

The Bimbo batted her false eyelashes and waved her hand in front of her nose. "I don't like snails. I find them repulsive."

Sure, but you'll eat a poor little duck's liver.

Casanova didn't look like he had much empathy for his date. This was getting amusing. Nikki stifled a smile.

"I'm certain there must be something on the menu you'd like," he chuckled.

"I wanted foie gras," she whined. "I don't know if I really want to eat here. It's not like the service has been spectacular." She looked Nikki up and down, finally glaring at her.

"I think the service is excellent," Casanova said mildly.

"Why don't you take another moment to decide, and I'll be right back. I might add that, if you'd care for oysters, we are serving them tonight, and they are divine, and we have a lovely Pinot Grigio to complement them with."

"Super," The Bimbo replied, her voice laced with sarcasm. "While you're back there, can you bring me a scotch and water? I'm not much of a wine drinker."

Boy, this woman was scoring points with Casanova. Was she the same gal who only moments ago asked Nikki not to blow it for her? Her man had plunked down a mean chunk of change on a superb bottle of wine. Now, because she wasn't getting her duck liver, she needed to make a scene. Nikki figured that from a man's point of view, she must be good in bed, because why else would anyone put up with that?

Nikki walked to the bar and ordered The Bimbo's drink.

"Hey, gorgeous, back so soon? Looks like you've got your hands full over there tonight." Maurice nodded in the direction of Casanova and The Bimbo's table.

"What else is new?"

"You tell me. How's the acting going?"

"Honestly? It doesn't seem to be going anywhere. It would appear I'm past my prime at thirty-four," she said. "Since the few shows I did as Detective Sydney Martini bombed so badly, I don't know, Maurice. Maybe it's time for a career change. I don't think I can handle working here forever."

Maurice picked up a butter knife and feigned stabbing himself in the heart. "Oh, my apple dumpling, how those words hurt."

Nikki waved a hand at him and giggled. She and Maurice did have a wonderful friendship, one they'd built over the past three years since she'd started work at the Chez la Mer. He was thirty years her senior and always a good listener. Nikki thought of him as the father she'd never had.

"Face it, you love it here. You've been here for what, ten years?"

"Twelve," he replied.

"Twelve. Okay. But bartending is like being a psychologist. Sure, people place orders, but I've watched you, and I know how great you are with people. They talk to you. With me, it's a rare smile and plenty of orders. If it isn't *just so*, then I'm the fall guy."

"Excuse me," The Bimbo sang out over the din, "Yoo-hoo."

Maurice handed her the drink. "I could put a little magic in there, if you know what I mean." He slyly took out a bottle of eyedrops from his shirt pocket. "She'd leave him high and dry and have to head for the drug store, for a box of Imodium AD."

"Nah, that's okay. That'd be bad karma, and I've racked up plenty of that already. I can handle her." Nikki placed the drink on her tray and walked back over to the table.

"It's about time. Did you enjoy your chat with the bartender?" The Bimbo asked her.

"Sabrina," the man chided gently. "She's doing her job."

Nikki smiled at him. The Bimbo cleared her throat, as if Nikki were committing a crime by smiling at her date. "I apologize. Consider it on the house," Nikki said, setting down the drink. But as she did, the woman shifted and started to stand. The drink spilled all over her short skirt.

The Bimbo gasped, her eyes wide with shock from the cold drink seeping down her scantily clad body. "You idiot! Are you totally incompetent? What the hell is wrong with you? This is a freaking Versace. You know Versace?" She rolled her eyes at Nikki. "Why am I bothering to say this to someone who buys her clothes at Wal-Mart?"

That hurt. Especially since she'd bought her shirt at Target, which she pronounced "Tarjay." *Don't go there. Don't tell her what she really is. Don't . . .*

"I certainly didn't mean to. I really am sorry. I'm sure it can be cleaned. Please send us the cleaning bill." Nikki could hear the trace of her Southern accent coming through. At that moment, she looked around and noticed the entire clientele was observing the scene, and that both the chef and manager had stepped forward.

The Bimbo pointed a finger at her and blurted, "No. It won't come clean. It's ruined. I can't go out like this," she said, then turned her focus to Nikki's manager. "She can't do her job, it's obvious. She's flirted with my date, had a gab session with the bartender, and now she spills a drink on me. I don't think so."

Casanova took The Bimbo by the arm. "Quiet down. Let's all relax. It was an accident, okay?"

The Bimbo yanked her arm out of his hand. "Accident, my ass. That clumsy woman spilled my drink all over me and ruined my fifteen-hundred-dollar outfit."

"I wouldn't have spent fifteen dollars on *that*," Nikki muttered. *Oops*. Self-control was another issue Nikki was working on, but a person can only take so much abuse, and this broad had tried her patience. Not to mention she'd insulted her fashion sense.

"I heard that. Now she insults me. Unbelievable," The Bimbo said, spinning back around to face Steve, the restaurant manager. "I want her fired. I have a lot of friends in high places. I'll tell all of them how terrible this place is, if you don't do something about *her*." She pointed a long lacquered nail at Nikki.

"Nikki," Steve said, his face beet-red.

Casanova pulled The Bimbo to the side and was saying something to her. Even though the manager beckoned Nikki, she couldn't help notice out of the corner of her eye that the cute guy seemed to be chewing out The Bimbo.

"Listen—"

Nikki held up her hand before her manager could continue. "Don't bother, Steve. I know what you're going to say. I'm sorry I caused such a problem tonight. It's not a big deal. I'll make it easy for you."

Nikki could see by the look in Steve's eyes that he did feel bad, but she knew he had no choice. She couldn't blame him at all. She went into the kitchen and grabbed her purse.

Maurice followed her. He held out a drink to her. "Hundred-year-old scotch, princess. Drink it with me."

She smiled and fought back any emotion. Why was she so upset anyway? She hated this job and its bad sound system. It was a miserable job. Well, except for Maurice. Steve was okay, too. "You have customers."

"Forget 'em. They can wait a few while I have a nip with you."

"I don't think that's such a good idea. I certainly don't want to get you canned, too. Actually, I wasn't fired, not technically. I quit," she said, half-laughing. She was trying really hard to fight back her tears, which were a mixture of anger, shame, and that feeling of failure that sticks in the gut.

He waved a hand at her like she was being silly, which she knew she was. Steve would never fire Maurice. He was as much a part of Chez la Mer as the pristine crystal chandelier in the entryway. He held up his glass. "To bigger and better things for the princess."

She clinked her highball with his and watched as the amber liquid swirled around inside the glass. She took a sip of the bold smoky drink. Very smooth—all the way down. Her stomach warmed. "That is good," she said.

The chef came in, poured himself a glass, too, and nodded at Nikki with a smile. He was a man of few words, but he could make dirt taste divine, and Nikki knew that he liked her. He was always giving her his latest dessert invention to try first or to take home with her. She'd miss him, too.

The chef took his glass, walked back over to the stove, and picked up where he'd left off. Nikki finished the contents of her glass, leaned in, and gave Maurice a kiss on the cheek.

"Don't be a stranger," he said.

"I won't."

"You shouldn't be alone. Are you going home?"

"In a bit. I think I'll stop off at the Liquid Potion and have another drink," she said.

"Be careful."

Nikki pulled on her sweater and went out the back entrance, not wanting to have any more contact with The

Bimbo or Casanova. She shut the door behind her and leaned against it, tears finally flowing freely. So she'd hated the job, wanted to move on . . . This was simply the catalyst to get her to do so. But the reality was, she had no prospects. Her acting career was pretty much sunk.

Now she'd have to figure out what her thing *really* was, because the rent would come due in a couple of weeks, and Nikki was already low on cash. She knew that Aunt Cara would help her out if things got completely desperate, but Nikki didn't want to put either one of them in that position.

She wiped away the tears, stood up straight, and started walking up the street. No more of this feeling sorry for herself. That Nikki Sands was far, far away. The new Nikki Sands was a survivor who could figure out what she wanted from life. She had to, because there was no way, no-how, Nikki was going backward after coming this far.

She walked a few blocks up the street and entered the wine bar off Wilshire Boulevard, looked around and found an empty seat at the counter bar. It was a bit early yet for the party crowd. She was glad, because the patrons who were already there were dressed to the nines, and her cheap white blouse, as crisp as it might be, along with her waitress's standard black crepe pants, were not working with this crowd. Yes indeed, wine was in order.

"What can I get you?" the bartender asked. Young, California-tanned, and athletic, he matched the decor of the place—faux-finish golden walls, candles in Gothic iron candelabras, crushed copper velvet draperies. Segovia's guitar music played in the background. Very Hollywood. Maybe she should've walked a bit farther east and found something more like a dive to drown her sorrows in. She was looking a bit pool-bar girl for such a swanky place. Screw it. She was here and ready for some vino.

"I'll take a glass of your Saddleback Sauvignon Blanc," she answered. "And can you fill that to the brim, please?" It was a bit pricier than what Nikki wanted to pay, but it isn't every day that a bimbo wanting desperately to be Paris Hilton turns your life inside out. So why not splurge?

"Nice wine," a deep voice from behind her said. "This seat taken?"

Nikki lifted her head to see none other than Casanova sliding onto the stool next to her.

"I thought I might buy you a glass of wine, as well as apologize for my date's rudeness. You ran out before I got the chance."

Silenced by surprise, Nikki shifted on the suede-covered bar stool and nodded, then shook her head. "Wait." She found her voice, ironed out the drawl in it before speaking again. "Let me get this straight. You're here to apologize to me and buy me a drink?" She searched the bar. "What's the deal? Where's Ms. Thing? Is she hiding in the wings? How did you find me, anyway?"

"Bring me a bottle of the Saddleback Cellars," Casanova said to the bartender, who set Nikki's glass down in front of her. Casanova then picked up the appetizer menu and scanned it. "Can we also have a plate of your goat cheese and mixed mushroom bruschetta?" He turned back to her and stuck out his hand. "I'm Derek Malveaux. I hope you don't mind an appetizer. Sauvignon Blanc goes so well with mushrooms."

Nikki hesitantly returned the handshake. "Okay." She couldn't think of anything more intelligent to say at the moment. She was stunned at the turn of events.

"I'm not here to prove anything. I felt terrible about the incident at Chez la Mer. My date treated you horribly. I called for a car to take her home. And as for finding you? Seems your bartender friend agreed with me that you would appreciate an apology. I got your job back, too, if you want it."

For the second time in less than five minutes, a wave of shock overtook her. Nikki shut her trap again, having to think hard for a response. She had no clue as to what to make of this man. Why on God's green earth would he do such a thing for her? After all, he had it in the bag with The Bimbo. What was his deal? "I get it. You've decided to go for the vulnerable girl, the one who's just lost her job." She knew she was far more of a challenge than The Bimbo, and men supposedly liked the thrill of the chase.

He eyed her. "No. I really am here to tell you that I'm sorry and buy you a drink."

"Okay." He was hot, he had good taste in wine, and she didn't have any other prospects. But Nikki wasn't a bimbo, and memories of her last breakup warned her to tread carefully. She promised herself to keep it all together, including blouse buttons and pants zipper. The next man she allowed to get her naked would most certainly be one she was in love with. Gorgeous or not, she was sure that Casanova was far more interested in getting naked than in experiencing love.

Nikki held up her glass of wine. "Here's to apologies accepted."

They clinked their glasses and brought them to their lips. Derek's lips were full, with a perfect cupid bow in the center of the upper one. They were very sexy, and kissable. The bartender set the bruschetta in front of them. They each took a bite.

"You're right. The Sauvignon Blanc works well with this. Good idea. So, tell me, Mr. Malveaux . . ."

"Derek, please."

"Okay, Derek. Tell me what happened to your date. She didn't exactly seem to be your type. And, to be blunt, are you hitting on me?"

"Sabrina, my date for the evening, was not someone I would have asked out. I can tell you that much. I don't live here in Los Angeles. I'm down for business, and one of my clients set the two of us up. Trust me. All I wanted to do today was have my meetings and go back to the Century Plaza, maybe have a massage in the spa, order room service, and retire for the night. And, no, I am not hitting on you. I'm apologizing to you over a glass of wine."

Nikki sized him up. Was this really the truth? Hard to say. There were plenty of men out there who knew how to tell a good story. This *was* L.A., and for all she knew, Derek was an aspiring actor with a bunch of fables ready to tell to any damsel he wished to bed. "Why didn't you cancel the date?"

"My client said she was a nice woman, and—"

"Had a nice bod."

"Yes, he did add that. I should've canceled, anyway, even if I might lose an account."

"I can't believe that. Over a defunct date?"

"She's best friends with my client's wife."

"Then he'd have to be one shallow jerk. I hope that's not the case. I'd feel even guiltier for losing you your client than for spilling a drink all over your date's designer outfit." She laughed. The wine was making what he was saying easy to buy into. He poured her a second glass. They polished off the bruschetta.

"Tell you what," Derek said. "Why don't we go back to the Plaza? Have dinner with me. I'll get you a car back to your place afterward."

Nikki shook her head. "I don't know about that."

"It's only dinner."

It wasn't like he was coming on to her. In fact, Nikki felt a bit irritated at the fact that he hadn't come on to her—at all. Was her getup that bad? *Oh, God.* Maybe she should've checked herself in the mirror in the bathroom. What if her mascara had run all over the place? And stress could make her break out in hives, too! What if Derek was staring at a red, rash-pocked face with a running black mascara mess? Not to mention, she hadn't taken a comb to her hair since walking from Chez la Mer to the bar, and there'd been a slight wind. This could not be good. She'd been dead wrong about Derek Malveaux. He really had only wanted to apologize to the pitiful waitress.

"What's the matter, Nikki?"

"I, you know, should really get home. I'm sure you're tired. I'm tired. It's been a stressful evening for me."

He frowned, and the few lines on his forehead crinkled together, as he appeared hurt by her response.

She touched his hand. "This has been great, and I really

appreciate the apology. But, please, you don't have to do any more for me tonight."

"I don't get you," he said. "One minute, you think I'm making a play for you. The next minute, I'm Saint Derek."

"I don't know. At first I thought you were trying to score with the ditzy waitress, which by the way, I am not. But, I've sat here with you for a while, and not once have you even tried to flirt with me."

"Let's start from the beginning, okay? I think you are a very beautiful woman. I'm sorry that the woman I was out with was so horrendous to you; so, yes, I felt that an apology was in order. Yes, I did, and do, want to get to know you better. However—" Nikki started to comment. He held up his hand to her, and she closed her mouth in response. "However, I am not trying to get you into bed. I'd like to have dinner with you, and I actually may have a proposal for you. Something you might be interested in."

"Are you some positive-thinking guru? You know, the kind who teaches that you can do anything you want as long as you try? Achieve your dreams, blah, blah, blah."

"No, but I believe in that way of thinking. I own a winery. That's how I make my money."

Then it hit her. Malveaux Estate. Some of the best Cabernets and Merlots to come out of the Napa Valley region. A major winery. They also produced a Chardonnay that was quite good. Nikki couldn't afford the wines, but working at Chez la Mer, she'd tasted a few. It now made sense to her why The Bimbo had made that comment to her about her wine expertise. Nikki was a threat to her.

"Derek Malveaux," she replied in wonderment. "Of Malveaux Estate?"

He nodded. "What do you say, we head over to the Plaza, have dinner, and I'll tell you my proposition?"

"I'd say you're on."

The evening hadn't gone as planned, but it certainly hadn't been boring. And, Nikki had to admit, she couldn't help wondering what Derek Malveaux's proposal might be.

Goat Cheese and
Mixed Mushroom Bruschetta

If you want to make an elegant but easy appetizer, try the
Goat Cheese and Mixed Mushroom Bruschetta. Sauvignon
Blanc is a good choice to accompany this treat. It is light
and fruity, which enhances the earthy flavors in the bruschetta. Nikki and Derek shared a delightful bottle of Saddleback Cellars Sauvignon Blanc with their appetizer. The
Sauvignon Blanc contains a citrus and hibiscus nose with a
wonderful gold/green color. The wine is crisp, with a clean
acid balance and light sweet oak; it's youthful and is a perfect food wine. It will give you the flavors of summer and
the pleasures that come from a well-crafted wine. Enjoy!

5 ounces Portobello mushrooms
4 ounces shiitake mushrooms
2 ounces oyster mushrooms
2 tablespoons olive oil
1 tablespoon unsalted butter
2 shallots
2 minced cloves of garlic
¼ cup chicken broth
⅓ cup dry white wine
1 teaspoon dried thyme
1 teaspoon dried basil
salt and red pepper flakes
12 slices of rustic baguette: sourdough, Italian, even
    whole grain for the health conscious
4 ounces goat cheese
2 ripe red tomatoes, cored & diced

Chop the mushrooms. Heat olive oil and butter over
medium heat in a sauté pan. Add the shallots and garlic and
mix for 1–2 minutes, stirring often. Add the mushrooms

and raise the heat a bit. Mix everything for about 8 minutes. Add chicken broth, white wine, and dried seasonings and cook until the liquid is evaporated. Season with salt for taste.

Preheat broiler. Spread the bread slices with goat cheese and spoon the mushroom mixture evenly over the bread. Place the tomatoes on top. Broil for 4 minutes, or until mushrooms begin to brown. Serves six.

Chapter 2

Nikki had been inside the Century Plaza only twice before; once to do a catering event for Chez la Mer, and again when she'd done her pilot for an inconsequential cable network. They'd shot a chase scene down one of the halls. It seemed so good at the time, but now when Nikki watched the outtakes, she realized how bad it really was. As painful as it was to admit it, she was not a great actress.

Inside the sunken lobby at the hotel a pianist at a grand piano played Frank Sinatra's "The Way You Look To-night." Talk about class and quiet good taste. Overstuffed sofas covered in sage-colored silk damask were strategically placed around glass-topped coffee tables. It all exuded elegance, style, and comfort.

Once seated at a booth inside the Breeze restaurant, Derek Malveaux looked even more debonair, his blue eyes sparkling in the candlelight.

"Here's the deal. I want you to order the wine tonight. With each course," he said.

"What? You're the expert. Is this some type of test?"

"You could say that. I was impressed earlier with your

knowledge of wine. Once dinner is over, I'll tell you my proposition."

"You are mysterious. I don't know if I can live up to your expectations. I know wine, but I don't know if I'd meet your criteria of a wine expert."

"Something tells me you can. Order anything you want."

Nikki shook her head. "Are you sure about this?"

"Humor me."

"Fine."

When the waiter came over, Derek ordered a Caesar salad to start for each of them, and Nikki ordered a half bottle of a crisp Fumé Blanc produced from a winery in Napa. "Why did you go with this wine?" Derek asked.

"Their Sauvignon Blanc pairs well with the salad because the tart, crisp fruit of the wine contrasts with the salty flavors of the anchovies and Parmesan in the salad. The winery that makes this wine is one producer that still believes in varietal character. Their Fumé Blanc actually tastes like a Sauvignon Blanc instead of the style of some other producers that over-oak their Sauvignon Blanc to the point that it tastes like Chardonnay instead of the grape it actually is," Nikki said when the waiter moved away.

"Off to a good start."

"This is very strange, Derek."

"Not really." He set his glass down and looked pointedly at her. "Why did you order a 375 instead of two glasses, since they pour it here by the glass as well?" Derek asked, referring to the half bottle by its other term.

"Why would I order two glasses of wine and pay more per glass, when I can get two and a half glasses in a half bottle for a little less and watch the waiter open it? This way, I know that it's *fresh* and hasn't been sitting behind the bar for three days."

"Good point."

They drank the wine, and Derek ordered the next course—Maine diver Scallops with lemon basil risotto. Nikki paired the main dish with a Pinot Noir.

"Explain yourself," Derek said.

"I always like to have a white and a red. You wanted the scallops, I want a red. The only red in my opinion that's versatile enough to pair with seafood is Pinot Noir. This Pinot should be Burgundian in style—I like lean Pinots. Tonight looks like an opportunity to try it. You did give me carte blanche to order the wine." She arched an eyebrow.

He smiled. "I did, didn't I?"

The waiter brought over and uncorked the wine. They didn't have half bottles of the Pinot, so she'd gone ahead and ordered them by the glass.

"Yes, you did." The wine was going to her head, indeed. She was feeling far more confident than she had in a long while. No more bad acting, but an interested winery owner asking her questions—and, was she *actually* living up to his expectations? Who cared? She was having fun. And, she had to admit, she did care that he seemed impressed. "What do you think of the Pinot?" Nikki asked, getting into Derek's little game. She motioned for him to try the wine.

"Oh, no, you first. That would be proper etiquette. You did order the wine."

"Yes, it would." She laughed, and brought the glass up to her nose. "Oh."

"What?"

Nikki looked up at the waiter. "I'm sorry. This wine has been corked."

"But it wasn't opened, ma'am."

"True. However, some say that in the bottling process, on average one in twelve are corked, and therefore they go bad."

The waiter apologized and went for another bottle.

Nikki leaned into Derek. "He must be new. Most waiters who wait at these types of places know that."

"They can't all be aficionados. Not like you."

She shook a finger at him. "You're giving me too much credit."

In between ordering, Derek said to her, "Tell me about yourself. I know there's more to you than waiting tables."

Where to start, and where not to? She would have to tip-toe around this one. "Actually, I do some acting."

He snapped his fingers and pointed at her. "I don't watch a lot of TV, but I thought I might have seen you before."

"I doubt it." She shrugged. Nikki didn't want to bring up her embarrassing stint as Detective Sydney Martini. "I did a pilot and a handful of shows, but it didn't make it. It was on one of the cable channels. It was supposed to be like a *CSI* meets *Alias* kind of thing, but my acting wasn't exactly worthy of an Emmy."

"I bet you're too critical of yourself. Are you doing anything else? Any new shows?"

"Nope. Nada. My agent isn't calling. She's probably forgotten my name." Nikki laughed, trying to make light of it. "I'm thinking that maybe acting isn't my bag at all."

"It's not a passion, then?"

"I didn't say that. But I'm thinking that maybe being on the other side as a writer might be a better fit for me. I've always loved writing. I've even thought it would be fun to create a dinner theater. For the moment, it's looking like I'd better find another day job."

"You're not going back to Chez la Mer, then? They said it wouldn't be a problem for you to come back."

"I'd rather not. I think I'll be much happier if I can get away from waiting tables."

The waiter arrived with their entrées, arranged their plates before them, and poured them their selected glasses of wine from a new bottle of the Pinot.

Derek held up his glass. "My turn to toast. To a fascinating lady, and to the prospect at hand."

Nikki held up her glass. "And to whatever that might be."

He set the wine down. "You've made some very nice selections tonight. Can I ask you how you know so much about wine?"

"When you work in the restaurant industry, you learn a lot about good wines."

Derek shook his head. "No, it's more than that. You know more than the average waitress. What gives?"

"It interests me. The one thing I did like about my job was that my manager always let us join in on the wine tastings. I quickly learned that if I had knowledge about the wines I could up the bill by a decent amount."

"And by doing so, you got a larger tip." Derek finished her sentence for her.

"A girl has got to make a living. I follow the credo that knowledge is power, and as a waitress, that can equate to money. Believe me, when I first started working at the restaurant I had to fake my way through. All I knew was that red wine came from red grapes and the white, well, it's obvious. So, once I started doing the tastings, I'd head to the library and check out books on wine, and then once my brain was trained I was able to train my palate."

"The library, huh?"

That was the truth. She'd spent a lot of time in the library. Wine and food magazines were not the only "interest" Nikki had. She'd studied many things and had given herself what she liked to refer to as her own private school education. "Yep. The library. I love to read, research, and learn new things."

"Uh-huh. Kind of a Renaissance *woman*."

She held up her glass before taking another sip. "If you say so."

"I do, and I like your answer. Anyone who has a desire to keep growing and educating themself fits okay into my book, which I thought you might anyway. Here's the deal. You're out of a job. I have a job for someone like you, who knows wines. I'm looking for a new sales manager and personal assistant at my estate in Napa. I lost my last one to a maternity leave. She ended up wanting to stay home permanently after the six weeks were up. I couldn't blame her. I think you would be perfect for the job."

"No, no, no." Nikki shook her head. "I don't know *that* much about wines. And I certainly don't know the first thing about sales." Her head whirled due to the buzz from the wine and from the scotch earlier in the evening, which was suddenly coming on really strong.

"You're right for this job. And yes, you do know about sales. What do you think you do at the restaurant?"

"Listen, Derek, I appreciate the offer. I really do. But I don't think so."

"All right, a deal then. You fly back up to Napa Valley with me in the morning. Stay at the vineyard for a few days. Learn about our wines and what the job entails. If after that time you still don't feel confident with the position, you fly home. No harm done. Can I add that the job pays close to six figures, with bonuses and benefits?"

Okay, now that was an attention getter. Nikki cocked her head, studying Derek across from her. That kind of money could change her life. What would it hurt to get out of L.A. for a few days? She'd never seen Napa Valley. Oh, yes, the wine was working nicely on her.

She noticed Derek studying her, tracing his finger around the rim of his wine glass. Nikki touched his finger with hers. "What time does the flight leave?"

Maine Diver Scallops

Maine diver scallops are always a winner. For this dish try Estancia Pinnacles Pinot Noir. This wine is fruity with ripe cherry and strawberry, layered with sweet oak and aromas of dried flowers, leaf, and spice. It has a silky mouth-feel and leaves a long finish.

2½ tablespoons extra virgin olive oil
2 cloves garlic, minced
4 tablespoons leeks cut into julienne strips
1 cup shiitake or oyster mushrooms cut into large pieces
½ cup shallots, minced
1 teaspoon kosher salt
1 teaspoon fresh thyme, finely chopped
½ teaspoon white pepper
2 tablespoons Armanac, or brandy or cognac
2 lemons
1 cup heavy cream
8 fresh Maine diver scallops
½ teaspoon Balsamic vinegar

Heat one teaspoon of the olive oil in a medium skillet over high heat. Add garlic and sauté until golden brown. Add leeks, mushrooms, and shallots and cook for two minutes, seasoning with kosher salt, thyme, and pepper. Deglaze the pan with Armanac and fresh lemon, reducing by half. Add heavy cream and reduce until the cream thickens as a glaze. Remove the ragout into separate bowl. Add the scallops to the skillet, and cook for about three minutes on each side. Place the ragout on dinner plates, top with the scallops. Drizzle Balsamic vinegar over the top. Makes either 4 appetizers or serves 2 as a dinner entrée.

Risotto with Lemon and Basil

3 tablespoons olive oil
1 onion, chopped
5 cloves garlic, chopped (or 1 tablespoon chopped garlic from a jar)
1 shallot, finely chopped
2 cups Arborio rice
½ cup dry white wine
3½ cups simmering chicken broth, with the addition of 2 tablespoons finely grated lemon zest
3 tablespoons butter
½ cup grated pecorino Romano cheese (or Parmesan)
2 tablespoons parsley, chopped
¼ cup basil, julienned
salt and pepper

In a large saucepan, heat olive oil over medium-high heat. Add onion, garlic, and shallot. Cook until onion is translucent. Add rice, stirring constantly, and cook 5 minutes more, making sure rice does not brown. Add wine, stirring constantly, and let totally evaporate. When wine is evaporated, begin adding broth ½ cup at a time, letting each addition evaporate before adding the next addition.

After fourth addition of broth is added, begin tasting rice. Rice should be al dente when done. You need to keep tasting rice, because, depending on rice, you may or may not have to use all of the broth. Add lemon zest after fourth addition of broth is absorbed.

After last addition of broth is absorbed, remove from heat, and stir in butter, Romano, parsley, and basil. Season with salt and pepper. Serve immediately. Serves 6–8 as a side.

Chapter 3

Private planes, fancy cars, and mansions set among luxuriant vineyards. This place exuded wealth. Nikki watched from the car window as Derek sped past one vineyard after another, noticing the enormous Tudor-style and ranch homes. This kind of wealth captured a serene elegance from an age gone by, whereas L.A. seemed so artificial. That was the only way she could think of it. The people from this region knew how to be rich and carry it off. Old-school wealth at its most gracious.

Twenty minutes after landing at the airport in the Malveaux Estate private jet, Derek pulled his black Range Rover in front of an iron-gated fence. The name Malveaux was etched into the gate. Derek pushed a button on a remote he pulled from the overhead visor, and the gate opened. They entered and drove down a long dirt road surrounded by sections of grape vines, all twisted up like long manes on wild horses. Rows of chocolate brown soil—rich and vibrant, mixed with flowing areas of intense green, looking as though they would be soft to the touch, like silk or satin. A light fog hung in the air, drifting down from the clouds hovering above, appearing stormy and ready to explode—volatile in such a serene setting. Nikki cracked the window and took in the earthy fresh scent.

"Gorgeous, isn't it?" Derek inquired.

"Unbelievably so." Nikki feasted her eyes on the sights around them. "Do you ever work in the vineyard itself?"

"Sure I do. It's what I love the most about living here. You know, people come here and all they see is wealth, greed, materialism, and believe me, there's plenty of that. You'll see when you meet my family. I come from a long line of snobs, and for the most part, the tradition still holds. But for me, there's a lot more about this vineyard that gives me joy than just the money."

Nikki looked away from the scenery for a moment and over at Derek. She noticed that his hands gripping the steering wheel were sun-kissed and weathered. He told the truth. A man with hands like that certainly worked the land.

"It's really an art form," he said.

"What is?"

"Growing the grapes. You can liken pruning vines to the art of sculpting. It's that precise."

"Really?" He faced her, and the faint sunlight glistening through the fog caught his eyes and made them look bluer than any ocean Nikki had ever seen. Yep, the scenery around this place was A-okay.

"It's like pruning roses in relation to the time and consideration you have to give to each vine. Believe me, you have to know exactly where to cut."

"I had no idea. I know about tastes and what wine goes with what, but I've never really given much thought to the entire process, from the growth stage on." She crossed her legs and saw that Derek's eyes followed them, right to the hemline of her black skirt, above her knee. She'd paired the skirt with a teal V-necked sweater hoping it would complement her eyes. Her palms grew sweaty.

"You're going to learn a lot around here, then." He pulled the Range Rover up next to a cottage that was about half a mile away from what she assumed was the main house. It sat on a small knoll, surrounded by oak trees covered in Spanish moss. The cottage was a craftsman creation, with a porch and white picket fence to match. "This will be your home. For as long as you need it, in order to make a decision about the job."

Nikki got out of the car and looked around, noticing a pond behind the house surrounded by more oaks. Two Muscovy ducks were enjoying a swim. For a brief moment, the scene reminded her of back *home*—the trees and ducks, anyway. Although the cottage didn't look very large, it was larger by far and a thousand times nicer than the home where she'd spent her first several years in the foothills of Tennessee. "This is amazing," she said.

He opened up the back hatch of the SUV and took out her suitcase. "Come on, I'll show you the inside."

The porch had so much charm in and of itself, including a swing and roses on a trellis on each side, that if it hadn't been real, it would have had to be part of a Norman Rockwell painting.

The interior of the cottage carried the quaintness throughout, decorated in French-country plaids and florals in colors of black, peach, pink, cream, and green. A small kitchen opened into a nook with bench seating. Off to the side of the kitchen table was a small telephone table. On the other side of the kitchen was the family room with a pinewood entertainment unit complete with TV, stereo, and all the entertainment accoutrements one might desire. A fireplace in front of the sofa balanced out the room. There was one bedroom.

"Wow!" Nikki exclaimed when she opened the bedroom door. The room was an absolute dream, decorated in pink with black-and-white traditional toile. Pink roses filled several vases on the dresser, along with an antique bookcase containing the classics. "Consider me your new tenant."

Derek laughed and pointed to the French doors, which opened out onto a balcony overlooking the pond. "Look through there. You see that?"

Nikki went to the window and saw across the pond another home, similar in style, but more like an old barn. "The barn?"

"Not a barn," he replied.

"No?"

"My house. I renovated it when I came home from college." He crossed his arms and leaned back on his heels. "By myself, I might add."

"No kidding? But why? Why don't you live in the mansion I saw up on the hill as we drove in?"

"You mean the insane asylum?"

He said it so seriously that for a second Nikki wasn't sure if he were joking or not. "What's behind that statement?"

"Trust me, you'll see. I'm hosting a charity event for the Leukemia Foundation tomorrow night. You'll get to meet the inmates who live in the mansion, otherwise the people who I loosely refer to as my family. They're a *special* bunch." His reply heavily laden with sarcasm was not lost on Nikki. "There's my half brother, Simon, my stepmother, Patrice, and my ex-wife, Meredith. Oh, did I forget Simon's partner, Marco? He's at least got a sense of humor."

"You should have told me about the party. I'm sure your family isn't that bad, but it's bad for me that I don't have anything dressy to wear."

"As long as you have something black, you'll fit right in."

She did have that. The every-woman's requisite simple black dress was packed away, and though it was nothing to be worn to a charity event, it would have to do.

"Why don't you get settled in, and I'll be back by in half an hour. I need to make sure everything is on schedule for tomorrow. I'd like to show you around the place and have you meet my winemaker, Gabriel Asanti. He's amazing. What he can do with a handful of grapes is nothing short of a miracle. I assure you, your taste buds will never be the same."

"I'm looking forward to it." Nikki locked the door behind Derek after he left, and then laughed out loud for the ridiculous act. What could happen in a place like this?

She started to unpack her suitcase in the bedroom when, out of the corner of one eye she caught something moving outside by the pond. She went to the doors and saw a rustling in the bushes across the way, but then it stopped, as if someone were there and knew they'd been spotted. Nikki locked the French doors, and once again laughed at herself. "My overactive imagination. Maybe I should be writing screenplays instead of trying to star in them." She looked at herself in the mirror over the dresser, and ran her fingertips over the tiny fine lines on either side of her eyes. "Yuck."

She went back to unpacking. Once again she noticed movement from outside, but all she saw was the pair of ducks. "Ducks, dingbat. That's all it is. Ducks." She went to the French doors and peered out. The ducks flew off, leaving ripples in their wake on the pond's surface. She started to turn back around, and there it was again. This time it was unmistakable; she saw a flash of green, and it wasn't leaves on a bush. This was green fabric, like someone's shirt.

She opened the door, stepping out into the cool air. A frenzy of goose bumps ran down her arms, and she rubbed her hands briskly over them. She sang out, "Hello. Anyone there?" Curious by nature, she took a step outside and called out again, to no avail. "I know I saw someone," she muttered under her breath. Screw it. Nikki wasn't a fraidy cat. Besides, she did Tae Bo, and if Billy Blanks had taught her anything, he'd taught her how to throw one damned good roundhouse kick.

She walked the hundred or so yards around the pond where she knew someone had been only moments before. The brush grew dense and grabbed at the skin on her bare arms, scratching her. A mosquito landed on her, biting her before heading off to its next victim. She slapped her neck, but missed. "Ouch." She knew she should turn around and go back to the guest house. But she'd grown up reading Nancy Drew books, and she'd be damned if she'd turn back now. Nancy wouldn't walk away. She'd pursue.

Her shoe got bogged down in some mud, and she had to

yank to pull her foot out, losing her shoe in the greenish muck. "Damn!" Her foot covered in mud, her arms scratched up, and mosquito bites rising along her neck, she was foolishly looking for some phantom juvenile delinquent who got his *cojones* off spying on unsuspecting women. Could it get any worse? Only if Derek found her like this.

But even worse than that was when her bare foot brushed against something that didn't feel like a prickly bush. It tickled, but not in the way a bush would. She looked down and saw a hand. She screamed as her eyes followed the hand deeper into the bushes. There was the body of a man with thick grape vines pulled tautly around his neck, his brown eyes bulging out of his purplish face. His dark, longish hair covered in mud. He wore a green shirt, and across the right side of his chest on the shirt was his name—Gabriel Asanti. With a flash of recognition, Nikki knew she'd just met the winemaker.

Chapter 4

"I am so sorry," Derek murmured, taking off his navy blue knit sweater and pulling it over Nikki, who hadn't realized until she felt its warmth that she was trembling. His Rhodesian Ridgeback, named Oliver, lounged in between the two wicker chairs, where they were seated on Derek's porch. Every once in awhile, the dog lifted his head to watch the commotion going on in the distance across the pond.

"If you'd like, I can call my pilot and have you flown home."

"Afraid you can't do that," a young woman police officer said, approaching them. Oliver barked as she walked forward.

Derek stretched his arm over the chair and stroked his dog's head. "It's okay." The dog quieted down, and the officer climbed the steps. "Nikki, Jeanine Wiley. Or Officer Wiley."

Officer Wiley stretched out her hand to shake Nikki's, and they greeted each other. "Miss Sands has to stay until the chief says that she can leave. She's a critical part of this investigation." The freckle-faced redhead pulled out a pocket-sized notepad. "Mr. Malveaux, I hate to seem rude, but I need to ask Miss Sands a few more questions, and it's important we have some privacy."

Derek looked questioningly at Nikki.

She shook her head. "I'll be fine. I planned on staying anyway. We still have a job interview."

He gave her a warm smile. "Can I get you anything? A cup of tea, coffee, wine?"

"Tea would be nice."

"Officer Wiley?"

The policewoman, whose face was already ruddy, turned bright red. Such a deliciously good-looking man had obviously never asked her anything so kind. "No. No, thank you."

Derek went back into the house, Oliver in tow, while Officer Wiley opened up the notepad and took a pen from her shirt pocket. "I know you went over this before with one of the other officers, but, now that you've had some time to relax a little and think about it, perhaps other details have come to mind."

Nikki shook her head and told Officer Wiley the same story she'd explained when the police first arrived. She looked past Officer Wiley's shoulder and saw Gabriel's body being wheeled into the back of the coroner's van.

"You didn't know the victim?"

"No. As I've already explained, I arrived this morning."

"What compelled you, if you were frightened by seeing something move in the bushes, to take a walk to check out what it might have been?"

Nikki eyed the young cop. Was she insinuating something, or was Nikki simply being paranoid because she'd been the one to find the body? She sighed, worn out from the freakish experience.

"Here's the deal. I wasn't exactly scared. It bugged me, yes, when I saw the bushes move, and I had a creepy feeling that maybe someone was watching me. The last thing on my mind was that someone might actually be killing someone else."

"Uh-huh." The officer jotted something down.

Nikki got the distinct feeling that the officer was keeping something from her, but that was what the police were supposed to do—keep the details of a murder investigation under wraps. Nikki knew that much from her short-lived TV show.

"Can I ask you something?" Officer Wiley asked.

Nikki nodded.

She hesitated and glanced around. "Um, are you by any chance *the* Nikki Sands, the one who did that show about Detective Sydney Martini?"

Nikki shrunk down in the wicker chair and wrapped her arms more tightly around herself. She gave a slight nod.

Officer Wiley lowered her voice almost to a whisper. "I *loved* that show. I was so mad when they took it off the air. I mean, there were only what, five episodes?"

"Four."

"It was *so* good. You were awesome."

Great. Nikki had actually come across one of her ten fans, and she *had* to be a policewoman investigating this murder.

"I loved the way you kicked butt on the bad guys. You can throw some great kicks."

"Tae Bo. Get the advanced tapes. Look, you know that character I played wasn't really me. Shouldn't we finish here?"

"Right. Sorry, I'm just really excited to meet you," she gushed.

"Thanks, Officer Wiley."

"Call me Jeanine, except you know . . ." She glanced around. "Except when one of the other officers is present. One other thing, would you mind giving me an autograph?"

Derek walked out in time to witness this, and handed Nikki her tea. "It's kind of hot, so be careful. Are we about done here, Jeanine?" he asked.

A blushing Jeanine Wiley nodded and stood up to go. "Thanks for your cooperation. As I said before, we need you to hang around for a bit."

"No problem," Nikki replied. "Am I a suspect?"

"Miss Sands, we have to look at all the angles."

Nikki and Derek watched as the policewoman descended the porch steps. Nikki put down the cup of tea that had been warming her hands nicely. "Did you say you had wine?"

Derek laughed. "The tea not strong enough for you?"

"Don't get me wrong. It's very good, but after this afternoon, and your Napa Valley police force interrogation, I think I'd like something a bit stronger."

"Can't blame you. Why don't you follow me in and warm yourself by the fire."

That did sound very inviting. His place was as cozy as her guest cottage, but in a very masculine way. The furniture was done in distressed leathers and warm woods, the walls were painted a golden tone, and a Navajo rug blanketed the hardwood floor in front of the fire. Nikki fell into an oversized chaise. Oliver plunked himself in front of the fireplace and wagged his tail at her. Derek handed her an aperitif glass. She looked at the tawny colored contents and couldn't help but ask, "Port?"

"I'm going against the grain here. Port, as you know, is usually an after-dinner dessert drink, but in this case, something with a higher alcohol content might do you some good."

"Hmmm." She took a sip. The slight sweetness of the port added to the warmth it sent down into her stomach.

"I am a Napa Valley vineyard owner, and for me to serve you something from Portugal is not exactly protocol."

"It's good. You can't tell me that all you drink is California wines."

"Shhh. No, of course not. It'd be ridiculous of me to do that. There's so much to experience in wines. Gabriel understood that." Derek walked over to a corkboard in the kitchen and pulled a photograph from it. He came back over to Nikki and handed it to her.

"You and Gabriel?" There was Derek, his arm around the other man in a brotherly fashion, along with a slew of

other folks. A golden-haired, attractive woman was on the
other side of Gabriel. They were all covered in dirt, everyone holding a glass of wine up into the air. Gabriel had a
brooding, Italian look about him, with hooded dark eyes
and a gaunt face, his nose pronounced and very Roman. He
was thin, but manly looking. His smile appeared honest
and bright.

"At last year's crop planting."

"Is the woman his girlfriend? They look pretty cozy,"
Nikki remarked, noticing that the woman hung onto
Gabriel tightly."

"Tara Beckenroe? No." Derek kind of laughed. "Well, I
shouldn't say no. I think in Tara's mind they were pretty
close at the time. They spent a few nights together, and
Tara became kind of obsessive. She gets that way when she
decides to go after something."

"You sound like you speak from experience," Nikki
said.

"In regard to Tara? Yeah. Let's just say she doesn't play
coy. She's a barracuda, and she's made a few attempts at
getting to me. I'm not interested. Gabriel showed her some
interest, and she was all over it. But Gabriel wasn't the kind
of man a woman could tie down easily. Tara is the kind of
woman who likes to get her man. Gabriel liked to *date* a lot
of women. She wasn't exactly thrilled when he told her to
back off."

"Looks like a quite a celebration." Nikki flapped the
picture in a slight motion.

"We were celebrating the planting of grapes that we
both felt could revolutionize California dessert wines."

"You two were close?"

Derek nodded. "We are, I mean. . . ." He took a sip from
his port, obviously not knowing how to finish the sentence.
He set his glass down on the end table next to Nikki, giving
her a saddened half smile. "Gabriel was getting closer and
closer with each season to making a dessert wine that almost copied the exact taste of wines from the Porto area in

Portugal. We'd developed a neutral grape brandy along with a couple of grape varietals that, once mixed together, would have been a phenomenon. But now . . ." Derek brought his glass up to his lips and took a slow sip.

"Did you know Gabriel for a long time?"

"A while. He came to the vineyard about a decade ago, about five years before my dad died. I liked him right away. He was funny, with a real stereotypical Italian macho attitude. I got a kick out of him. He was a great chef, too. He didn't know anyone here, and I met him in a wine shop down the road when I was delivering some wines. That was back before Malveaux Wines really took off, and I was doing a lot of the footwork myself."

"Admirable."

"No. Not really. Hard work is how it gets done. My brother, really my half brother, doesn't even come close to understanding that concept. But he's another subject. Anyway, I overheard Gabriel talking to the shop owner, asking why he didn't carry any Italian wines. I laughed at that, because being in Napa at a smaller wine shop, it was obvious why there were no Italian wines there. Gabriel took my laughter as an insult. But it got us talking about wines, and we wound up corking a bottle of mine and drinking it. He bragged, claiming that he could make a better bottle than what I'd shared with him, and again I laughed. He said that he'd prove it. So I took him up on it and brought him here. Before long, our old winemaker who never got along well with my dad was out, and Gabriel was in. I worked alongside him for a bit, but then I was needed more on the business end of things when my dad began showing his age and grew quite fragile."

"I'm so sorry. It sounds like you've had quite a bit of loss in your life."

Derek set his glass down on one of the wooden tables and walked back into his kitchen, which overlooked the family room. His back was to her as he opened the refrigerator. "I think we all have."

She heard the deep emotion in his voice, signifying to her that he was choked up. In such a short time, the story of Derek Malveaux and his vineyard had grown quite complex.

Derek came back out of the kitchen after a few moments, refilled her glass, and set down a tray of blue-and-green veined cheeses, walnuts, and pear slices. "I'd hoped to invite you out for a nice dinner, but I don't think I'm up to it. I don't know what to do about tomorrow night."

She reached across him for a piece of cheese, her arm grazing his chest. "Please, don't worry about me and dinner. This is perfect. The day has gone by quickly. I suppose when there's a murder involved . . . Sorry, I didn't mean to sound crass."

"You didn't. You didn't even know Gabriel. I'm sorry that you're here under these circumstances." He grabbed a handful of nuts from the bowl in the tray.

"Don't worry about it. I'm still interested in the job, that is, if you still want to consider me."

"Nothing has changed. In fact, more than ever, I'm going to need some help around here. Gabriel was one of the finest winemakers in the country, not to mention my friend. It'll be hard for me to concentrate, and I'll need a pair of eyes to watch over my shoulder."

Nikki wasn't sure what he meant by that, but she decided to let it go for the time being. "You mentioned something about what to do concerning tomorrow night. Are you referring to the benefit?"

He nodded. "I don't see how I can cancel. It's not only to raise money for the Leukemia Foundation, but it's an annual tribute to my mother's memory. She passed away from the disease when I was a kid. I hold the event yearly, and we raise a great deal of money. It's also when we release the new vintages for the season. Gabriel usually does it. He makes quite a toast." Derek brought his hands up to his face. "This is very hard."

"No worries. I understand. I hope I'm not overstepping my boundaries here, but I think you should go forward with the benefit. From what you've told me about Gabriel, that's what he would've wanted, and in a way, you can extend the idea of celebrating his life by showing off his latest creations."

Derek looked over at her. "That's a really nice thought. Thank you."

Nikki could feel the port making her senses buzz in a fuzzy but good way. She was no longer cold, but very warm, and she knew that for everyone's good, she'd better get the hell out of his house. With Derek in such a vulnerable state, the alcohol doing its job, and his musky cedar scent wafting its way toward her, she was about ready to initiate something she might regret later. "I'd better go. It's almost dark, and I think that maybe you could use some time alone."

He didn't answer right away. She wondered if his mind was on the same track that hers was, but how could it be? He'd just lost his partner and dear friend. The last thing on his mind would be getting frisky. Plus she had that rule thing about mixing relationships and business. A major no-no.

"Let me walk you back. And, I'd feel better if Oliver went with you."

"You don't have to do that." She said it, but she did kind of like the idea of having his large dog sleep in the same room with her.

"I insist."

Derek walked her back over to the guest cottage, Oliver following. "In the morning you can just let him out. He knows his way around here, and he certainly knows where the food bowl is," Derek said, after checking throughout the cottage.

"No problem. We'll be fine." Nikki closed the door behind him, this time bolting it and not laughing at the idea of doing so as being ridiculous.

Stilton Cheese & Port

If you ever find yourself in the position Nikki was just in, where you've discovered a dead body, been interrogated by the police, and been offered a spot to warm yourself by the fireplace in the home of a gorgeous, interesting man, you should really ask for a nice bottle of port.

Port comes only from a region in Portugal called Porto. There are two types of Porto. The first is called a wood port. This type includes Ruby Port, which is dark and fruity, blended from young, non-vintage wines. It's the least expensive of the two.

Another wood port is called Tawny Port, which is lighter and more delicate, blended from many vintages, and aged in casks for sometimes up to forty years and longer. This port is moderately priced.

Finally, the second type of port is Vintage Port. This wine is aged two years in wood and will mature in the bottle over time. It is expensive, but well worth it.

Port always goes nicely with Stilton cheese, a salty, blue-veined cheese that provides great contrast for the lush, sweet wine. Dark chocolate truffles, crisp pears, and a handful of almonds complement port nicely, too. You can't go wrong with a port produced by Warre's or Dow. They're both excellent producers of this tasty treat.

Chapter 5

Derek did his best showing Nikki around the vineyard, explaining the operations of the winery. She could see the pain in his face; he'd changed in a matter of twenty-four hours. She could feel his sorrow in the way he walked and talked.

They were now inside a barreling room, walking between row upon row of wooden barrels. It wouldn't be hard to get drunk off the fumes alone inside the room.

"Not all wines are meant to be aged once they come out of the barrel and into the bottle." Derek said, rubbing his hand on one of the barrels. "It's a misconception that wine will improve if it sits in the bottle longer. In reality, only ten percent of wine improves while it's in the bottle. The rest of our wines should be enjoyed within a year of purchase."

Nikki nodded. She'd noticed that today he was all business. She'd told him when he'd come by the guest cottage that morning that she'd be fine, roaming around on her own, and that when he found time and felt up to it, he could give her a tour. But he'd insisted on getting it out of the way. He'd said that he needed to keep things functioning.

Showing her the ropes kept him on task, and Gabriel would have expected nothing less of him.

"So you age the wines in the barrels?"

"Yep."

She noticed that his eyes looked especially blue today. He wore a caramel-colored turtleneck sweater with jeans. She liked his down-to-earth style, not something she'd expected from a vineyard estate owner and multimillionaire.

"We use oak barrels because there's a biochemical interchange of phenol from the oak in the aging of the wine, which adds more flavor to the final product. There's a difference between American barrels and French barrels, in that American barrels have a narrow belly compared to the French, which can hold as much as 3.3 gallons more wine. It all depends on the type of flavor you're going for."

"These labels here, I assume they're the type of wine in the barrel?" Nikki asked, trying hard to focus on Derek's words, but having a difficult time not allowing lustful thoughts, as well as morbid ones from yesterday's aftermath, to distract her. The combination of the two had her all tied up in knots, and she was wishing she hadn't had a half a pot of coffee that morning. Her nerves were abuzz.

"They are. If they're a combination of grapes, say it's a mix of Cabernet, Merlot, and Syrah grapes. We list them by the content of which is the strongest grape in the barrel. See here." He pointed to another label on the barrel. "This defines the wine. We list the appellation, which is of course Napa Valley, then the varietal composition, which for this wine is Chardonnay. The alcohol content is 13.9 percent. The list continues with the pH, the brix at harvest, which means the sugar content, what the residual sugar is, how many months the wine stays in the oak, the case production, and, finally, the winemaker." Derek turned his face away from hers for a moment.

"Are you okay?" She knew he wasn't, but she couldn't help asking.

"It's hard. This was where Gabriel's work came to fruition. This row we're walking down is where he was putting together some new and interesting wines. He liked to experiment. You see, we sell a good share of our grapes to other wineries, and they in turn use their vintners to make the wine they desire. It's how we make the bulk of our money. But what you see on this row here comes from the grapes we don't sell off, which is about ten percent, and that ten percent happens to be the best of the best on the vineyard."

"Sort of like the cream of the crop," she said. Derek smiled, and her stomach did that flip-flop thing again. It was good to see him smile; even better that she'd caused him to do so.

"Exactly, the cream of the crop. I've got plenty of people in this valley wanting to purchase grapes off that particular section of my land, but no matter what the offer, I keep saying no. The fact is, that small percentage of our grapes is what sets us apart from all the others here in wine country. The grapes that come from that section are grown in loam soil. Loam soil is the perfect mixture of silt, sand, and clay. It drains well and produces supreme grapes, which in turn obviously produce superb wines. Every vintner wants to grow grapes from loam soil."

"Jealousy runs thick, I take it?" They walked through the large wooden doors of the barreling room and found themselves outside. Bright, warm sunshine hit their faces, even though the air was still quite cool. It was nearing noon. The sweet smell of wet soil and fruit filled the air. It was fresh, lush, and nearly intoxicating.

"I suppose it's possible that there are some folks out there jealous of what we have here at Malveaux. And, I'm sure I've been the topic of gossip once or twice around town."

The soles of their shoes squeaked slightly against the damp soil. She was glad she'd brought her Keds. "Do you think its possible that one of the locals with a bad case of jealousy could've murdered Gabriel?"

"I've thought a lot about that, and, yes, I think that's possible. Gabriel was a renowned winemaker. He won awards continuously through the years, and I don't like saying this because he was my friend, but Gabriel could be somewhat of a braggart. He didn't hesitate in letting on to people about who he was and how many awards he'd won. That kind of thing."

"Is there anyone in particular you can think of that this might have really bothered?" Nikki asked, thinking she could be on to something here.

Derek nodded. "It's a far reach because the man I'm thinking of appears to be a good man. He kind of keeps to himself, is a hard worker. He's liked around town. I don't know him well, though. But I do know that he and Gabriel had this competitive thing going."

"Who is it?"

"His name is Andrés Fernandez. He's from Spain and works down at Spaniards' Crest Estate. The owners are a group of Spanish businessmen, most of whom reside in Europe. They produce small but elegant production wines around the world. They own and operate some of the best wineries, especially in Spain and various locations in Europe. Andrés runs the show here in Napa."

"What was the rivalry between Gabriel and Andrés?"

"I'm not certain. He and Gabriel got into it at a wine-makers' dinner a few months ago. I also heard that they got into it again not that long ago at the opening of Andrés' sister's new restaurant. I couldn't make the event, and Gabriel didn't want to talk about it afterward, saying it was just hot air between two winemakers. I didn't push it. It was none of my business. Plus, I'm not one for gossip. Gabriel had his issues, and there were things that I didn't like about my friend, like the way he used women, at least that was in my opinion. He claimed that the women he dated understood his *rules*, and everyone was happy with that situation. I don't know about that. He seemed to have a way of mes-merizing women, people in general. He was very charming that way, and there were also a lot of other wonderful things about him. I suppose we're all a bit like that. Complicated."

"Hmmm. Yes. Most of us do seem *complicated*. With

this Andrés, do you think whatever the problem between them was could be enough to motivate him to murder Gabriel?"

Derek shrugged. "It's no secret that both men didn't care for one another. Andrés doesn't strike me as the murdering type, maybe a recluse, but not a murderer."

Nikki made a mental note of this, knowing she'd have to go visit Andrés Fernandez.

"I have another thought for you in regard to your special ten-percent lot of grapes."

"I'm all ears." He smiled.

And blue eyes, and strong shoulders, and kissable lips. Get a grip. "Here goes. With Gabriel gone, so is the *production* of your premier wines. Face it, you've told me several times now that he was one of the world's renowned winemakers. To replace him will be no easy task. You'll lose at least a year's worth of profit from your premier wines, maybe more, and thus have to consider selling that special ten percent of grapes off to the various wineries around town."

Derek stopped walking for a minute and faced her. "You're good. And thanks for reminding me of the road I have ahead of me in replacing Gabriel," he said.

She winced at his bluntness. "I'm sorry. I guess I was rattling off theories."

"No, it's all right. The truth hurts. Not only is my good friend gone, I now have to find someone who can make wines the way he did, if I want to maintain the reputation of Malveaux and not become merely a wine-box winery."

"I doubt that would ever happen."

"I know. I'm feeling sorry for myself. I've got to say, your theory is a decent one. You should've studied law. Where did you learn so much about this stuff?"

They started walking again, heading for the tasting room. "What I'm saying is mainly common sense. But when I did those few episodes of my terrible TV show, I researched a lot. I may be a bad actress, but I am a good researcher. I was also raised by my aunt, who used to be a homicide detective for the LAPD. She just retired a couple of weeks ago. I used to scour all her books and go over cases with her, when she'd bring work home. It always fascinated me."

"Why didn't you go into law enforcement?"

"I guess I always wanted to be an actress."

"Really?"

"Why do you say it like that?" She crossed her arms in front of her, as they walked up to the front door of the tasting room. He held the door open for her, and she nodded her thanks.

"I don't know. You don't strike me as the actress type."

"You must've seen my show," she replied sarcastically.

"Like I told you over dinner the other night, TV isn't my thing. Occasionally, I'll rent a movie. By the time I get in at night and wind down, I want to go to bed, or I'll read a bit. It used to be that Gabriel and I, and sometimes Minnie, our accountant—who you'll meet at the party tonight— would get together and mix up some dinner, drink good wine, and visit, but not that often."

"You're not a real social type, then?"

He shook his head. "No time. This is the tasting room. We won't open today because of the party, but we usually open at lunchtime. You'll see that we have tables out on the patio for people who want to bring picnic lunches and taste wines. We also have a restaurant here on the property, which is really a bistro-type of place, where we serve mainly cheeses, fruits, pastas, salads and sandwiches, and an amazing French onion soup. We only open for lunch. Part of your job will be overseeing the restaurant. There's a full-time manager there, but you'll be her boss, which she probably won't care for." He shrugged. "But that's the way it goes."

"Do I get to meet *her* today?"

"You will tonight."

"I'm going to meet everyone tonight, aren't I?"

He nodded. "I won't lie to you, the manager of the bistro is my ex-wife, Meredith. It was part of the settlement that she stay on here, since she's the one who came up with the bistro idea, anyway."

"You're not putting me in charge out of spite, are you?" Nikki didn't think he was that kind of man, but one never knew.

"No. Actually, I suspect that Meredith is lying about the profits and the wine inventory."

"She couldn't get that much from it, could she?"

"Enough for her weekly spa treatments and a few vacations a year. We do a good business, but even if the Malveaux Estate makes millions, it doesn't give anyone the right to steal. A percentage of the profits from the bistro go to the Leukemia Foundation. We also have our Wine of the Month Club, which takes in quite a bit in proceeds for the foundation. Minnie, my accountant, who I mentioned earlier, oversees that venture. Hopefully Minnie sticks with me. She's got this dream of going to Tuscany and she mentions it often. But I need her to watch over Meredith. If Meredith is doing something sneaky with the bistro profits, it's not a matter of stealing from me or the estate, but from the very ill people I want to help."

Nikki nodded. She could see his point, and she had to agree. If his ex was stealing money from the bistro, she was both coldhearted and calculating. "What about your accountant? Has she found anything off in the accounts? Have you asked her to look into it?"

"She hasn't found anything concrete yet, but Minnie agrees with me that something isn't adding up. I'm hoping that with new pairs of eyes and ears around here, someone with a fresh perspective can help figure it out." Derek's cell phone rang. He pulled it from his jeans pocket and flipped it open. "Hello? Yes. Okay, I see. Yes, I'll be right down." He flipped shut the phone. "I'm sorry. That was the police. They need me to come down to the station and answer some questions."

"Do you want me to come along?"

"No, no. I feel bad enough already. Last night I wanted to take you to dinner, and since that didn't work out, I thought we'd have lunch today. But, I don't know how long I'll be tied up, and when I get back, I'll have to make sure we're set for tonight's party. Take a rain check?"

"Of course. You do what you need to do. Mind if I hang in here and look around?"

"No. Why don't you stop by my place around four-thirty? If I have everything for the festivities all sewn up, we can take a quick walk down to the vines and have a glass of wine before getting ready for the party."

"Sounds good." He waved at her, and she watched him leave. With Derek gone, she took notice of the tasting room and all its beauty. The architecture itself was amazing, with rounded walls and arches that led from the sitting room into the area where the wine was poured. Fantastic art by Miguel Nuñez adorned the walls, showing the gilded golden beauty of the women in his paintings. Mocha-colored leather chairs covered in vine-and-grape-tapestry patterned seat cushions were grouped around wrought-iron and wooden tables. This room alone she could live in.

As she wandered around appreciating the art and the room, an eerie sensation came over her. She glanced all around the room, which was dead silent. That same sensation of being watched that she'd had the other day, right before discovering Gabriel's body, caused her adrenaline to start pumping. Nikki told herself it was mere paranoia. She moved toward the door to leave. As she did, she heard a loud commotion from the back room, where she presumed the wines were kept. She and Derek hadn't ventured that far back into the room. She'd been working her way toward taking a look at it, when the feeling had come over her. Goose bumps snaked down along her arms.

"Hello?" She had the choice to get out of there fast or do what she'd done yesterday and see who was behind the crashing noise she'd heard. Should she go and see what the hell had happened in the back room, or run? Common sense told her to run, but her curiosity took hold, and just like an idiotic teenage girl in a bad horror flick, Nikki couldn't control herself.

She flung open the door leading to the back room, where the wines were stored. Several of the bottles were shattered on the ground. A mixture of glass and pale yellow and red liquids swam together, blending into a dark pink.

She looked around. There was no one in sight in the small room. It was necessary to walk carefully around the rows of wine bottles stacked on racks, because they could be knocked over with little difficulty. Someone had just been in here. Either the wines had been deliberately destroyed, or knocked off accidentally while someone attempted to get out. She carefully treaded around the shards of broken glass. Something in the mix that didn't fit caught her eye. It was a small piece of gold. She bent down and picked it out from among the broken glass and wine. Holding it up to the light, Nikki saw that it was a gold charm piece. Strange as it was, it was a half of one of those charms in the shape of a heart. One friend took half of the heart with "best" on it, and the other friend took the part that read "friends." She'd shared one almost exactly like it with her friend Tessa back home when she was a little girl. They'd saved up all summer working a lemonade stand when they were six and bought it as a gift for each other that Christmas. Seeing this one tugged at her own heart. Child Protective Services had removed Tessa from her home only two months after that. Nikki never saw her again.

All the same, the charms were kind of a hokey thing to have. Nikki held the "best" half of the charm in her palm and realized her faux pas as she did. She'd picked up what could be evidence. Not a smooth move. Because she'd made the move without thinking first, she decided that maybe she'd leave the police out of this. She didn't want to get into any trouble. Besides who was to say that she was in harm's way in the first place? And furthermore, that the trinket in her hand meant anything to anyone?

Whoever had been inside the stockroom may not have even known she was in there. Who was she kidding? If that were the case, then knocking over the wines wouldn't have necessarily caused someone to run . . . unless they were stealing a bottle of wine for themselves, or maybe they didn't want to get busted for killing several good bottles of vino. That had to be it. Yep. No need to alert the cops.

Nikki could see the door the intruder escaped through, which now stood wide open. Whoever had been here had left in a hurry. She pocketed the charm, feeling that whoever had been inside the stockroom had definitely been watching her and Derek. Then a chilling notion came over her as she realized she didn't have the Peeping Tom vibe when Derek was around. She fidgeted with the charm. She didn't want to think what she was thinking, but the thought refused to be shoved aside. What if it had been Derek who'd been in the stockroom, taking a peek at her? He'd left only moments earlier. He could've easily snuck around through the back. She didn't know why he would do that, unless he didn't trust her for some reason. The goose bumps on her arms prickled as the hairs on the back of her neck rose. *Maybe* Derek Malveaux was the one with something to hide.

Chapter 6

Derek pulled into the police station parking lot. He hadn't liked the sound of Jeanine Wiley's voice on the telephone, telling him that the chief had a few questions for him. He'd known Jeanine all her life, and she'd never spoken to him like that.

Jeanine's father had worked for the winery as a security guard years ago, after he'd retired from the force in San Francisco. The winery had fallen victim to a few break-ins back in the early '90's, specifically in the tasting room, where a hoodlum who knew good art was stealing it and selling it cheap. Old Raymond Wiley had caught the thief, and they hadn't had any problems since—not until now.

Derek stepped out of his Range Rover. He spotted his brother's silver convertible with Marco in the driver's seat. Derek sighed and walked over to him.

"What are you doing here?" Derek could at times appreciate Marco's sense of humor, but for the most part was usually aggravated by the presence of his brother's partner. Marco had a knack for stirring up all sorts of gossip and chaos at the winery, just for his own entertainment. He'd given Derek more than a few headaches. He was looking forward to Marco and his brother flying off for their annual fashion shows.

"Oh, hello, Derek. It is so terrible what has happened to our poor winemaker? No?" he said in his thick Italian accent.

Derek ignored the "our" part. Marco had no say or proprietorship in the vineyard. "Let me ask you again—what are you doing here?"

Marco shrugged in an exaggerated fashion. "I am thinking that I am doing the same thing here that you are doing here. I had to bring Simon over to answer some questions. He is so saddened and angry about this horrible killing. That Jeanine Wiley policewoman called him in for a talk. You do not think they will want to speak with me?" Marco pulled out a cigarillo from an expensive leather holder.

"I think you're probably on the list somewhere. I'm sure they're speaking with anyone and everyone who was at the winery yesterday."

Marco lit the cigarillo. The bitter stench wafted into the crisp air. Derek took a step back from the car. "Well." He waved the smoke around with his hand. "I do not know why they would ask me a question. I do not know anything. I have nothing to say. Do you think they will want speak to your new *amante*?"

This fool was priceless. "She's not my lover. She's considering taking employment with the winery."

"Hmmm. Vintner, perhaps? No?"

Derek ignored the remark, turning to walk away.

"Derek, you need to be careful with what people are saying. There is a tale traveling at the winery that says you may have had a reason to send Gabriel to meet the angels."

Derek kept walking, refusing to buy into the viciousness Marco was peddling—the kind of bullshit Derek knew could cause him problems.

He walked up to the reception area and was told to take a seat, that someone would be with him in a moment. A few minutes later, he watched as the redheaded Jeanine Wiley showed his brother out of an interrogation room. The two of them came his way. Simon wore a smirk on his face. Derek remembered a brief time, when Simon was only a toddler, that he actually thought his brother had an angelic face; now, it looked anything but, with his high cheekbones and spite radiating from his eyes—spite Derek knew was directed solely at him.

Derek stood. "Hey, little brother."

Simon kept walking. "Hey, yourself," he said, his tone singsong and dripping with sarcasm. "Be careful in there. Watch what you say." Simon turned around and winked at him.

Jeanine Wiley looked at Derek curiously. Derek shook his head. He didn't have time for this, not today.

"Follow me, Mr. Malveaux," Jeanine said.

"Jeanine, you can call me Derek. I've known you since you were in diapers."

She lowered her voice. "Not here. I'm working. I'm a professional, you know."

Derek smiled at her, following her into the same room where she'd questioned Simon. He could still smell his brother's strong cologne—some overrated, grossly expensive stuff he special-ordered from France every month. That was his brother, always figuring that if something cost more, it must be the best.

Seated at the far end of the table was Police Chief Horn. Stan Horn had been the police chief in Napa Valley for the past thirty years. Even at sixty-five, Stan would probably have to be forced out. With his grandfatherly face, crinkly lines across the forehead and around his eyes and mouth, and head full of white hair, Stan Horn's resemblance to Santa Claus didn't go unnoticed by many. His hair was all white, but all there. Stan also had warm brown eyes, and a smile that drew people in to smile right along with him. But he wasn't smiling now. "Have a seat, Derek."

Derek sat in one of the cold metal chairs and crossed his arms in front of him. "What can I do for you, Chief?"

"You got yourself quite a problem out there at the vineyard."

Derek nodded. "What do you know about Gabriel's murder?"

The chief set his gnarled hands on the table and folded them together. He sat up straight in his chair. "How about you tell me what *you* know?"

"I told you what I know yesterday," Derek replied calmly.

"You were in your house filling out some paperwork for the winery, after escorting Miss. . . ." The chief glanced down through his spectacles at his notepad. "Miss Sands to the guest cottage."

"Yes. I was finishing up paperwork I needed to complete before I could travel to Europe with an extensive wine collection. I'd like to take it to London next year to sell, which requires a list for shipment, and that's what I was doing. The deadline to get it in is early next week."

"No one can vouch for you, or was with you at that time, when you were filling out this paperwork?" Chief Horn asked.

"Unless you consider Oliver someone, which I do, but as far as a human someone goes? No. I was alone. What's this all about, Stan? You're not considering me a suspect, are you?"

"You know I can't rule out anyone, and there's a situation here I have to discuss with you, which is rather delicate. You may want an attorney present."

"I don't need an attorney, Stan. I haven't done anything wrong. I loved Gabriel like a brother. He was the main reason for Malveaux's success. The last thing I would want would be to see him dead. Ask your questions. I have nothing to hide."

The chief shifted his head from side to side. Derek heard his neck crack. "Were you aware that Gabriel had a job offer out at Sumner Winery?"

"Cal was always trying to woo him. Gabriel never would've gone. Cal doesn't have much to offer a winemaker like Gabriel. Certainly not the money. Besides, Gabriel was totally loyal."

"You sure about that?"

"Positive. Who told you this, anyway?"

"That's confidential."

"Right." Derek figured that it was Simon who'd been doing all the talking.

"We do have it on good authority that Gabriel was considering another position, and that you and he had recently had a row of some sort."

Derek shifted in his chair. "That's ridiculous."

"You didn't accuse him of any underhandedness going on at the winery, like maybe skimming the profits?"

"I'm not going to deny that I suspect that someone is taking money from the accounts. They don't add up, and both Minnie and I have been confused by it. But as far as Gabriel was concerned, I didn't consider him the culprit. I did ask him what he thought about it."

"What did he say? Did he get upset?"

Derek shook his head. "I don't believe this. Yeah, okay, he did get a bit defensive. Why? I don't know. But we talked about it later and cleared the air. I never meant him to take it the wrong way."

"There's something else we need to talk about."

Derek stared at the chief. He had a feeling he knew what was coming next.

"Meredith."

"I know the rumors. They're not true," Derek insisted, waving his hand, dismissing the suggestion.

"You sure about that? More than one story going around says that they *are* true, and that the two of them were carrying on during your marriage, and that they only recently had a falling out."

"I know Meredith was not faithful to me, and that in itself is a total embarrassment. The fact that she's still residing on my vineyard is an even bigger embarrassment. I don't believe that my friend had anything to do with her. But even if he had, trust me, it would've been *her* I would've killed, not Gabriel." Derek was sorry he'd said that, the minute the words escaped between his lips. The chief looked at him with disbelief. Maybe he *should* have had a lawyer present. "I'm sorry. I didn't mean that. This is all so crazy. You've known me for a very long time."

"Since you were a boy." The chief nodded.

"Right. Do you really think I'm capable of murder?"

The chief didn't answer right away. He sucked in his breath and finally said, "No, son, I don't think you're capable of murder. But there are some signs, and they aren't good ones, I have to say, that point in your direction."

"You're listening to hearsay and gossip."

"That's about all I've got to go on for now."

"Fine." Derek stood up. "If you don't need me any longer, I have a fund-raiser to prepare for."

"Yes, indeed. Grace and I'll be there, in honor of your mother."

"Thank you."

Derek walked to the door. The chief called out after him. "Be careful, son. I don't think you're capable of murder, but someone on that vineyard *is*, and my gut says it might be someone trying to set you up."

Derek closed the office door behind him and headed for the front entrance. Jeanine Wiley lifted her head and gave him a wan smile.

He got behind the wheel of his car and couldn't help wondering if the chief was right. Was someone trying to set him up? If so, who and why? Well, there were people with reasons. For starters, his own family. Simon couldn't stand being low man on the totem pole. Could Simon have murdered Gabriel with the intention of setting Derek up? He knew Simon loathed him, but was he intelligent enough to plan and execute a murder, and then divert the focus from himself and frame his brother?

Then there was his stepmother, who despised him for the same reasons his brother did. Derek knew that his father's will stated that if Derek were incapable of running the vineyard, then his percentage would fall into the hands of Patrice, and she would finally have total control. Being behind bars would certainly cause him to lose his grip at the vineyard. However, like Simon, Patrice was no rocket scientist, either. As much as his relatives disliked him in control, he found it difficult to believe that they would go as far as murder. Then again, anything is possible.

Craziness. Sheer and utter craziness, and now it was causing a sense of paranoia that disgusted Derek. He needed someone to talk to who had a brain and sound ideas. And if she had a gorgeous smile, well, all the better. That someone was Nikki Sands.

Chapter 7

After finding one of the maintenance crew to help clean up the mess in the wine room, Nikki headed back to the cottage. She took the charm from her pocket, fingering it, then tucked it away inside her travel bag.

She kept coming back to the theory that she and Derek had discussed before her scare in the wine-tasting room. Nikki refused to believe that Derek had any part in the murder or anything else that had gone on since she'd been at the vineyard. What she couldn't shake from her head was the idea that Gabriel had made an enemy of Andrés Fernandez, and why. She looked at a map of Napa Valley that was hanging in the living area of the cottage.

Spaniards' Crest was only a mile away. Good. She'd kill two birds with one stone. She'd clear her head by taking a run down to Spaniards' Crest Estate. Hopefully Andrés Fernandez would be around and willing to talk with her.

"Okay, Oliver, I'm going to need some backup. You game?" The dog cocked his head to the side. "How about this, then? You wanna go? Wanna go for a run?" These particular words elicited a response, as Oliver did a dog dance with a twirl that Nikki assumed meant "yippee, let's go."

A few minutes after donning a pair of shorts and a T-shirt, with Oliver frolicking beside her, she set out for Spaniards' Crest Estate. It was almost two o'clock, and the air was cool in the early-November afternoon. The sun shone through a small section of clouds and beat down on the blacktop, reflecting some warmth. The beauty of the surrounding area continued to amaze her as it had the day before. The autumn colors of olive, sienna, and rust weaved together like silken threads within an intricate tapestry. Awe-inspiring and breathtaking in its glory, so much so that Nikki almost forgot where she was headed and why, until she spotted the sign in front of the Spaniards' Crest Estate.

Spaniards' Crest was far less assuming than the mega-glamour of Malveaux Estate. Oaks and evergreens bordered the extended drive leading up to the Mission-style winery and estate home. Arches with fuchsia-colored bougainvillea growing tall and spreading across the adobe-tiled rooftops opened out into what looked to be a patio area. The baritone voices of the Gypsy Kings singing one of their Spanish melodies echoed through the covered arched hallway.

Nikki scanned the vineyard, seeing a handful of workers spread throughout the vines. Someone cranked up a tractor in the distance. She thought her best bet was to walk toward the patio where the music was coming from.

Oliver followed at her heels up a set of brick steps and onto the patio. A dark-haired man in a plaid shirt and jeans was seated at a picnic table with his back turned toward Nikki. He was speaking into a cell phone, and the way his free arm was waving wildly, she bet that he wasn't having a pleasant conversation. "I know," he replied in a Spanish accent. "I was in Spain. I was unable to get the contracts dealt with. I have a problem here. I need to have these grapes harvested. Fine. Call me back." He shut the phone and mumbled something in his native tongue that she was sure wasn't a nicety.

"Excuse me," Nikki said.

His head snapped up, and he turned around to face her. His plaid shirt was open and exposed a sleeveless under-shirt that didn't hide the fact that the man was built.

"I'm sorry, I didn't mean to startle you." She stretched out her hand. "Hi. I'm Nikki Sands. I'm looking for Andrés Fernandez."

He sat up straight. Nikki couldn't help but notice his re-markable looks. Hazel eyes framed by a thick fringe of eyelashes, an angular face, his high cheekbones reddened by the sun, and a small beauty mark high on his right cheekbone. One thing Napa Valley wasn't lacking, besides a plethora of grapes and fancy estates, was handsome men.

"That would be me. What can I do for you?" He faced back around at a bizarre glass instrument on top of the pic-nic table, sounding as if he had no interest in her.

Nikki knew she was going to have to try and give one heck of a performance, because she sensed that Andrés wasn't the trusting type from the get-go. "I'm here with a new wine magazine coming out called," she paused and cleared her throat, "excuse me, something caught in my throat, anyway the magazine is called the *Vine Times*, and I'm writing a story about the winemakers here in Napa Valley."

He frowned. "In jogging shorts and with a dog? Don't you people usually call when doing a story?"

"Yes, we do. But you see, I was out on a jog, and I passed by your winery here, and thought since you were on my list to talk to, I'd see if I could at least stop in and say hi, maybe set up an appointment." She studied him, shift-ing her weight from one foot to the other.

"Hi," he replied sarcastically. He crossed his arms in front of him. "Nice Ridgeback." He motioned to Oliver.

"Yes, he is a really good dog."

"Your dog?"

Nikki nodded. "Sort of, kind of. Yeah. A friend gave him to me."

"A friend? Nice friend. Expensive dog." He smiled. "Not too many Ridgebacks around. There are a few Mastiffs, a couple of Dobies up the way, but I only know one Ridgeback here in Napa Valley." Andrés pulled a pair of sunglasses from his shirt pocket and put them on. "Why don't you tell me the truth, Miss Sands?"

"What do you mean?"

Andrés pointed to Oliver. "I only live a mile away from Malveaux. I've even returned that dog back to their place a time or two. You're not a reporter. This *is* a small valley."

"Can I have a seat?" She motioned to the picnic table.

He shrugged. She sat down by him. "You didn't buy any of that, huh?"

"Not even if you didn't have the dog, but he makes it obvious."

"And to think I'm an actress, or I used to be."

"Not a very good one." He turned back to what looked to be a science experiment on top of the wooden table. It was a piece of blown glass with a bulbous bottom and narrow stem. Liquid flowed down to the bottom and pushed the scaled numbers on the narrow part of the tube upward. Nikki suddenly realized what it was—a hydrometer used to measure the amount of sugar in must or wine. The instrument allows the winemaker to predict and adjust his recipe depending on the readings taken. She remembered reading about hydrometers in one of her wine books at home, but she'd never seen one.

"Ouch. Thanks. That's why I said 'used to be.'"

"Alright, Charlize Theron. By the way, how do I even know that your real name is Nikki Sands?" He waved a hand at her. "It doesn't matter. What do you want, and why are you making up stories to get at what you want?"

She crossed her legs and held her head up high, flicking hair that had fallen from her ponytail out of her face. She looked pointedly at him, deciding total confidence would be the only possible way of getting to this man. "I'm considering taking a job with Malveaux."

"How nice for you."

"I'll be honest with you. I'm the one who found Gabriel Asanti murdered."

"Great. Did Malveaux send you here as some private investigator? Because I already spoke with the police. I didn't care for Gabriel, but I didn't kill him."

"I'm not a P.I., but I am curious, and I thought I'd get an outsider's perspective of Malveaux Estate and the folks there, plus Gabriel's murder has me shaken up."

"So you come talk to me?"

"Why not? I've heard all the rose-colored-glasses stuff from Derek Malveaux, now I want to hear if there's any dirt. I don't want to make a bad decision. I'm considering uprooting from L.A. and leaving family behind. This is a big deal for me. I wouldn't have thought twice about taking the job before this murder, but now . . ." Half-truths were not half lies, but half-truths. From the look on his face, her acting had improved, because he stopped looking at her with darkened suspicion.

"Working for Malveaux is fine, I suppose, if you view making wine as only a business deal."

"What do you mean?"

"Maybe I shouldn't be so harsh on Derek Malveaux, because I believe he's tried through the years to maintain what his father started. I think Gabriel Asanti brainwashed him and the rest of the world into thinking his wines were a cut above the rest."

"Are you saying they're not? The man has won tons of awards. I've tasted his wines. They're delicious."

"The taste is good, I suppose. It's the attitude that Gabriel had that angered me. Wine is not supposed to be about how much and how many. Dollars and cents, awards and kudos. That's all Gabriel cared about. He didn't appreciate the art form. He didn't understand the beauty of the culture."

Andrés was proving to be not only a recluse, but maybe a bit eccentric, too. "I'm not totally sure I understand."

"How could you? Are you a farmer? Do you grow grapes? I would guess, no. You're someone who sees dirt, soil, as messy, filthy."

"You don't know what I think." *Wasn't dirt dirty?* Did someone know something Nikki didn't, because she'd been called dirt as a kid, and it hadn't been used in a nice way.

"Making wine starts from the soil. It's like a painting. The soil is the canvas. The roots of the grape vine are like a paintbrush. The grape grower, winemaker, all of us on the land here are the painters. Our product should be about divine taste and art and culture. The greatest miracle-maker of all turned *water* into wine. Need I say more? Someone like Gabriel comes along with his big-business attitude, and he dilutes the art."

There was some definite deep-seated resentment going on within Andrés toward Gabriel. "I see. Gabriel didn't take what he did seriously?"

"No." He shook his head and grimaced. "The irony is that he won awards, he is known, he's a superstar, when he doesn't deserve to be."

"Do you think you deserve to be?"

He didn't respond right away. Nikki shifted uneasily. "I am a man, Miss Sands. Therefore, I do have an ego. I can't say in all honesty that I don't think I shouldn't be a recipient of certain awards or cheers from the sommeliers and oenophiles around the world. That would be a lie. However, my ego isn't about money or even myself, but about maintaining what I do as the art form it's always been."

"Big wine business has been around for years. Why the beef with Gabriel? Why Malveaux?"

"I don't know. Maybe because they're the biggest, or maybe it's because Gabriel Asanti liked to throw all of his accomplishments in my face." He took his glasses off and adjusted them.

"That would be upsetting." She wasn't totally buying

his reasons. There was something else going on behind those eyes as to why Andrés didn't like Gabriel.

"Yes." He turned toward his uncompleted task. "I think we're done here."

"Right. Thanks."

"By the way, Detective Martini. . . ." He winked at her. "I think you'll be fine working with Malveaux. Derek himself is a nice guy, but the rest of them are a bunch of lunatics."

"You called me Detective Martini."

"Yeah, I'm a bit of an actor, oops, I mean liar myself. The dog didn't give you away. There's a handful of Ridgebacks in the area. They make good watchdogs. I saw your show a few times. You weren't really that bad. Also, gossip travels fast around here. Apparently, there's a certain policewoman who's a bit starstruck with you." He smiled at her. "I've got business in town. See you around. If you decide to take the job, come down and we'll celebrate with a *really* good bottle of wine."

Nikki's body grew warm as embarrassment filled every nerve ending, and she was at a loss for words. Before she could open her mouth again, Andrés stood up and walked inside the winery. Shaking off the feeling, Nikki started running, Oliver staying in line with her. When she hit Highway 29, she realized she'd forgotten to ask Andrés one more question. She wanted to know where he'd been the other day about the time Nikki spotted the disturbance in the bushes over by the pond. She turned around to question him about it.

Cresting the top of the hill and heading back toward the winery, she heard a car engine start on the backside of the vineyard. She watched, out of breath, mouth open as Andrés sped down the dirt road toward the highway. He apparently hadn't seen her coming back up the hill.

Nikki hung her head and sighed. The rest of her questions for Andrés Fernandez would have to wait.

Chapter 8

Nikki had quite a bit to think about. Her scare in the tasting room, which led to the discovery of the charm, and now the bizarre conversation she'd had with Andrés that only led her to more unanswered questions, confusing her. Oddly enough it also set her adrenaline to pumping, as if she was onto something and it was exciting, in a weird way. She still had plenty of energy and a little time to kill, and as Oliver was still hanging in with her, she continued on her run after reaching the Malveaux property.

Rounding the pond, Nikki was suddenly aware of the morbidity that now surrounded the serene area and decided to take a rest. The Muscovy ducks that were in the pond yesterday, before they were scared away by the killer, had returned. They took to the sky as she approached. She thought about jogging by the site where she'd first discovered Gabriel. Maybe she'd missed something. Who was she kidding? Miss something? She wasn't Nancy Drew. Hell, she wasn't even Detective Martini from her defunct TV show. And even if she *had* missed something, the cops certainly hadn't. They'd done their job. They'd been out there for hours. It was one of the reasons she'd fallen asleep so easily the previous night, because she knew Jeanine and another officer were still combing the area when Derek dropped her off.

But Nancy Drew or not, she once again went against her better judgment and coaxed Oliver along with her. He followed at her side as she headed back into the deep brush and twigs, again getting scraped and scratched, but driven all the same. She was careful, especially with Oliver at her side, to walk around the perimeter of the yellow police tape. She didn't want to corrupt the crime scene in any way.

Nikki hadn't a clue what she was looking for, only a morbid sense of curiosity. She sat down on a log outside the taped-off area. Oliver flopped down at her feet. Having him there was calming, and the spot would've been glorious if someone hadn't been killed there only the day before. Something about wanting to enjoy the serenity and the beauty didn't seem right to Nikki. More than that, though, something wasn't right about the theory that Gabriel had been killed at this location.

Nikki watched the ripples across the pond, and the sunlight cast shadows around the area where the oak trees grew tall and thick. Then, it hit her what wasn't right about Gabriel being murdered at this spot. She forced herself to picture him again in her mind—swollen purple face, crusted-over eyes, and matted hair. Gabriel had been dead far longer than mere minutes when she'd found him. He'd have to have been dead for quite a few hours, maybe even a day. She'd learned enough from Aunt Cara to know the states a decomposing body goes through. And when her bare foot had grazed his hand, his body temperature had been cold. The police had to know this information, and Nikki knew she should really leave it up to them to figure it all out, but maybe it was simple curiosity, or maybe some of Aunt Cara's influence had rubbed off on her. Whatever it was, Nikki couldn't help but be intrigued by the mystery of it all, and she had a strong desire to figure this thing out.

She smacked herself in the forehead. Oliver lifted his

head and whined. "Don't you worry. I may be slow at times, but when I get cooking, I start to sizzle. All we have to do, Ollie—you don't mind if I call you Ollie, do you?" Oliver nuzzled her free hand. "Good. The next thing we have to do, Ollie, is find out exactly where Gabriel was killed, and how someone was able to drag him here. What is close enough, a place where other people on the vineyard wouldn't notice someone unloading a dead body?" She turned her head from side to side, scanning the entire area, until she focused on what was exactly across from her, and large enough to block someone's view—Derek's house.

Yikes. She didn't like that one bit. Okay, there was no way Derek killed Gabriel. She'd already decided to her own satisfaction that he was a good guy. He hadn't been watching her from the stockroom, and he certainly hadn't murdered his winemaker. No way on earth. If Derek's place was the scene of the crime, then maybe someone had killed Gabriel and hidden the body in Derek's garage. *Oh, yeah, no garage. But wait a minute.* Nikki's eyes focused on what appeared to be a small toolshed, big enough for a body to be stored in, maybe even murdered in, off to the left of the house. *Could the murderer have killed Gabriel in that shed?*

"C'mon, Ollie." Nikki jumped to her feet and sprinted over to the shed. Ollie outran her and headed for Derek's porch, until she whistled for him. The dog bounced back to her side. Nikki quickly scanned the area and didn't see Derek's Range Rover or signs of anyone else. Even though she knew in her gut that Derek wasn't the killer, he might not approve of her snooping around.

She pulled open the door of the shed. It screeched, like fingernails on a chalkboard. There was nothing unusual inside, just some tools and a lot of dust bunnies. There was a spiderweb that looked like it had been there for years, and way in the back there were a couple of rows of wine racks. She walked over to them and noticed that for the most part they were dusty, and a few even had remnants of a dangling spiderweb. She did notice that one bottle in the middle of a neatly organized row was missing, and thought that was kind of odd. A few other bottles looked as if they'd recently been fingered and turned around, maybe pulled out of their spot and the label read.

She walked over to the other side of the shed, rummaging around the wooden planklike table top that at one time could've easily been an area for someone to play fix-it man. "Hoo, hoo, hoo," Nikki said aloud. Ollie cocked his head. She glanced down at him. "What do we have here?" She picked up an opened pack of cigarettes. Benson and Hedges Menthol. *Wonder who smokes the ciggies?* Nikki turned the pack over. She brought it up to her nose, smelling the tobacco inside. A couple of the cigarettes were gone. By the look of the pack, Nikki figured they weren't that old. She wasn't a smoker, but it wasn't a difficult assumption to make.

After scanning the area of the shed further to see if she'd missed anything, Nikki decided to put the pack of cigarettes back where she found them. She couldn't help being curious about who they might belong to. Maybe whoever the smoker was, could also be the killer. Maybe whoever that person was came to the shed to plot, or had a smoke to ease their nerves after murdering Gabriel. Or they could've even hidden his body inside the shed until they could think of where to put it. It was something to consider.

She felt pretty smug with herself after her day at detecting. There was indeed, the possibility that it would all lead to nothing—the charm, her talk with Andrés, and now the pack of cigarettes. Or, the thought stuck in her mind that all of these little things could add up and lead to something or someone, and that someone could be a murderer. Nikki had the distinct feeling that she was getting in over her head, but she also didn't want to go to the cops, not yet anyway. She was sure it wouldn't be in her best interest if the police knew she'd been semi-conducting a private investigation on her own. Nikki knew that Carolyn Keene would be proud of her, as she thought fondly of Nancy Drew in her favorite in the series-*Number 49—The Secret of Mirror Bay*. Aunt Cara on the other hand might not be so proud of Nikki if she knew what she was up to.

Nikki checked her watch and saw that it was closing in on the four o'clock hour. She was short on time, as Derek wanted to meet her around four-thirty. She'd have to put her detective hat away and go on to Derek's, but first she wanted to finish her run, because she wasn't willing to cheat herself out of any of the food that evening.

She trotted onto one of the side roads, hearing her own heartbeat and the pounding of her feet against the dirt, almost in sync with one another, as her mind went over the events of the past twenty-four hours.

A big gust of wind blew dirt up to the left of her, several hundred yards away, startling and distracting her. Out of the dust came a red jeep, speeding down the dirt road, headed straight for her. It pulled up next to her, with two women as its passengers. One was probably in her mid to late twenties, with dark hair, eyes of the same color, and lips so full of collagen, Nikki had the urge to touch her own. The other woman was a redhead, mid-fifties, light green eyes, and attractive in an artificial way. They'd both spent some money on quite a bit of plastic surgery.

"You must be the latest," the younger one said.

"Excuse me?" Nikki replied, out of breath.

"Derek's. You must be his newest conquest," the redhead said.

"What?"

The younger one turned to her counterpart and commented, "She's good. Coy. He likes that."

"Mmhmm. Blonde, too. Must be from L.A." She shook her head in an exaggerated fashion. "You'll wise up. They all do. You've heard about the murder, haven't you?"

"She's the one who found poor Gabriel."

"Excuse me, but who are you, and what are you talking about?" Nikki asked.

"You don't have to pretend with us, sweetie. Derek's got

deep pockets. Anyone can see that. But he's also got some serious charisma, and some other nice assets." The woman winked at her. "Just when you think you're getting close to the payoff, you start to fall for those baby blues and those nice strong abs, and wham-bam-thank-you-ma'am."

"It's not pretty. He can turn women into putty," the older one added. "And, he's had plenty to do it to."

"Maybe he turned Gabriel into putty, too. That best-friends act of his was only a ruse. I should know. We women need to stick together, which is why we thought we'd give you a bit of a warning about Derek. He's not all that he pretends to be. So watch your step, because he'll love you and leave you, like that." The younger of the nip-and-tuck duo snapped her fingers together.

"Well, I'm sure we'll see you tonight. Look at the time, Meredith. Gotta go, sweetie."

The woman driving turned the car around and pressed down on the gas, leaving Nikki in a cloud of dust. She closed her eyes. When she opened them, the dust was clearing. "What the hell was that?" she said to herself.

She decided to go to Derek's house and see if he'd returned yet. She'd been running for almost forty minutes. It was nearly four-thirty, the time that he'd asked her to check in with him. She needed that glass of wine he'd promised right about now.

"What happened to you?" he asked as she jogged up to him. He stood on his porch as the sun started to descend.

"Don't ask," she replied, dusting herself off. Ollie came up next to her, panting. He quickly found his water bowl, half of which he lapped up, splashing the rest onto the porch.

A loud squeal followed by a hoop and holler came from the jeep as they spun out on the dirt road closest to Derek's place and went flying past them at an even higher speed.

"Don't you get it? She met the Botox buddies," a young, prim woman remarked walking out onto the porch, a note-book in hand. She wore glasses and looked every bit the li-brarian with her severe chin-length page boy. She stuck her ivory-colored hand out to shake Nikki's. "I'm Minnie Lark. I'm the accountant here at Malveaux. Derek tells me you're considering a job with us."

"I am." Minnie definitely moisturized. Her hands were silky soft, and that complexion was perfect. Not even a damn blackhead or enlarged pore. Nikki wondered for a second what her skin-care regimen consisted of. She'd have to ask later.

"Great. We'll have to talk, because you'll be working closely with me. I know Derek has told you about our suspicions concerning certain portions of the books. He says that you have good instincts. Maybe together we can figure out the cash-flow leak. It'll be good to have you here. Maybe the boss will give me time off to go on a Tuscan holiday."

"Only if you promise to come back. I don't want you buying a villa like that woman in the movie," Derek said.

"Like in *Under the Tuscan Sun*?" Nikki asked.

"Exactly. You never know, I just may up and relocate there and fix up my *own* villa. The book inspired me, and the movie, well, the scenery alone is to die for. Did you see the movie, Nikki?"

"Actually, no," Nikki replied, hating to admit that she hadn't, not wanting to see Diane Lane play a part she'd tried out for and bombed at. "I'd like to, though." Now that her green-eyed monster had been tamed and she'd accepted the fact that an Academy Award was not in the cards for her.

"I better get a move on if I'm going to be ready for tonight's benefit. I'm also making the preparations for Gabriel's memorial service on Tuesday. Did you want to use our usual caterers?" Minnie asked Derek.

"That's fine. It'd be too large for the bistro to handle."

As Minnie started down the steps, she turned back to Nikki. "Don't worry about those two in the jeep. They're harmless. They've both had so much plastic surgery, the anesthesia has killed off whatever brain cells they had left after all the alcohol they've put away."

Nikki couldn't help but laugh. "Thanks." She watched as Minnie got behind the wheel of her Nissan Maxima. "She's very nice. I'm relieved to come across someone normal around here. Besides you, that is."

This time, Derek laughed.

Nikki tucked some fallen strands from her ponytail back behind her ears. "I've pretty much made up my mind. I'd like nothing more than to catch the. . . . What did she call them?" Nikki pointed to the dirt road, where only minutes before, the red jeep had sped by.

"The Botox buddies."

"Right. I'd really relish catching the Botox buddies doing something dastardly."

"I'd relish that myself," Derek replied. "Yes, that's our pet name for my stepmother, Patrice, and my ex-wife, Meredith. Believe me, though, I have a few other names for them."

"I'm sure. I came up with one or two myself. So, that's your ex-wife, huh?"

"Yeah, that she is. Hey, you know, it's been a hard day, and tonight is probably going to be very long, too. How about we open a bottle of wine and take a walk? I'll tell you all about this crazy place and the bizarre family who—against my wishes—resides here. You should be prepared, anyway."

"They don't live in the main house, do they?"

"Afraid so. Remember how you asked why I lived here, and not at the big house?"

"Because they live in the big house?"

"Them, and the rest of the hangers-on."

"Wow. Why, though? If the winery is yours, what are they doing hanging around?"

"When my dad died he left the largest portion of the winery and vineyard to me. He left the other half to be divided between my half brother and stepmother. However, he left the house to my stepmother. Believe me, if I could, I'd have them all carted off. Instead, I've learned to bite my tongue, and respect my dad's wishes. I love this vineyard, and I refuse to let them push me out of here. He left me something worth more than the house."

"What's that?"

"A tremendous wine collection, along with my mother's diamond from her engagement ring. They're both worth more to me than the house. After having the entire crew living there tainting it, I would have to demolish it and re-build before I could ever live up there."

"That's a shame."

"Not everything is fair in life," he replied. "Come on, Oliver, let's go for a walk."

Oliver didn't even open his eyes. "Let me try. C'mon, Ollie, let's go." Nikki slapped her hand against her leg. Ollie lifted his head and flopped it back down. The poor dog was exhausted from keeping up with Nikki.

"At least he responded to you."

"I think he likes his new nickname."

"Nah, I think he likes you. Who could blame him? I'll go grab our wine." He returned a few minutes later with plastic wine glasses, filled with an oaky-flavored Chardon-nay. "Full-bodied," Derek said. Nikki knew she was blush-ing, and realized that he'd noticed when he said, "I mean the wine."

"Of course you mean the wine," she replied.

"I mean you, too, but . . ." Now he was the one blushing. They both started laughing, releasing all their tensions. "Ready for that walk?"

"And that talk."

The setting was perfect for a walk with a charming man—rolling hills of grape vines, separated by rows of colored earth in variations of brown, ranging from terra-cotta to deep chocolate. With the sun continuing to make its descent, a light mist came over the valley, mixing in with the pastels already blanketing the area. Everything re-sembled a Monet watercolor.

Nikki liked it that Derek genuinely wanted to educate

her about wines. They walked for a bit, comfortable together in the peace and quiet, except for the sound of their footsteps on the bare earth.

Derek broke the silence. "How was your day? What did you do after I left?"

She shrugged, not sure if she was ready or up to revealing all the aspects of her day yet. She put her free hand inside her shorts pocket. The idea of organizing her thoughts before rambling on about what she'd been up to throughout the day was probably the best course of action here. Besides, she really wanted to get to know Derek a little better. "Not much. I went for a run, took in some sights. You know, it was a pretty easygoing day. I'm more interested in your sordid tale, and don't leave out any of the details."

"You sure?"

"Sure about what I did today, or sure about wanting to hear about your nutty family?"

"The latter." He arched his eyebrows at her and gave her a bemused look.

"Of course I'm sure," she replied, relieved that he wasn't going to pressure her or doubt her about what she'd done earlier that day.

"Take notes. I might give you a pop quiz later." He winked at her.

Her stomach did that flutter thing, then sent the willies all over, but the good kind. This man was going to be frustrating as all get out.

"Meredith and I were happily married for only a year."

"Unlucky in love. What happened?"

"She's not the faithful type. I took a business trip, and Meredith was convinced that I was messing around and decided to even the score. Crazy thing was, screwing around on my wife was the last thing I was interested in doing. I was truly taking care of business, trying to make the money that kept her in Tiffany jewels and designer clothes."

"Not good."

"It gets worse. Today, the police chief informed me that

there are rumors floating around, about Meredith and Gabriel."

"What do you think about that?"

"I don't. I knew Gabriel well enough, better than anyone else did. At least I think I did, enough to know that he'd never do that to me. I refuse to believe it. Maybe other men's wives, but not with mine."

"I take it you've become a suspect in the investigation."

He nodded but didn't say anything, and then took a long drink of his wine. "I don't know what to think. Those rumors have been around for some time, but Gabriel denied them, and I can't fathom him lying to me. The chief also said that Cal Sumner, one of my competitors, had been trying to lure him away, and that Gabriel was tempted."

"Getting sticky, isn't it?" She swirled the golden contents in her glass.

"You haven't heard it all. Chief Horn says that someone may be trying to set me up for Gabriel's murder. For what reason? I don't know. I've run a few scenarios through my brain, even considering my half brother or stepmother as suspects. But neither one of them is smart enough to commit murder. They're a part of the whack pack up at the mansion, but killers? I can't see it."

"What about other winery owners, or a distributor? Someone you do business with? It could be someone jealous of your success, like we discussed before, of how big the Malveaux name is in the wine industry." Nikki's mind flashed on Andrés' face. Could he have had resentful feelings not only toward Gabriel, but Derek, too? He spoke strongly of his belief about winemaking being an art. Could he want to bring down everyone involved with Malveaux Estate? Andrés was eccentric, yes, but crazy? Nikki wasn't certain yet.

"I'm sure somewhere along the line I've angered a few folks, but nothing stands out. People are funny, though. You never really know what makes them tick, or gets their goat. It concerns me that the chief could consider a setup a possibility. He warned me to watch my back."

"That's probably the first intelligent thing the chief has said to you. I think he could be right about that. There's something I need to tell you." Nikki proceeded to tell him about her experience in the tasting room, keeping her find of the charm to herself, thinking that was safe. She wanted to get his reaction, see if there was something he was hiding. Then maybe she could put any doubts about him out of her head.

"Are you all right?" he asked, sounding truly concerned. They stopped walking. He placed his hands on her shoulders and rubbed her arms.

All doubts vanished when she looked in his eyes.

"Sure. I was shaken up, but I'm fine. I was thinking that whoever was in that room watching me, perhaps was a threat to me. But now that you mention someone setting you up, I think that maybe somebody is following you, and couldn't get out fast enough to stay on your heels when you left me in the tasting room. Or, whoever it was wants to figure out who I am. They may have seen me cruising around here with you."

"If someone is setting me up, then you could also be in danger. They might try to use you to get to me," he noted.

That was a thought she did not want to entertain. "I suppose," she reluctantly admitted.

"You suppose? Nikki, I don't want you in any danger. I certainly don't want to be the cause of any harm to you. I'm sure I can get Chief Horn to let you go on back to L.A. We can discuss a job position when this thing dies down. Bad choice of words, but you know what I mean. I can even give you an advance on your salary, as a good-faith incentive."

Nikki took his hands from her arms, squeezing them. An electrical charge traveled through her as she stood there in the open vineyard holding Derek's hands. "Nope, and no way. I'm not leaving. I want this job, and I want it now. If you're in trouble, I'm going to help. You asked me to join you here for a few reasons. You need a good assistant, someone who can help manage the place. You need someone to look after your best interests, and to figure out if you're being cheated. I am your woman." The strength in her commitment amazed even Nikki. "I have to tell you, no one has ever treated me as kindly as you have. The other night, you could have done what others might have, join your date in ridiculing me, or just ignore me. But not only did you give her the boot, you tracked me down and apologized. You have a heart, and I like that about you. I'm not going anywhere, boss." She heard the twang in her voice that can only come somewhere from the Deep South, and for once it didn't really bother her.

"Are you for real?" he asked.

"I am."

"Okay, then. We may have to work out some new sleeping arrangements, if we're both possible targets."

"What did you have in mind?"

"I was thinking about moving you into the big house. I know I mentioned my thoughts on my stepmother and half brother, but I really think they're harmless. Whoever planned this is smarter than they are. There's a security alarm and so many people there, it would be awfully hard for anyone to hurt you."

"Oh." She couldn't help but hear the disappointment in her own voice. What had she expected? Hey, baby, join me in my pad, and we'll hide out under the covers from the bad guys?

"I know it's sending you into the snake pit, but I do think you'll be safer. Just to piss everyone off, I'll send you up there with Ollie. Simon and Patrice are both allergic to animals."

"Then who will protect you?"

"I've got a gun right next to my bed, under lock and key."

"Reasonable enough." But why couldn't he have said, "Blondie, it's you, me, and the Colt .45 waiting it out— together." Wanting to change the subject and her lustful focus, she said, "Whatever you think is best. So, tell me about your dad."

"My dad was the king in this industry. But it also brought him a lot of heartache. We lost my mother when I was seven. The vineyard had produced a few bad crops, and then there was a year when the frost got us. We also had some problems with phylloxera many years ago. It wiped out many of the vineyards here, and it cost a fortune to get things going again for everyone in the valley."

"Phylloxera?"

"It's a grape louse, one of the grapevine's worst enemies. It will eventually kill the entire plant. An epidemic infestation came close to destroying all the vineyards in Europe back in the 1870s."

"Then how did it become a problem here in the 'eighties?" Nikki asked.

"The pest is native to the U.S. However, the grapevines that were grown naturally here were resistant to the louse. Some East Coast grape-growers unknowingly shipped infested vines to France. The French grapes were grafted and imported back to the United States. Grape-growers take precautions to prevent phylloxera, but once you have it, it's like an incurable disease."

"Sounds horrible. What did your dad do?"

"He grasped for the goose with the golden egg. Her name is Patrice. She bailed him out of trouble, but then, after he rebuilt this place and earned millions of dollars more than it took to help him out, she nagged him for the next twenty-something years until his heart finally gave out. Personally, I think he couldn't wait to see my mother again. They had quite a love affair until she became sick. Even through her illness, he did the best he could for her. He doted on her." Derek finished off his wine.

"But Patrice is a totally different person than my mother," he continued. "She gave my dad nothing but grief and a sniveling, spoiled brat of a son who never appreciated how hard Dad worked.

"He always treated me a lot more like an adult than a kid, confiding everything in me, for the most part. He even saved me from boarding school after a few years. Patrice started sending me away each August to some stuffy boarding school back East with the belief system that children were to be seen, not heard unless called upon. When the winery started to make a profit, my dad put a stop to her sending me away. Then along came Simon to take her focus away from controlling me. Poor Simon. Guess he wasn't what she'd hoped for. Serves her right." He looked away forlornly and then back at Nikki. "You know, I'm not even sure what it's like to be a kid. But you get over that stuff, I suppose."

"I wonder if you really do." Nikki heard the melancholy in her voice and hoped he didn't realize that it was coming from her own memories.

"I suppose my dad must have loved Patrice to a degree, or he wouldn't have been so generous with his will and stayed with her, but I think there was some guilt factor at work there."

"Because she'd bailed him out way back when."

"Exactly. I don't believe that Dad ever had a real close relationship with anyone after my mom passed away. And, honestly, I have to wonder if I'm not following in his footsteps."

"You can't be serious," she replied, beginning to understand the mystery of this man.

"I don't know. Things sure went wrong with Meredith. I don't know if I ever want to travel that path again. Apparently, she's got her eye on Cal Sumner."

"The same one who was trying to lure Gabriel away from you?"

"Supposedly so. I don't believe that. Cal has tried hard to get Gabriel to come to work for him, but he doesn't have much to offer. Frankly, I'm surprised at Meredith's interest. Sumner isn't the wealthiest boy in town. Nice guy, though. Can't blame him for trying to steal my winemaker. He and I have even joked about it together. He's not the first vineyard owner in the valley to do so. I hope Meredith doesn't get her hooks into him. The poor man will be ruined."

"If that's the case, why does she continue hanging out

here? Why not move out? She must have some cash from the divorce settlement. What does she get out of being here?"

"She'd like more, and she says that the bistro is important to her, claiming it's her baby. Wait until she finds out that you're her new boss."

"She's going to love that."

"I don't care. We recently signed the divorce agreement, after fighting for a couple of years over it. I agreed to keep her on, but her attorney didn't read between the lines. My lawyer wrote in the final decree that Meredith could maintain her interest in the bistro, but it doesn't say that she is to manage it. I've allowed her to do so because it's never been a priority for me, until I started seeing the bottom line slip and got suspicious. I wish she wasn't a part of any of my businesses. And before you ask, no, I didn't have a prenuptial. At the time, I believed in everlasting love. Now I call myself stupid."

"Sounds more like jaded to me."

He laughed. "Anyway, Meredith would like to get a larger sum from me, but it's impossible. We weren't married long enough for her to collect alimony, and in this state, she can only get her hands on what I made during the year we were married, which I'm happy to say was the vineyard's worst year in the last five. So the joke's on her."

"I think I get it. She hangs out with Patrice, because Patrice owns part of the vineyard. She buddies up with Patrice because, maybe somewhere, there is a benefit to her."

"It's got to be something like that. What I don't get is what's in it for Patrice. And trust me, after knowing that woman for about thirty years, Patrice is always in it for something. Those two aren't Botox buddies because they love each other's company. They're up to something. I'd put money on it."

"You weren't kidding when you said it was like an insane asylum around here, were you?" And, now in some sordid way Nikki knew that she was contributing to it. She glanced down at her watch. "We'd better start back so I can clean up. Something tells me that workout attire covered in dust isn't exactly appropriate for the occasion."

"Why not? You'd make a scene. It'd be entertaining."

"Thanks, but no thanks. I don't think I want to be the butt of your evil step-mother's and her protégée's jokes."

"We'll head back in a sec. I want to show you something first."

They walked down a row of vines and stopped.

"These quadrants of grapes will be harvested and bottled next year, and sold in our first Syrah. I am so excited about this crop, I can't tell you how amazing it's going to be. Vineyards are usually noted for one type of wine they do really well, whether it's a Chardonnay or Merlot. It used to be, back in the day, that wineries did try to make as many varieties as possible. We do have a good collection here, but what I'm really working toward, is being known as the winery that produces big, bold reds.

"More and more, our reputation has been building with the reds, and we sell far more reds than whites. White wine became a big hit in the 'nineties because of the upswing of people watching their health, and nutrition starting to take priority here in America. People could pair the wine with fish or chicken. But now, the consumer realizes that red goes with everything. Like you did the other night. And folks aren't so intimidated by eating red meats anymore. Steak is in again, especially with Atkins and the surge in popularity of protein diets. It also hasn't hurt those of us who make red wines that the media has reported the positive health statistics among the French and other red-wine drinkers."

There was something endearing and childlike about his passion for his life's work. He reveled in it, enjoyed it. He walked the vines, and Nikki knew that at harvest, he was picking alongside his workers. However, Nikki could also see the difference in his philosophy in winemaking versus Andrés' concepts. Derek loved and appreciated it, but the bottom-line dollar and recognition was important to him too. It was still a passion for him, only slightly different from the way Andrés perceived it as a passion.

"I would really love to learn everything I can about the process, what makes one crop better than another. I know a lot about the bottled wines already out there, but the actual day-to-day stuff that goes on behind the scenes in making the wines really interests me."

"Good. If there's anything I love talking about, it's wine and the vines used to make wine." He turned his head for a second. "Wait a minute," he said, turning back to her. "Manuel, hey, Manuel," he called out.

A worker a hundred feet or so away waved at them. Derek took her by the hand, as they walked over to him. "Manuel, this is my friend Nikki Sands. She's going to be working with us."

Manuel was strong and muscular. Although he looked young from a distance, his face bore creases from what she assumed to be the sun and hard work. He was one of those people whose age you couldn't tell by looking at them. Somewhere within a twenty-year span, because, though he had a young man's body, he also exuded a sadness in his deep brown eyes. Life had been difficult for this man.

He took off his thick work glove and shook her hand, enveloping it in the largeness of his own. "Nice to meet you," he said in a thick Spanish accent.

"You, too."

Derek pulled him aside and said, "I've got a box of clothes for your children up at the house, if you want to stop by in the morning. I also found some toys and books I thought they might like."

"*Gracias, Señor*. You're too kind."

"Let me know if you could use anything else."

The man nodded. Although he sounded gracious, Nikki also recognized that look of swallowed pride. Taking a handout was a hard thing to do, but sometimes necessary. Manuel didn't look like it was something he enjoyed.

They started to walk back to the house, the fog drifting

deeper into the valley. Nikki hugged herself, a chill seeping into her.

Derek took off his navy pullover and handed it to her. "Put this on."

"Thanks." She took it, appreciative for it. She pulled it over her head and that same woodsy, cedar scent of his from the night before hit her. She breathed in deeply.

"Manuel lost his wife and youngest child last year in an accident. She was driving to the school to pick up their other two children, and it was raining. One of the trucks that haul wines from here to a distribution warehouse hit a slick spot and collided head-on with her. Manuel hasn't been the same since. I doubt he ever will be. Recovering from something like that is almost unimaginable."

She heard the emotion in his voice and wasn't sure how to respond. "That's terrible." An old memory stirred from within. She shoved it down. This was not about her trauma.

"It is," he whispered, nodding his head.

They walked the rest of the way in silence, reaching the guest cottage. She wanted to tell him about her thoughts on Gabriel, the charm, Andrés, and the pack of cigarettes she'd found in the shed, but her instinct, which was something she'd counted on from the time she was a little girl, told her to hold off. Besides, Derek had been through quite a bit of trauma himself, and she didn't know if any of it meant a thing, or if it was prudent to talk about Gabriel with him yet.

"Say an hour?" Derek asked.

"You got it." She went inside the bedroom of her quaint quarters and put the "best friends" charm in the side pocket of her travel bag. Then she headed into the bathroom, stripped down, and stepped into the shower, wanting to wash the day down the drain, except for the walk she'd taken with Derek.

The steaming water hit her, warming her bones. She couldn't help feeling anxious about seeing Derek again. And to think that only forty-eight hours ago she thought he was a man with one thing on his mind. He'd proven her wrong, and she couldn't help wishing that he hadn't.

Nikki needed to get it together. A man like Derek Malveaux would want nothing to do with the likes of her, if he knew the truth about her.

She sure wasn't a blueblood. Hell, who knew if she was even pureblood? That was always the insidious little joke in her house growing up, although she knew they all liked to tease her, because it got to her, and her family loved to get to her.

The memories that went along with her childhood could still sneak up on her and hurt, no matter how hard she tried to shove them down.

What she remembered about that day so many years ago: the smell of bourbon that permeated the air as she walked into the ramshackle house off the dirt road; the ugly pair of high-water jeans that she was wearing that were nothing like the Dittos all the little girls who lived in town wore; her shoes with holes at the end of them because they were hand-me-downs and too small at that. Everything Nikki wore was a hand-me-down. She was the youngest and by no means her dad's favorite, and therefore the last to ever get anything good, if anything at all.

"Where's your mama?" her dad asked her.

"I don't know, I just came from the school bus," she replied in her six-year-old voice. She wasn't happy about the bus ride because she was made fun of on the bus, as she was at home. The poorest of the lot in more ways than one.

"You don't know, huh?" He held a drink of what Nikki knew to be bourbon in one hand and a cigarette in the other. The remote to the TV was in his lap.

He sat slumped down in a chair covered in burn holes from the constant flow of cigarettes hanging from his hands and mouth. It always amazed Nikki that he never burned the place down. There'd been nights when she'd been afraid to go to bed with Mama off working at night, and Daddy watching TV through drunken eyes. Nikki couldn't remember the last time he ever worked, if he ever had.

"Well, I got me an idea where your mama is, and you know what, I'm gonna tell you," he said slurring his words.

Nikki never liked her dad much. Sometimes he was okay and would once in awhile read a story or play around with her and her brothers and sisters. He played more with them than with her. She had the distinct feeling that he didn't like her much, either. She made it a practice to keep out of his way. At least he didn't hit her like he did her mama. So many nights of screaming and pounding and heart-wrenching sobs. Nikki would try to comfort Mama after he'd pass out in his chair. She never understood why they all couldn't leave him behind. Nikki knew in her heart from the time she was a young child that none of it was right, and that there had to be a better way.

"Actually, kiddo, I'm gonna show you where your mama is."

He stood up and grabbed her by the hand, nearly yanking her arm out of its socket. She let out a small scream. Where were her brothers and sisters? They should be home soon. They were all older and went to the junior high or high school. She hated that she got home first. Maybe Penny, if she got home, would help her. She was the nicest one, and the only one who ever stood up to Daddy. She was tall, kind of round and almost as mean as he was, but Nikki knew that Penny sort of liked her. She hugged her sometimes.

"That hurt," she said in a quiet voice not wanting to make him madder than he was, because he was mad and she had no idea why. She was sure she hadn't done anything. He was mad at her mama, but he also seemed mad at her, too. But then, he always did seem mad at her.

He opened up the door of the Pinto, the rear end bashed in from one of his last ventures out. He shoved her into the front seat, slammed the door to the car, got behind the wheel, and cranked the engine. Before long they were bumping rapidly down the dirt road that led away from their two-bedroom house.

As they sped away she saw a group of five of her siblings walking home. They all watched, and she turned, trying to see their faces through the dirty windows of the car. Penny waved her hands frantically at them, but Daddy didn't stop. This could not be good.

"You know what, girl? I've been hanging on to this year after year, trying to do my best by all you kids, even you. But I get no thanks for being a decent father and husband. None," he roared.

Nikki recoiled in her seat, trying to get her legs up under her.

"You know where your mama is when she should be home tending to you? You don't mean nuthin' to her, and you don't mean nuthin' to me, and you definitely don't mean nuthin' to that fool she's been messing around with all these years, kiddo. That's your daddy." He weaved back and forth, in and out of his lane. The windows of the car were now down, blowing hot humid air through it. Her lungs burned. She wanted to cry but was too afraid. She didn't understand him and didn't want to. His words were too ugly for her.

"I put up with her and her cheating on me for years, 'cause I loved her. But no more. No more. Every time you come home from school, and I gotta look in those eyes of yours and know you ain't my kid, I about go crazy. You're just lucky you ain't no boy."

Nikki covered her ears.

"Game's up, kiddo. It is u—" He didn't finish the word, and Nikki opened her eyes for a split second. In that second she saw a blur of blue coming at them, and then nothing. When she woke up in the hospital, her father was dead. Her mother sent her off to L.A. right before her tenth birthday. She hadn't been back since.

Her mother had finally given her the gift of having a good life by sending her away to live with her Aunt Cara. Nikki had replaced her mother with her aunt, and was grateful every day for Aunt Cara. Without her love and care, and the offer to raise her, who knew where Nikki might've ended up. Aunt Cara had taken her in without batting an eye, and even though her job as a cop with the LAPD was time-consuming and stressful, she rarely missed any of Nikki's school events or anything major in her life. Yes, her aunt had always been there for her—a willing parent and friend.

Cara had been married once, before Nikki came to live with her, to another cop. He was killed in the line of duty, and her aunt sadly enough never remarried, or dated much for that matter. She'd always wanted a child, but during the five years she'd been married had been unable to get pregnant. So, as much as Cara filled that maternal void for Nikki, it was apparent that Nikki also filled a void for Cara. God, how she missed her, but this was her aunt's time, and with any luck maybe she would let loose, relax, and even, fingers crossed, find love again.

Nikki stepped out of the shower and dried off, shaking out the demons in her head. How had she made it? A huge part of it was because of Aunt Cara—one of the few sane ones in a long line of crazies.

She tried desperately to push those thoughts away as she slipped into her black dress. It did the trick, making her look sophisticated and showing enough cleavage to sexy her up some.

After applying a bit of nectar-colored lipstick, along with some blush across her cheeks and eyelids and a couple of coats of mascara, she figured she was as ready as she was going to be. Nikki shut the door to the guest cottage behind her and walked out into the chilly evening.

Chapter 9

Nikki tightened her black shawl around herself while waiting for Derek out on the front porch of the cottage to attend the evening's grand soiree.

"I like a lady who's on time," he said approaching the front steps, looking amazing in a charcoal suit, burgundy shirt, and tie. "And one who looks absolutely beautiful, I might add."

Her face and a few other areas warmed to the compliment. The strange day with its clues, weird interviews, and her hunches all vanished as Derek held out his arm, and she took it.

"Are you ready for this?" he asked.

"Are you kidding? I'm dying with anticipation."

"Let me assure you then, that if you've ever enjoyed a soap opera in your life, and I'm not admitting to anything here other than I did watch an episode or two of *Melrose Place* back in the day, before I turned a new leaf and took a hiatus from the tube, then what you're about to witness would put that show to shame."

"As I said, I can't wait. And, if what I experienced today

was a preview, well I'm certain this will be damn good. However, I'm curious about how you got mixed up with this crowd if they're as ludicrous as you say."

"What's the saying—you can't choose your family? In my case, I didn't choose half of these folks to be involved in my life. I am guilty of Meredith, that I will confess to." He sighed. "But love is blind."

"You are a man of clichés."

They laughed together. "That I am, my dear. Hopefully, you'll find that I am also a man of substance, or at least I like to think so."

They entered the old mansion that overlooked the vineyard. It was a Tudor straight out of the English countryside. Bach was being played quietly in the background through the house's sound system. The whole place oozed fancy-schmancy. Everything was done in dark woods, fabrics of damask and velvet in burgundy, gold, and hunter green. Apparently no one had told Derek's step-monster that 1992 was more than a decade past. Someone had spent a lot of money on decorating the house, but someone sure in heck needed to spend some money updating it. Still, the home was remarkable.

The architecture held true to its seventeenth-century English style, with all its charm and beauty, from high ceilings to stained glass windows, and even a turret that surrounded the staircase leading upstairs. "To live in a home like this, if you can call it a home—it's so amazing. God, how lucky," she said turning to Derek.

"It used to be. I haven't lived here since I was seventeen. That's when I went away to college. When I came back, I moved into the farmhouse. I couldn't live here. It'd be like *One Flew Over the Cuckoo's Nest*. Speaking of which, here comes one of the asylum inmates now."

She watched as Derek plastered on a phony smile for Botox buddy number one. This close up, and without dust in her eyes, Nikki could really get a good look at just how lavishly paid Patrice's plastic surgeon must have been. She made Joan Rivers look tame in comparison. Her low-cut black beaded dress showed off what one could only assume were a pair of store-bought boobs. A matching beaded purse hung from her shoulder.

Nikki crossed her arms in front of her, suddenly becoming very aware of her lack of haute couture and the fact that her bra size was a B cup, even with a Miracle Bra.

"Lovely you could make it, Derek," Patrice cooed.

He leaned in and coldly kissed his stepmother on the cheek. "Last time I checked, Patrice, I was the host. Let's play nice tonight and remember the reason we're all here is to battle leukemia."

"Yes," she said sounding rather snakelike as she placed a long emphasis on the *s*, her eyes darting around the room. "But I am allowing you to host it in *my* home. By the way, have you seen Meredith? She looks gorgeous, especially on Cal Sumner's arm. I'm so pleased she's found someone who can satisfy her." She leaned in to him and lowered her voice. "Maybe if you could've satisfied her, she wouldn't have wound up in another man's bed." She winked at Nikki, who looked away, unsure of exactly what to do.

"It's always a pleasure to see you," Derek replied, noticeably holding back his anger as his jaw clenched around his response.

"I think I'd like a drink, please," Nikki said, trying desperately to break the tension between them, and to get as far away as she could from the hideous woman.

"Of course she would like a drink." Patrice looked aghast at Derek. "Sometimes Derek forgets his manners. It's something I've worked on for years with him, but not even expensive boarding schools helped."

"Patrice Malveaux, this is Nikki Sands," Derek said with a nonchalant smile, remaining as cavalier as he could.

"Yes, Nicole, nice to formally meet you."

Nikki stifled a retort and instead smiled. "Nice to meet you, too, Patricia."

"Patrice, darling."

"I'm terribly sorry. Shall we get that drink now?" She

faced Derek, who hooked her arm as they walked away from the wretched hag's piercing eyes, which Nikki could almost feel burning a hole through her back. "I'm beginning to get the picture. Whew. That was ugly."

"That's nothing. She was just winding up."

Nikki glanced back over her shoulder at Derek's stepmother and caught her breath to see Patrice digging out a pack of Benson and Hedges from her purse. *The smoker.* Could Patrice also be the owner of the "best friends" charm? Nikki doubted it, fairly certain that Patrice's best friends were diamonds. Derek interrupted the thought process starting to roll in Nikki's head.

"Here, I want you to try this." He took a glass of white wine from one of the butler's trays. "This is our latest Sauvignon Blanc. It's a little young in my opinion, but it's fresh and tangy." Taking a pita-type appetizer from another tray, he thanked the waiter, calling him by name. "And it goes nicely with this appetizer," he said, handing her a pastry tart off the waiter's tray. "This is a recipe my pal Bob Hurley gave me. He owns one of my favorite restaurants around here. I'll have to take you there. This is a goat cheese and red onion tart with apple-smoked bacon. It's delicious. Bob's a great guy, so I asked him for the recipe. A lot of times at events we do here at the winery, I'll give the caterers my own recipes to prepare."

"Your recipes?" she asked, surprised. "Aren't you talented?"

"I don't know about that. I like to cook, and I learned a lot from my mom. She was a wonderful cook. In fact, when my folks had parties, she never allowed them to be catered." Nikki thought she saw him tear up, but the dim lighting made it hard to really tell. "She was funny that way. Fantastic cook, but when she was in a kitchen, or anywhere else for that matter, it was a disaster. Cooking she could do. Cleaning was not her thing. You know how you see characters on TV cooking with flour on their nose, and all over the place?"

Nikki nodded.

"That was my mom. She marched to her own drumbeat. I think that was why she was so special."

"You really miss her."

"More than anyone will ever know. We were really close, and that's why I do this each year, and stay as involved as I am in the foundation. Leukemia is a wretched disease. I want to do what I can to help find a cure. But tell you what, I don't really want to talk about it right now."

"I understand." Nikki wanted to help lighten things up for him, so she decided to talk about what he loved the most. "Pairing the wines can be pretty intricate at times," she commented.

"You should know. You've done a good job yourself suggesting pairings."

She liked the sound of that. "Thanks." They finished off their tarts and glasses of wine.

"Hey, there's Minnie." He pointed through a pair of French doors at the woman she'd met earlier. "It might be nice for you to acquire a perspective other than mine about the winery."

A twinge of guilt traveled through her with the knowledge that she'd already gotten another perspective on the winery from Andrés.

They stepped out onto the patio. The area was absolutely glamorous, like something from a movie set. Lanterns filled with candles illuminated the scene, and the scent of orange blossoms filled the air. A group of musicians played big-band music in the gazebo on the other side of a lap pool. The effect was from another era, and far different than the stuffiness in the interior of the mansion.

They walked toward Minnie, who smiled as they approached. "I really think that you'll like it here. As I explained earlier, I could use some help," she said, holding out her hand.

"While you two ladies chat, I'm going to head over to one of the bars and bring another wine for you to try. Minnie, anything for you?" Derek asked.

"If your hands aren't too full, I'll take whatever you bring out."

Nikki could be friends with this woman. She was warm, yet conservative enough to give off an air of respectability. Usually people like that intimidated Nikki; however, Minnie Lark did not.

"Sorry that you came here at such an awkward time. It's been horrific losing Gabriel, and then having to pull this party together. Usually, it's a mellow scene at the winery, minus all the misfits. I don't know how Derek does it, and is able to keep the gluttons at bay at the same time." Minnie nodded her head in the direction of a small cluster of people.

They included Patrice, who was puffing away on her cigarette, and Meredith, as well as a man Nikki assumed to be Cal Sumner. He had his arm around Meredith, and now she could see why Derek's ex was infatuated with the vineyard owner down the road. He looked a great deal like Johnny Depp, once again affirming Nikki's findings that the men occupying Napa Valley weren't passed over in the looks department. She didn't recognize the other two men, but they were quite a pair. Both handsome and dressed as if they'd stepped out of a Banana Republic ad, the dark-haired one clad in a white silk shirt and khaki pants, his counterpart wearing an olive-green silk shirt and black pants. Nikki thought that they were probably Simon, Derek's half brother and his partner, Marco.

As she watched the group, Minnie rattled on in her ear about the winery and the types of wines they produced, becoming noticeably quite tipsy. "Gabriel was great. I mean fantastic, you know. He was such a genius with the wines. I can't believe he's gone." Her eyes brimmed with tears.

"I take it that you knew him pretty well?" Nikki got the distinct feeling by the way the woman acted that Minnie knew Gabriel as more than just a friend.

She nodded and sucked back a deep sob, lowering her voice. "I did." Minnie looked down.

"Minnie, are you okay?"

"No one knows this. I don't even know why I'm telling you. I shouldn't tell you. I don't know you, but you seem like a nice person, and I have to talk to someone." Nikki gave her an encouraging nod. "Gabriel and I were lovers. We kept it under wraps because it's not always the best idea to mix love and work, if you know what I mean."

"I do."

"I'm sure Derek would've been fine with it, but it was kind of fun for us to have a *secret*. It seems silly now that he's gone. So do the dreams we shared. My idea of going to Tuscany was real. We talked about it one night after we watched *Under the Tuscan Sun* together at my place. Gabriel always wanted to go back to Italy. Get away from here, maybe have our own vineyard." A tear fell down her face.

Nikki touched her shoulder. "I'm so sorry. I can't believe that you're here tonight. Gosh. If there's anything I can do to help you through this, please let me know."

Minnie nodded. "Thank you." She brushed away her tears.

Nikki hesitated for a moment but figured there was no time like the present, since Minnie had been the one to open the door and let it all out. "I don't want to upset you, but do you have any idea as to who might have done this?"

Minnie looked away from her and out past the dance floor and gazebo. When she turned back to face her, tears had flooded her eyes again. For a second, Nikki was sorry she asked, until Minnie sighed and again nodded. She lowered her voice. "That's another reason why I'm feeling so horrible."

"What do you mean?" Nikki asked.

"I, uh, I have a friend, a dear friend. His name is Andrés Fernandez. He's a winemaker down the road, at Spaniards' Crest. He's a good listener, you know?"

Nikki nodded, not sure where this was going, but having a gut-wrenching feeling that it was going somewhere *good*. She didn't think it was a bright idea to let on to Minnie that she'd already heard Andrés name mentioned more than once in regard to Gabriel's murder, or the fact that she'd already had personal contact with the man. If Minnie knew this, she might change her mind about telling Nikki whatever it was she wanted to tell her.

"He and Gabriel didn't get along, and well, they went a few rounds more than once."

"You mean fighting?"

"They had a few yelling matches. I saw Andrés push Gabriel once, not that long ago at a party. Gabriel went to swing at him, but Andrés' sister tried to break it up. She actually wound up getting hit by Gabriel, accidentally, because she got in the way, and you can imagine Andrés' reaction. He pretty much vowed to *get him.*"

"What was the fight over?"

Minnie traced the rim of her wine glass and then took another large gulp before answering. "As much as I loved Gabriel, it was no secret to anyone that he was a womanizer. He tried to tell me that he was changing and he loved me, and you know men, all of that stuff. But, I knew that he loved beautiful women. And, Andrés' sister is a beautiful woman."

"Are you saying that Gabriel was also sleeping with Andrés' sister?" Man, did the guy get around or what?

"No. Isabel, that's Andrés' sister, wanted nothing to do with Gabriel. But, according to Andrés, who talked to me about the incident at the party, Gabriel would not leave Isabel alone. He'd call her, and when they'd run into each other around town, come on to her, and this really bothered Isabel, who complained to her big brother."

"Who reacted like most protective big brothers would."

"Exactly."

Aha! The key to the clue as to why Andrés really despised Gabriel so much. Nikki also couldn't help wondering about Minnie. Why wouldn't an intelligent, lovely woman like her send someone like Gabriel packing? What wonderful quality did this guy have that everyone around him fell prey to his charms? That is, apparently everyone but this Isabel and her brother. She couldn't help thinking poorly of the deceased, however; the more she learned about Gabriel, the more she didn't like about him. "Have you told the police any of this?"

"No. Of course not. Andrés is my friend. I like his sister. They're good people. There may have been bad blood between him and Gabriel, but I don't think he could do something like kill Gabriel."

"But you can't help wondering, can you?"

She shook her head. "No, I can't. But I can't go to the police, and besides I'm sure that they're aware of the difficulties between them. There were a lot of people at that party, and someone must have said something to the police by now."

"What was the party for?" Nikki already had a feeling she knew from her earlier conversation with Derek.

"Isabel recently opened a restaurant over in Yountville. It's called Grapes. It was her opening night."

Nikki nodded and took a sip of her wine.

"I'm sorry to tell you all of this. I couldn't take it anymore."

"I'm happy that you feel you could trust me and I could be here for you."

Tears streamed down Minnie's face. "Gabriel really loved me. He did. It wasn't like with him and Tara or whatever he wanted Isabel for, or Meredith for that matter." She covered her mouth. "You didn't hear me say that. Please. That did not come from me. Deal? Besides, I don't even know if it's true. Gabriel insisted that the rumors about them were false, but the gossip was brutal. Someone got that idea about him and Meredith, and the stories became more exaggerated with each telling. I'm sure it put a strain on Gabriel and Derek's relationship."

Derek was right, the goings-on at the vineyard would have put any and all soap operas to shame. Gabriel apparently had played the starring role as the gigolo. Just like Raoul Bova, who'd starred opposite Diane Lane in Minnie's favorite flick. Yes, that would've been a great role. Bova was luscious and had reeled in Lane's character,

Frances. Granted, Nikki hadn't seen the movie, but she had
read the screenplay and she also knew Bova from *Avenging
Angelo*, a Stallone stinker that Nikki had actually enjoyed,
mostly because of Bova. Bova's character in *Under the
Tuscan Sun* was the womanizer on screen that Gabriel was
in real life. Lane's character fell hard for Bova and then
caught him screwing around. The difference here was Minnie hadn't been willing to let go of her Italian charmer, and
of course, no one was murdered in *Under the Tuscan Sun*.
Minnie had been sucked in and romanticized her relationship with Gabriel, excusing his bad behavior.

Minnie wiped the tears from her face. Nikki wanted to
ask her more questions, but Derek appeared at her side
with a new glass of wine.

"This is our Cabernet Sauvignon. I think this is one of
the best we've ever produced. Gabriel did a great job."

Minnie glanced away and then back at Nikki, her eyes
pleading with her to keep silent. She wondered if that was
what the woman *really* wanted.

"Here, try these. I'm going back in to bring some for
you, Minnie," he said, handing Nikki a plate. "They're delicious. Broiled oysters with a jalapeño pesto. They've got
a bit of a kick to them."

"Don't worry about me. I think I'll mingle a bit. It was
nice talking to you, Nikki."

Nikki smiled back at her. Derek looked questioningly at
her and led her to a nearby table. She ate one of the warm
appetizers before setting them on the table, discovering
that Derek was right. They were delicious.

"What was that all about?" he asked.

"She's pretty distraught over Gabriel's death."

"I'm sure she is. We all are. Most of us are, anyway. My
brother and his partner, on the other hand, don't seem to be
unhappy." Derek pointed to the boys of summer doing the
swing on the dance floor. "That's Simon and Marco, and
the only pleasure I get from those two is the knowledge
that Patrice can't stand it that her only son is gay. If you
look at her right now, she's trying very hard to avert her

eyes from the dance floor. She can't even admit that Simon is gay. He sleeps in the same room with Marco, they travel together, they kiss in public, I mean *c'mon*. But, because Simon hasn't come right out and told his mother that he prefers men, then to her he's just *artsy*."

"You still think I should move in here?" She pointed to the mansion.

"Yes. They may all be loonies, but they're harmless loonies. You'll be safe here, and I'll feel better about that."

"If you insist." She didn't feel good about it at all, and she wasn't in the least bit convinced that any of them weren't capable of murder, as she thought about the cigarette pack she'd found earlier and the charm. It did look more and more like Andrés could be involved in Gabriel's murder. She wondered what the police had determined in regard to Andrés.

"I do."

"Here, have another oyster." He picked up the appetizer and fed it to her.

She was pretty tipsy from all the wine, but not too tipsy to recognize that when a man feeds a woman, it hits a ten on the flirting-Richter scale. The band switched from the big band music and started playing the Rolling Stones' "I'm Just Waiting on a Friend."

"I love this song," Derek remarked.

"Me, too," Nikki replied as the saxophonist started in.

"Will you dance with me?" Derek stood and extended his hand. Nikki thought she might melt right there. But, before it could get any better, a fortyish woman wearing a low-cut gold-colored gown with a slit up the side that would give even Samantha from *Sex and the City* a run for her money, rudely interrupted them.

She pulled a chair right up to their table and reached for Derek's hand. The one intended for Nikki. "Don't mind if I do." She set her wine down, splashing it around, just missing Nikki's dress. Brushing back her hair, the same color of the dress, with an exaggerated flip of the hand, the woman batted her thickly coated eyelashes in their direction. She sat down and grabbed an oyster from the platter at the table, tugging at Derek's hand.

"Sit down, darling. I want to talk to you. You've gone over the top once again. What a lovely event. I am blown away. It's marvelous, absolutely marvelous." She leaned over and gave Derek a kiss on the cheek imprinting the side of his face with her lipstick. The woman's raccoon eyes gave Nikki the once-over.

"So anyhoo, darling, I love the new wines and can't wait to write about them in *Winemaker Magazine*. They're fab, fab, fab. When are you going to give me a little private tasting, hmm?" She scooted her chair closer, nudging him on the shoulder.

Nikki was sick to her stomach. She had no idea that women could be so totally obnoxious. Well, yes she did. That TV show *The Bachelor* kind of proved it.

"I'm really busy these days, Tara. But it's nice to see you," Derek said, obviously as annoyed by her presence as Nikki.

"You can never be too busy for those who help you on your way up the ladder, now can you? And you have to admit I always write a very nice article about you, your winery, your wines—ah. Fab, fab, fab, darling. I simply wish I could say that to Gabriel. We were *so* close. He was such a darling. It is so horrid. I am mortified that anything like this could happen in our quaint little valley. I've heard the memorial service is on Tuesday. He deserves a toast. I'd like to give him one, darling." She sloshed back a gulp of wine, set the glass down, and reached her hand out, sliding her long red nails down Derek's arm in what could only be construed as a pass.

"That's okay, Tara. I'll be doing that later on this evening. Have you met Nikki Sands?"

The woman stuck out her hand. "Nice to meet you, darling. I'm Tara Beckenroe, *Winemaker Magazine*. And what did you say you do?"

"I didn't." Her name clicked in Nikki's mind as she recalled the picture Derek had shown her the evening before. *This was one of the women Gabriel had been seeing.* No wonder he'd rid himself of this one. And now it looked as though Tara was gunning for Derek.

"Of course, darling. Would you be a dear and grab me one of the Merlot? It's absolutely divine." She ran her tongue across her lips and took Derek's hand, and held it tightly in hers. He turned bright red.

"Certainly," Nikki replied.

Derek grabbed her by the arm as she stood up. "No, you don't have to do that. I can go, or one of the servers should be out in a minute."

"Don't worry about it." Nikki touched his shoulder and caught Tara's gaze. "I need to visit the rest room anyway."

"Thanks. You're such a dear."

She overheard Tara comment as she walked away, "My, she's a cutie pie." Nikki winced.

She did have to go to the rest room, that wasn't a lie, but she also needed some fresh air. She didn't think the vulture was going to remove her talons and fly away anytime soon.

Nikki stepped into the house. Most of the guests had migrated outside and were enjoying the band and the festivities. She grabbed a glass of water to clear her mind a bit, and headed up the spiral staircase after looking around to make sure no one was watching.

The upstairs was in as much need of a good decorator as the downstairs. She peeked inside one of the bedrooms. Ooh, scary. She shut the door. The burgundy and hunter green colors had migrated their way upstairs as well, and in this room, they came in the form of puff valance window treatments.

She moved down a long hallway, lit by candlelight, which gave it the feeling of a haunted house. Nikki wanted to get a good picture of this loony bin, if she was going to be spending her nights here. The classical music, piped through the house, mixed with the muffled band music and voices through the open French doors.

Nikki couldn't help reflecting upon everything that Minnie Lark had told her earlier. She and Gabriel had been lovers? That being the case, why did she mention Tara or

Meredith? Current girlfriends usually didn't like to freely bring up past bedmates of their boyfriends. And why tell Nikki about them, especially Meredith? If they truly had been left in the past, which Nikki doubted from all accounts she'd heard in regard to Gabriel and his passion for women.

Minnie was sweet but different. Maybe she was simply trusting and needed a shoulder to cry on. After all, love was a funny emotion, and women have put up with worse things than a philandering lover. Nikki could kind of understand Minnie telling her about Andrés. He did fit in the suspect category as far as she was concerned, and even though he and Minnie were friends, Nikki was pretty sure that Minnie felt the same way. Nikki had gotten the feeling that was something the woman really did want to get off her chest. Maybe Minnie did feel a certain comfort level with her, and that was why she'd divulged as much as she had. Or maybe she suspected one of the other women who'd been in Gabriel's life at one time or another, and that's why she'd let all their names come rolling so easily off her tongue.

What if the whole thing about Meredith and Gabriel *were* true, and she couldn't blame Derek for believing that it wasn't. Gabriel *had* been his best friend, but there were those best friends who back stabbed by sleeping with their pal's spouse. Now, if Minnie were also sleeping with Gabriel, maybe she got a little jealous. Maybe Meredith and Gabriel had not been through playing house. Was it possible that Minnie could've murdered her lover?

This was getting out of control. The list of suspects was growing, and so were their motives.

Nikki wished she could pick up a phone and call Aunt Cara. Maybe she could. She did have a cell phone in her handbag. If Aunt Cara were somewhere in range, she knew she'd answer. But it was the middle of the night in Spain. The heck with it. Nikki had to take the chance. Cara would advise her, help her put this puzzle together. She also would probably tell her to get the hell out of there.

She walked all the way down the hall to the last door. The sound of a door closing from the other end of the hall caught her attention. She turned to see who it was, but there was no one there. A draft filled the hall. Just the wind.

Uneasily, Nikki decided to open the door to the room. It was unlocked. She stepped inside. The room hadn't been used in years. It was enormous, dust-filled, and hadn't been updated since disco was hot. The bed was a white wrought-iron queen-size, with a canopy covered in pink ruffles everywhere. It almost looked like a little girl's room. A dark wood vanity table was over in the corner, with powders and silver brushes on top. Nikki moved toward it, hoping to find a phone there.

As she walked around the side of the bed to the vanity, a sickening surge struck her in the stomach, seeing that someone else had also wanted to use the phone in this room. Nikki quickly realized that Minnie Lark was not going to get that vacation she'd longed for in Tuscany, and she doubted she'd murdered Gabriel. Because there, on the floor by the side of the bed, lay Minnie with a spilled glass of red wine next to her and the phone cord wrapped around her neck.

Goat Cheese and
Apple-Smoked Bacon Tart

The goat cheese and red onion tart with apple-smoked bacon is a good starter dish. Luckily, Nikki and Derek were able to finish theirs before they were so rudely interrupted by another kind of tart—that Tara Beckenroe—and just when things were starting to warm up between them. A nice wine to pair with the tart is Grgich Hills Chardonnay. The enticing aroma of this wine displays a subtle combination of varietal fruit and oak, followed by a cornucopia of delicate tropical fruit flavors such as pineapple, mango, and lemon. This recipe was so graciously passed on from Bob Hurley, owner of Hurley's in Yountville.

TART DOUGH: 9-INCH TART PAN

> 1 cup all-purpose flour
> ½ teaspoon salt
> 4 tablespoons cold sweet butter cut into small pieces
> 1½ tablespoons solid vegetable shortening
> 2½ to 3 tablespoons ice water

In a bowl combine flour, salt, butter, and shortening. Quickly work ingredients together with fingers until evenly mixed. Add 2½ tablespoons of water and gently work into the dough until it comes together. Form into a ball and let rest, covered in plastic wrap, in refrigerator for 30 minutes.

Roll the dough out on a lightly floured surface into a circle about ⅛ inch thick. Place into tart pan, trim the edges leaving a 1 inch margin so that you can fold it under, and crimp edges.

Bake at 425°, using buttered foil and beans or pie weights to keep the crust from rising. Bake 8–10 minutes until the edges are set and slightly brown.

FILLING:

> 1 teaspoon cooking oil
> 5 ounces diced apple-smoked bacon
> 3 cups sliced red onions
> 1 tablespoon fresh chopped thyme
> 1 whole egg
> 1 yolk
> 6 ounces Chevre-style goat cheese
> 1 pinch nutmeg
> 1 pinch salt
> 1 cup half-and-half

Cook bacon in 1 teaspoon oil until most of the fat has rendered. Pour off excess fat and add onions. Cook slowly until soft and translucent, add thyme.

Mix eggs with goat cheese, nutmeg, and salt until it has a smooth consistency. Add half-and-half slowly so as to prevent lumps, until it is all incorporated.

Spread bacon and onion mixture evenly throughout tart. Pour on the goat-cheese mixture and bake in at 350° until custard is set, about 35–40 minutes. Let cool to room temperature before serving.

Broiled Oysters
with Jalapeño Pesto

There is a theory that oysters are an aphrodisiac. It really was too bad neither Nikki nor Derek got the chance to find out if the theory holds true.

However, if you want to give it a try, open a bottle of Napa Valley's Cakebread Cellars Vin de Porche and see if Aphrodite's charms go to work on you and your loved one. This wine has an inviting floral fragrance. On the palate, the overall impression is one of a smooth refreshing dryness with flavors that resemble a mix of fresh strawberries and cherries. This recipe serves 10, so you may want to invite some friends over. Don't be surprised if they leave early. And, don't be even more surprised if eight months later you're asked for your oyster recipe to make for a baby shower or two.

    ½ cup (packed) fresh basil leaves
    ½ cup cilantro leaves chopped and pucked
    2–3 jalapeño peppers
    ¼ cup plain dry bread crumbs
    ¼ cup freshly grated Parmesan cheese
    ¼ cup water
    1 tablespoon fresh lemon juice
    2 garlic cloves, peeled
    ½ cup (1 stick) butter, room temperature
    30 fresh oysters, shucked, shells reserved

Combine basil, cilantro, jalapeños, breadcrumbs, cheese, ¼ cup water, lemon juice, and garlic in processor. Blend until mixture is finely chopped. Add butter and process until smooth paste forms. Season pesto to taste with salt and pepper.

Preheat broiler. Arrange oysters in half shells on 2 large

baking sheets. Top each oyster with 1½ teaspoons pesto. Working in batches, broil until pesto begins to brown, about 1½ minutes. Place 3 oysters on each plate and serve. Serves 10.

Chapter 10

What seemed like forever was really only a matter of a few minutes or so, from the time Nikki spotted Minnie's body, to letting out a bloodcurdling scream that sent a few people dashing into the room. The next thing she knew her eyes were meeting Derek's, whose jaw dropped open at the sight of Minnie. He looked at Nikki, and her hands began to shake. She could see it in Derek's eyes, and knew he had the same thought in his mind that everyone else did who had come into the room—what the hell was she doing in there? Right now, she couldn't find words to answer anyone. They weren't asking it out loud—yet. But she knew that they would be.

The one person standing off in the corner actually looking rather smug was Tara. She gave Nikki a smarmy smile, or at least Nikki thought she did. In all the confusion, on top of the three glasses of wine she'd had, she knew she wasn't thinking straight.

"Oh, my God, how did this happen?" Patrice yelled at no one in particular, her arms raised above her head and flailing around.

Before anyone could answer her, Chief Horn was herding people out of the room. Jeanine Wiley showed up after a few more minutes and followed the chief's lead.

Derek grabbed Nikki by the arm. "Come on, they'll definitely want to talk to you, but I'd like to speak with you first."

Nikki didn't care for the tone of his voice. He'd never sounded harsh before. He led her outside, where he passed by Simon, asking him to please let everyone else know that the party would be rescheduled, and to thank the guests for their contributions.

"Why me?" Simon asked. "Aren't you the big man around here? Isn't this your gig?"

Marco sidled up to Simon. "I am thinking it would be a good idea to listen to your brother," he said sweetly.

Nikki couldn't help wondering, by the look the two of them exchanged, what they had up their sleeves. She didn't have time to think about it, since Derek tugged on her arm again. They walked out past the gazebo, into the rose garden, where they sat down on a bench away from the crowd and the chaos. Car headlights bounced off the nearby hillsides, with people pulling out of the estate and down the road leading through the vineyard and back to the main highway.

Derek sat slumped over, his head in the palms of his hands, shaking his head. "I can't believe this. I really can't. Who is doing this, and why?"

She could hear the gravity in his voice and the distinct tone of sadness.

"What were you doing in that part of the house? I thought you were going to the rest room. Did you know that room had been my mother's when she got sick?"

This could get dicey. She didn't want to tell him what Minnie had said to her about Meredith and Gabriel, or what was behind Gabriel's conflict with Andrés. Before she divulged that information Nikki knew she needed to go back and speak to Andrés. That would be the first item on her agenda in the morning.

She didn't know fact from fiction at that moment, and before she started talking to anyone she wanted to know that what she'd discovered were indeed facts.

As far as what might have gone on between Gabriel and Meredith, Nikki didn't know if Derek's ex would cop to it if it were the truth, and the only way to really know the truth about the possible affair between the two of them would be from Meredith's mouth. Something told Nikki that Meredith wasn't going to say a word to her about her love life.

Nikki decided to do the best she could, by staying as close to the truth as possible. "I wanted to take a tour of my new digs and see what I was in for. I'm sorry. And, no, I had no idea it was your mother's old room." That said, what had *Minnie* been doing in *there*?

"I would've shown you around. All you had to do was ask."

"I know. I didn't want to bother you. You had a lot on your plate this evening, being the host and all. Besides, I also wanted to try and reach my aunt in Spain. I told you that she's on a backpacking tour, and I had a real need to speak with her."

"It's the middle of the night there. You could've asked me for the phone, too," he replied.

"I could have, but honestly, it was such a sudden impulse. I'd been thinking a lot about Gabriel's murder, and since my aunt was in law enforcement, I thought of bouncing around a couple of theories with her that you and I have already discussed."

"Have you had any new revelations now that we have two people—both of whom I cared about—dead?"

"I can't say that I have. Maybe someone really wants to run you out of business. Either that, or someone had it out for Gabriel and Minnie." Andrés was in the back of her mind. There was something dark, mysterious, yet endearing about the winemaker down the road, and Nikki didn't want to serve him up on a silver platter. Her gut said that he was innocent, but he sure did have motive. At least in

Gabriel's case. Minnie claimed they were dear friends, so Andrés murdering Minnie did not fit. "I also think we really need to look into your suspicion that the books were being doctored. Maybe whoever is skimming profits killed Minnie and Gabriel because they found out who it was."

"Meredith?"

"Maybe, maybe not. The winery is quite an operation, with more than a handful of employees, family included. It's kind of easy to point the finger at Meredith, isn't it?"

Derek shook his head again. "I can see Meredith as a thief, but a killer? No. I was married to her. I think I would've known if I was sleeping with the enemy, someone who is a sociopath."

Nikki didn't want to remind him that Meredith was also a manipulative liar and philanderer. Those criteria from what she knew fit that of a sociopath.

"I can see where Gabriel might have made enemies. I mentioned Andrés Fernandez to you, and I know there were others. But not Minnie. Everyone liked her. Gabriel could be a loose cannon. At least he was in the past. He had a lover-boy rep around town, and a temper. Say the wrong thing, and he could blow up. He was a real ladies' man, and I know that didn't make everyone happy around here. But Minnie, she couldn't have done a damn thing. She was a very sweet lady. You met her."

Nikki nodded. "It looks like it's clearing out up there. I've got an idea that the police will want to talk to me. If they can't find me, I doubt it'll bode well."

They started walking back toward the mansion. Nikki knew she should bring up what she thought about the possibility of a love triangle. "You know, I *do* have a new theory, but I don't think you're going to like it."

He shrugged. "There's nothing to like about any of this. Friends and employees of mine are dead, and someone around here killed them."

"It may be difficult to consider, but jealousy is a huge motive for murder. I know that you don't want to think about the possibility of Gabriel and Meredith having an affair, but I think you might want to reconsider that." She paused, waiting for his response. When he continued walking, his hands shoved into his pockets and didn't appear to have any reaction at all, she decided to continue. "For some reason, Minnie confided in me tonight. She claimed that she and Gabriel had been lovers." This revelation did get a reaction.

He stopped and faced her. In the moonlight, she could see he wore a look of incredulity. "I don't believe that."

"Why?"

"I don't. I hung around the two of them all the time. There was the typical friendly flirting, but nothing that indicated they were sleeping together. I don't think they could've hidden it from me. They would have both known that I would've been fine that the two of them were together. I mean, I do have an unsaid rule about dating amongst employees. But rules can be broken. I'm certainly no dictator."

"Apparently, the secrecy of it all lent to the romance and fun for them. And, you said yourself that Gabriel was a real ladies' man. Maybe he wanted to keep their relationship hush-hush for fear of another woman he was seeing finding out. I don't know. Minnie indicated they liked it that way. Gabriel even told her that the two of them would go to Tuscany together, for more than just a vacation. If it's not true, why would she say something like that to me? Why make up something like that?"

"I don't know." He took his hands out of his slacks pockets and crossed his arms.

There was now a definite edge to his voice. Nikki pulled her shawl tighter around her. He appeared to be almost angry at her suggestion. But she pressed on. She was already in deep, so she might as well unload another tidbit. "Hear me out. Say they didn't want anyone to know. The real reason why? You got me. But if Meredith was sleeping with Gabriel at one time, and discovered that he and Minnie had gotten together, is it possible that she might have killed the two of them out of jealousy? Jealousy combined with the possibility that she could be stealing money from you, and afraid Minnie would or did find out? Maybe Meredith had a real thing for Gabriel. For a woman to stray on her husband, even a woman like Meredith, I would think the man would have to be pretty special." That was not a good thing to say, and she knew it right after it rolled off her tongue.

There was no more edge to Derek's voice. He was downright angry. "Nikki, I'm hiring you to help manage this place, and be my assistant, not an amateur detective. I think I know my own people pretty well. I may be naïve in some ways, but not in this one. To be honest, I can't help wonder why the hell dead bodies started turning up around here, right after you arrived. It's also curious that you're the one who keeps finding those bodies. Why don't you twist that one around in your brain?" Derek hurried his step and walked on ahead of her.

His words stung. Tears filled her eyes, as her ears started ringing and her gut flipped over in a bad way. She wanted nothing more than to go and pack her suitcase and get out of there.

She could see Derek's silhouette in front of her. He'd stopped. She didn't know what to make of it, but kept walking toward him.

"We need to talk some more about this tomorrow," he said.

She sighed heavily. "I don't know, Derek. I think maybe it would be best if I head back to Los Angeles."

He shook his head. "Please don't. Let me digest this. Stay at least through tomorrow. If you want to go home after that, fine."

Nikki decided she'd give him that much. She didn't like the way the situation was souring. Funny thing was, though, she wanted to see this thing out because she was in so deep. Nikki was determined to see someone behind bars for these murders. She may not have known Gabriel, but she'd met Minnie and genuinely liked her. Moments ago she'd also genuinely liked Derek. At that moment she wasn't so sure how she felt.

They didn't say anything else on their walk back to the mansion.

Jeanine Wiley approached the two of them as they walked through the front door, running her hands through her wavy hair. "We've been looking for you. I'd like you to have a seat in there." Jeanine pointed into the living room, where Patrice, the boys of summer, the vulture, and Meredith, along with her Pirate of the Caribbean, were busy chatting, presumably about the evening's events. Cal Sumner caught Nikki's eye, and again she noticed his resemblance to Johnny Depp.

In the dining room, the catering crew milled around the formal table, looking unhappy that they had to remain until given the go-ahead to leave.

Nikki took a seat in a wing-backed chair next to the sofa where Meredith, Patrice, Simon, and his partner were seated. Cal Sumner and Tara Beckenroe were leaning against the mantel of the fireplace, having an animated conversation. Derek took a seat opposite Nikki. As she sat down, the conversations ceased. All eyes on her, she couldn't help but shift uneasily, fidgeting with her hands, wanting to sit on them. She'd never been such a focus of attention. Derek quickly and formally introduced Nikki to everyone in the room.

"How ghastly that you found that poor girl, Nicole," Patrice said.

"It's Nikki," Derek corrected his stepmother.

Patrice didn't appear to care, or even take any notice.

"Yes, darling, you must have been terrified," Tara Beckenroe added.

"I wonder," Meredith cut in. "What were you doing there in the first place?"

Jeanine Wiley came back into the room, followed by a hulk of a man with narrow eyes the shape and color of a raven's. Nikki thought she'd seen him in uniform the day before, helping with the murder investigation.

Jeanine walked over to Nikki. "That is what we'd like to know, too, Miss Sands. What were you doing in there?"

"I wanted to make a phone call." She looked up at the man next to Jeanine.

Jeanine followed her eyes. "This is Officer Mark Anderson. He's helping with this investigation."

Nikki smiled. Officer Anderson sort of grunted at her. Another brain surgeon for the team.

"We have phones all over this house. Why go all the way upstairs, to the very last room?" Patrice chimed in, her phony smile looking more and more like the snarl on a pit bull.

"Shouldn't we go somewhere private?" Nikki asked Jeanine. Here she was telling the cop how to do her job. Wasn't there a golden rule anyway, about separating suspects, witnesses, whatever?

"Good idea."

"I think I should question Miss Sands," Officer Anderson said.

Nikki rolled her eyes. The lug speaketh. What intelligent notation was going to cross his lips next?

"That won't be necessary. Chief Horn asked me to talk with her," Jeanine replied.

"I think I should do it," he said, placing his hands on his hips, over pants that were far too tight for him.

The sight was obnoxious. What was he trying to prove? Nikki immediately didn't like him.

"That's all right, Mark," Chief Horn interrupted, walking into the living room. "Jeanine can handle it. We have plenty here to keep us busy. Officer Wiley, why don't you and Miss Sands take it outside for a moment."

Nikki heard the chatter start up behind her before she was even out of the room. She also heard Derek trying to defend her. That helped ease her troubled mind somewhat about the conversation they'd had while walking back to the house.

"I don't know about your Goldilocks girlfriend. She seems to show up around dead bodies a bit too soon after they've expired, don't you think?"

"Simon, you're an idiot. Leave Nikki alone."

"Yes, Simon. Be nice. But I do like the nickname Goldilocks for her. It's truly fitting."

Nikki closed her eyes for a second and sighed, recognizing Tara Beckenroe's voice. Maybe she shouldn't have come up here. But, it wasn't like the decision to join Derek for a long weekend in Napa was a no-brainer. Cute guy wants to hire you for a new high-paying job at a world-renowned winery in Napa Valley. *Hmmmm?* Who knew there'd be dead bodies and lunatics involved?

"I'm sorry to have to ask you these questions, but you did find both bodies, and it is kind of odd," Jeanine said.

"I know it is. But, come on, what motive would I have? I didn't even know these people. I met Minnie once earlier today, and then spoke with her all of ten minutes this evening."

"No, a motive doesn't seem likely with you."

"Of course not."

"But. . . ." Jeanine Wiley crossed her arms in front of her, over her pink sweatshirt. She'd obviously been pulled away from her TV screen to drive out to the estate.

"No, no, no." Nikki stifled a laugh, because she could see exactly where Jeanine's interrogation was headed. "I am not, repeat, not, some freakish psycho serial killer. I may have some neuroses, and my anxiety levels do go a bit high at times. I'll even admit to having popped a Xanax or two in my day. However, I do not, and would never, go around killing people, especially ones I didn't know. But there's some wackadoo around here, playing all of you for suckers. If I were you, I'd start looking at the freaks who live inside that house." Nikki nodded in the direction of the mansion. She thought about mentioning Andrés, but shoved the thought aside for the time being. He'd told her that the police had already questioned him about Gabriel's murder. They would have already arrested Andrés if they'd discovered significant evidence.

"Do you know something about anyone in particular around here, Miss Sands?"

"No, and quit calling me Miss Sands." She knew that

she wasn't saying the right things to Jeanine Wiley, but she was extremely irritated. "Call me Nikki."

"Were you with Mr. Malveaux all evening, except for your escapade upstairs?"

This was kind of a tricky question, when Nikki thought about it, remembering the several moments Derek left her at Minnie's side to retrieve the oysters and more wine. Technically, she *had* been with him, because if asked the question of somebody on a date, one might say, 'I was with him last night.' Jeanine didn't word the question the way she might have intended, in the sense of continually being in his presence all evening. Nikki knew a lot about *technicalities*. "Yep. I was with him."

"I know we'll have some more questions, but for now why don't you join the others?"

Nikki went back into the house. Tara, Patrice, and Meredith's date were still in the living room. Cal Sumner was a pretty sexy guy with his longish hair falling just so in front of his deep, dark eyes. He immediately stopped talking to Tara as Nikki entered the room and approached her.

He stuck out his hand. She took it. His handshake was firm. She liked when a man shook a woman's hand like that. She hated those dainty handshakes that most men gave women, like if they squeezed, they would break the woman's hand. "I'm Cal Sumner. I own Sumner Winery down the road."

"Yes, Derek mentioned you." She'd been right on figuring that's who he was when she'd seen him with Meredith.

"It's terrible what happened here. I really feel for Derek."

Nikki didn't know what to say. The evening was wearing on her, and all she wanted to do was climb in bed and go to sleep. "Speaking of Derek, do you know where he is?"

"He's talking with the police. Meredith is also with one of the officers. I think Simon and his friend are as well. Derek asked me if I would walk you back to the guest cottage. He figured you're probably exhausted, and he didn't know how long he was going to be."

"That's okay. Thank you, but I can make it back on my own."

"That wouldn't be right of me. Derek is a friend. Believe me, I don't mind walking a beautiful lady to her door."

Nikki didn't exactly relish the prospect of walking alone in the dark. There may have been police officers around and plenty of people still, but the idea that a killer lurked among them didn't make being alone too appealing. "Sure, why not?" If Derek had asked him to do it, then it would only be right to oblige.

Cal grabbed his coat jacket off of one of the chairs and slipped it over a navy blue silk shirt.

"Ta-tah," Tara Beckenroe called out after them.

Nikki noticed her wink at Cal.

"She's a strange one," Cal said.

Nikki opened the front door and replied, "Yes she is. But who the hell isn't around here?"

He laughed in response. "I like your sense of humor."

They closed the door, and Nikki walked out of the mansion, Cal Sumner by her side.

Chapter 11

Cal escorted Nikki into the guest cottage and was kind enough to light a fire for her. "Would you like me to make you a cup of coffee or tea?" he asked her.

"No. You've done enough. I'm sure Meredith will be looking for you before too long." Nikki fell into the overstuffed sofa and put her feet up on the coffee table. She was getting awfully comfortable here.

"She'll figure I went home, unless Derek tells her that I'm with you. I needed a break from her, anyway. I'm starting to find that perhaps she's a bit too melodramatic and materialistic for me."

"Yes, I've heard she likes her designer clothes and expensive jewelry."

"That said, I may not be the right man for her. My parents were farmers. I don't buy into all that stuff." He walked into the kitchen and rummaged around the cupboards. Nikki was too exhausted to protest, besides, the thought of coffee sounded kind of good. He put on the carafe. Before long, the aroma of fresh brew floated through the cottage. "Cream and sugar?"

"Yes, please."

He brought it to her and set it down on the coffee table in front of her. It tasted good and warmed her to her core.

"Gotten much of a chance to see Napa Valley yet?" Cal asked, sitting down in the chair next to the sofa.

"Not really. I haven't been here long, and Derek has really only had time to show me around the vineyard. Then, with Gabriel and now—" Nikki's throat caught on Minnie's name.

"It's all pretty rotten, isn't it?"

Nikki bit her lower lip, nodding her head.

"When this passes, I'd love to have Derek bring you over to my vineyard so you can have a look around, see what we do at Sumner. We buy some of our grapes from Derek. He grows a primo product in the valley. I'm envious." Cal laughed. "But, we're friends, so jealousy has no room in our relationship. We even had a running joke going about me trying to steal Gabriel from him. I'd kidded Gabriel about coming to work for me more than once, but I knew better. A vintner like Gabriel would've never left Malveaux. Although, I do have a great setup. I think you'd like touring my place. There's quite a bit of history there."

"I'm sure of that. Most of Napa Valley seems to be rich in history," Nikki replied.

"Yes, but my vineyard is one of a handful that has a section of caves beneath it. They were used during Prohibition to store and transport wine."

"That *is* interesting. Kind of like the underground railroad, only fine-booze style."

"There goes that sense of humor again. I suppose that's pretty much the way it was. Come by and have a look when you get a chance."

"I'll do that." Nikki wanted to broach the subject of murder again with him. "Do you have any thoughts on the murders? I mean, I assume you know a lot of people around here and that you must have an opinion about what's happened here."

Cal tilted his head and glanced upward out of the corner

of his eyes as if he was deeply pondering her question. He shook a finger at her as he started to speak. "There are some different types working for Derek."

"You think it's an employee?" Nikki sat up in her chair, placing her elbows on her knees, fists under her chin.

"I'm not sure. I do know that Derek's half brother has always had it in for him. You know the scenario—typical spoiled rich kid who doesn't think he has enough to keep him happy. He's too full of himself with ego to see that he's completely incapable of running an operation like Malveaux Estate. It takes someone with intelligence to operate a big-business winery."

"Simon isn't too bright?"

"Simon is a pretty boy. You saw him."

Weren't they all pretty boys around here? "The man he was with is his lover, right?"

"Marco? Yes. He's a riot to listen to. He's funny and entertaining, but you wouldn't want to tell him any deep dark secrets. He's a bit loose lipped."

Cal appeared more down-to-earth than Nikki would have imagined anyone associated with Meredith could be. But Derek also had that same trait. Meredith must've had something alluring about her, if she could land men like Cal and Derek.

"He's a gossip, I take it?"

"Gossip doesn't even describe it. He's up there with Cindy Adams, when he's not starring in her column himself."

"He likes the limelight? I'm surprised that big media hasn't glommed on to this story yet."

"After tonight they probably will. Marco likes the limelight, but he also knows how to keep a low profile when he wants. He knows Simon doesn't care to be in the gossip columns, so he does it for him. I actually think the two of them are in love, and I also think Marco would do *anything* for Simon and vice versa."

"Where are you going with that?" Nikki asked.

"Don't quote me, because I'm not one to get into the

middle of things, and if I'm wrong I don't need the hassle. This isn't a big town. Bad blood doesn't get you far in this part of the world."

Those words—bad blood—were the exact same ones Minnie had used when referring to the rift between Gabriel and Andrés.

"But you asked me who I thought was behind these murders." Cal set his coffee mug down on the table beside him. "I'd put some money down on Simon and Marco. If Simon didn't do it because he didn't have the backbone, then Marco would've done it for him. Like I said, Simon is a big spoiled man who acts like a child. He wants to run this estate, and Marco wants for Simon whatever Simon wants."

Nikki remembered the sly look the two of them exchanged back at the party shortly after Minnie's murder when Derek asked Simon to hold down the fort. "Do you think they would set Derek up for murder?"

"I wouldn't put it past the two of them."

"Why choose Minnie and Gabriel? It doesn't make sense to set Derek up by killing two people he thought highly of."

"True." He shrugged his shoulders. "I don't know why they'd choose those two. I'm not the police. I only know that Simon might think he has a reason to want to see his brother behind bars."

"Interesting." Nikki wondered if Cal might not be right about his theory. She also wanted to ask Cal about Tara Beckenroe. "How well do you know Tara Beckenroe?"

"She's a bit of a wild one."

"No kidding."

"I know she and Gabriel had a thing for a week or two. That was about it. But I don't think she was as hung up on Gabriel as she is Derek. Derek just doesn't pay much attention to her, and Gabriel, well, if it had legs, you know the saying. I actually think she may have *used* Gabriel to try and make Derek jealous, but fat chance she had doing that."

"Do you think she's capable of murder?" Nikki asked cautiously, not knowing where Cal's loyalties lay.

He shook his head. "Your guess is as good as mine at this juncture. I really have no clue who could be behind these murders. Like I said, I think Simon Malveaux is a sneaky snake. Listen, not to change a morbid subject, but let's change it anyway. Where are you from?" Cal asked.

"Sure." Nikki hoped she hadn't made him uncomfortable or upset him in any way by speaking about the murders. "I'm originally from the South. The hill country in Tennessee."

"Cool." He crossed one leg over the other and took a sip of coffee. "I went to Memphis once. I thought I wanted to be a country-western singer."

"No way." She cupped a hand over her mouth, stifling a laugh. "I'm sorry, it seems out of character for you. I don't know why. You don't look like a Garth Brooks, you look more like—"

Cal held up a hand. "Don't say it. I know who you're going to say I look like, but I'm far from being *People* magazine's sexiest man. And, don't worry about laughing at the idea of me being a country-western singer. You wouldn't be the first to think it funny." He picked up his mug and took a drink of coffee. "I even cut a record with a band. That was about fifteen years ago, but we never made it. It takes quite a bit of change to finance something like that."

"Sure does. I've studied acting for years." She didn't like feeling so comfortable with Derek's pal; but they were just talking.

"I take it you know a thing or two about the entertainment business, then?" he asked.

"Two things is probably *all* I know." She set her cup down in front of her, and brushed her hair back behind her shoulders. As she did so, she caught herself. Her friends had mentioned to her one night at happy hour that the hair flip was one of her trademark flirting techniques. She wasn't flirting with Cal Sumner. He was a nice guy, and that was it. They were having a pleasant discussion over coffee, probably both of them hoping to forget about the evening's nightmarish events.

"After I flunked out at trying to be the next Rhinestone Cowboy, I came here to Napa Valley, because I always had an interest in wine. I was able to get a small-business loan, and started out with a gourmet food and wine shop, then some land came up for sale that was reasonable, and I bought it. I lost both of my parents in two years' time back home in Utah. That's where I'm originally from. My dad had a stroke one day, and my mom died of a broken heart. At least that's what I believe. They were so close, and my mother couldn't have gone on without him."

"That's so sad."

There was a knock at the door. Nikki got up and opened it to see Derek and Ollie standing there. "Hi." He kissed her on the cheek.

Dog and master entered. "Hey, Cal, thanks for walking Nikki down here. Sorry I took so long," Derek said.

"Don't worry about it. We've been having a nice chat. Nikki is good company." Cal smiled warmly at her. He stood up. "I better head out. I'm beat myself. Do they know anything more?" Cal asked.

"The police? No. And, if they do, they're not saying," Derek replied.

Cal slapped Derek on the shoulder. "I'm sorry, buddy. If there's anything I can do, let me know. I suppose I'll see you on Tuesday at Gabriel's funeral."

He nodded. "You might want to find Meredith. She's looking for you."

"Let her look," Cal replied.

"Her true colors shining through?"

"Pretty much. I should have trusted what you said about her. But I like to give people the benefit of the doubt. I'm an optimist who thinks that people can change, especially when they go through adversity."

Derek didn't reply.

"We should get together, the three of us, and have dinner," Nikki said wanting to change the subject of Meredith. She did not just say that, did she? Yes, she did. Unbelievable. As if she and Derek were a couple. She didn't dare glance his way to see what the look on his face might be.

"Great," Cal replied. He said his good-byes and stepped out the door.

"Nice guy," she said to Derek.

"He is. I take it you've decided to stay?"

"I suppose," she replied curtly, still not sure of his feelings toward her, much less her own about him.

"I'm sorry about earlier," he said taking her hands in his. "I didn't mean to take all of this out on you. You're only trying to help. I'm very sorry. It's all starting to get to me. When you told me what Minnie said, something inside me snapped. I had to really consider the possibility of Gabriel and Meredith. I know in my gut it could be true. I know it. The police brought it up, but for whatever reason, until *you* pointed it out, I could've continued shoving it down and ignoring it."

That was something Nikki knew a lot about—pushing away painful memories and thoughts into some dark void from within, until they got so far down they could be ignored.

"I don't care about Meredith. If she did have an affair with Gabriel, then so be it. I can't change the past. He wasn't the only one she screwed around with. I actually caught her in bed with another man, and it wasn't Gabriel. After getting over it and her, nothing else she did mattered. But to have Gabriel betray me, that's another story. If the rumors are true, and they were together while Meredith and I were still married, I don't know." He threw his hands in the air. "Well, even after the fact, it's troubling."

Her heart softened to see his pained expression and hear the heartfelt words he'd spoken. "I understand. You're under quite a bit of strain."

"You are, too, and I want to thank you for being so wonderful through all of this and for tolerating me."

She squeezed his hands. He leaned in and kissed her on the cheek.

At that moment, any fleeting thoughts of Cal Sumner disappeared.

"Do you want me to stay the night?" he asked.

"What do you mean stay the night?"

"Here on the couch, to make sure you're safe."

She shook her head. "You don't have to do that. I'm a big girl. Besides, I have Ollie."

"Sure?"

"Sure, I'm sure. But if you get scared, you know where to find me," she joked, trying to make light of their bizarre situation.

"I'm going to turn in." He reached into his pants pockets. "Here. These are the keys to the Ford truck parked over near the tractor garage. It's not a luxury vehicle, but it'll get you around. I figure you might want to check out the town tomorrow. I'd like to get together, but it'll have to be later in the day. I need to take care of some business, and sadly enough I also have to make some arrangements for Minnie's body to be transported back home after an autopsy is completed. She was from Maryland, and Jeanine Wiley has called her parents. They want to bring her home, and I promised to see to it for them."

"I understand. It's very kind of you to do that and also to give me the keys to the truck."

"No problem. You can either let Ollie out in the morning or take him with you if you want. He likes to tool around town."

"He does make good company."

She walked him to the door. He kissed her good night on the cheek. "Why don't we get together after five? We can go have a casual dinner and try to relax some."

"Sounds great. I'll be here, so come by around then, and we can make concrete plans." She closed the door behind him. Thinking of their earlier conversation about her living arrangements, she figured that Derek would deal with it later.

Nikki went into the bedroom, put on a pair of pajamas

and flopped down on the bed, tugging the covers up around her. Ollie jumped up a few minutes later.

None of it made any sense. She closed her eyes. Images of a dead Gabriel, then a dead Minnie came to mind, and the curious thought as to what had provoked Minnie to go into Derek's mother's room. Nikki knew why she'd gone exploring. But why had Minnie done so?

More disturbing thoughts followed with a smirking group of eccentrics, including all of those living up at the estate, along with Andrés Fernandez over at Spaniards' Crest. She tried to fall asleep because she was tired, but after a half hour and with the cup of coffee Cal had served her running its course, her mind was still abuzz. She decided to get some fresh air.

Ollie reluctantly jumped off the bed and followed her onto the porch, where she sat on the top step looking out at the night sky. Country nights were amazingly dark. The stars were clear and so far away, but they were the only light to be seen for miles around on the moonless night. The damp musty smell of the pond nearby and the fruit from late harvest floated through the valley. Nikki felt very alone. Ollie licked her hand. "Guess I'm not all that alone, am I?" she said to the dog, who flapped his tail.

She stared out across the pond into the darkness. Her heart stopped. "We are definitely not alone out here, Ollie," she whispered.

Nikki quietly stood and went back into the house, grabbing Ollie's leash and the Swiss Army knife that Maurice from Chez la Mer had given her last Christmas. He'd asked her to keep it on her at all times, fearful that someone could harm her when she walked to her car alone or to her apartment in Venice Beach each night. At the time she thought it a sweet gesture, but kind of ridiculous. Who knew that she might actually need to use it on a vineyard in Napa Valley? With the knowledge that her sleuthing for the day was not through, Nikki set out to see who was inside the shed across from the pond.

Chapter 12

Nikki walked stealthily, holding Ollie on the leash close to her side. There was someone out at the shed, and she'd had a sneaking suspicion as she'd watched from the porch that *the* someone lighting up a cigarette might be none other than Mrs. Patrice Malveaux.

Not wanting to alert Patrice or whoever was at the shed, Nikki took her time walking around the area until finally she reached the back of the shed.

The smoke of the cigarette rose into the fresh air, clouding it. Nikki heard muffled voices. Ollie panted slightly next to her. She sat down in the grass alongside of him. He gave her a slobbery lick across her face. She caught herself from almost saying "yuck," out loud. Ollie lay down in the grass. Nikki put her ear up to the shed to see if she could hear what was being said inside.

"I don't like any of this."

Yep. That was definitely the step-monster.

"Do you think I do? I certainly didn't expect any of this to happen."

Another *woman*, and Nikki was banking that it was Meredith.

"It interferes with everything we've planned, Meredith."

"No one can know the truth about us," Patrice said. "It will fall apart if Derek finds out. You have to get back into his good graces and not screw up this time. He is a means to an end, and that end is a great deal of money. More than I currently have right now."

Wow. This was getting good. Could they be lovers? The mother who was so staunchly conservative that her gay son embarrassed her was also gay? Nikki pressed her ear harder against the cold metal of the shed.

"I'll take care of Derek," Meredith said. "I think if I play him right, then maybe I could lasso him back into my lair. I'll admit I messed up, but he's a man. He shouldn't be that hard to win back."

"What about Nikki Sands?" Patrice asked.

"She's harmless. I'm not threatened by her."

"I wouldn't be so sure about that. I saw the way he gazed at her at the party before everything happened."

"Easy prey," Meredith replied. "I'll be back in Derek's bed in no time."

"I hope so, and I hope the timing is right. Remember, we have one goal where Derek is concerned, and once he's served his purpose, then things will change dramatically around here. But watch yourself with Nikki, Meredith."

"Fine."

"I wish Gabriel had listened and taken the job at Cal's," Patrice said.

"Yeah. I guess if that had happened the way we planned, then I wouldn't even have to worry about getting on Derek's good side again." Meredith sounded odd, not as polished as she did when inside the mansion.

"Gabriel would've made Sumner Winery a five-star company. Cal has no clue how to make wines," Patrice replied.

"I don't know if Gabriel would be alive or not if he'd

moved to Cal's. What I do know is that Cal can't find out you talked to Gabriel about going to work for Sumner Winery. He would be insulted by that."

"He won't hear it from me," Patrice said. "Now what about Minnie? Do you think she was on to us and our situation?"

Nikki shifted in the grass.

"Shhh. Did you hear something?" Meredith asked.

Nikki stood and turned Ollie loose off the leash, hoping that if they came out and saw anything it would be the dog.

"What is it?" Patrice asked. "We need to go. I don't like it out here."

"Aren't you being a bit dramatic?" Meredith asked. "Stay here. I'll have a look around."

Nikki scrambled to get up, then sprinted back behind a set of bushes near the pond. Ollie soon found her as she ducked down. She couldn't see a damn thing and hoped that Meredith couldn't, either.

She stayed hiding in the brush for several minutes until she heard the two women walking back up toward the mansion. Nikki could no longer hear their conversation. She breathed a sigh of relief knowing that they hadn't spotted her.

After several more minutes Nikki stood and headed back to her cottage, her mind reeling, Ollie following along at her side. Once inside her temporary abode she headed straight for the kitchen cupboards. Not finding what she was looking for, she tried the hutch set up in the dining room. *Aha. That'll work.* She took out a bottle of Jack Daniels and poured herself a tall glass of the amber-colored liquid over ice, with a splash of water. It wasn't fine wine, but at that particular moment Nikki didn't think fine wine was going to help her get any sleep, exhausted or not.

She walked into the living area, flipped on the small stereo inside the entertainment unit and sat down on the sofa, grabbing a crocheted blanket off the back and covering her legs, which she curled up under her. "Murder by

Numbers" by the Police was playing on the radio. Nikki rolled her eyes at the irony. Ollie gingerly climbed up onto the sofa, as if hoping she wouldn't notice.

"Don't worry, I'm not gonna kick you off, Scooby. There's a murderer or two running around here and at least a half a dozen people with secrets they're keeping. I think your place is right here." She patted Ollie on the head, laughing at her own joke, then leaned back against the sofa, bringing the whiskey to her lips, and made friends with good ole Jack.

Chapter 13

The sun peered bright through the windows of the cottage the morning after the party and Minnie's murder, finding Nikki and Ollie still on the couch. Nikki struggled to open her eyes against the blinding light. An emptied highball on the coffee table and the Beastie Boys belting out "So What'cha Want" on the stereo added to the hangover she was beginning to feel, making her groan. It was not cool to wake up to a pounding headache with heavy rap music coming from the stereo and having Ollie breathing gnarly dog breath on her. Jack Daniels was no longer a pal. She grabbed one of her shoes on the floor next to her and tossed it at the stereo, hoping she would miraculously hit it. It bounced off the pinewood entertainment unit instead.

Nikki felt a tidal wave of nausea as she struggled to get up and walk over to the stereo, turning the power button off. Ollie lifted his head. *Must have coffee.* After several ice cold splashes of water on her face, the coffee was ready, and Nikki poured herself a large cup.

Deciding that she couldn't let a hangover get in the way of the day, she got dressed in a pair of jeans and a light yellow knit sweater set. Since she wasn't going to meet with Derek until dinnertime, she would take him up on his offer to use the spare truck he'd given her the keys to the night before. After setting out a bowl of water for Ollie, she decided to give the big dog his freedom and let him outside to do his thing for the day, remembering that Derek had told her Ollie's food bowl was out on his porch.

The truck was parked where he'd told her, down near the tractor garage. It wasn't a Range Rover, but it would do. She turned the ignition key on the old Ford. It roared to life, and before long she was bumping down the road and heading for Spaniards' Crest.

She drove up the long drive and found Andrés getting ready to drive his tractor out to the vines.

"Hey there," he said as she climbed out of the truck. "Did you already take the job and decide to come celebrate with me?"

"No." She shoved her hands deep into her jeans pockets and stopped for a second, studying him. *His eyes.* Dark and mysterious—yes, but the eyes of a murderer? She didn't think so. She knew she didn't want to think so, because something about him intrigued her, and she couldn't help but want to have that glass of wine with him, if she did wind up staying.

"What is it, then? Why are you looking at me like that?" he asked.

She sucked in a deep breath and blew it out before continuing. Maybe she shouldn't do this. Ask him these questions.

"Yes? I'm waiting."

"Sorry. I actually . . . well, I've got a few more questions to ask you," she replied, starting to walk toward him again.

"Really now? Okay. But you're gonna have to do it while riding on the tractor with me. I have work to do. I need to collect grapes from all the quadrants to bring back and check the brix."

"Check the what?" she asked.

"The brix. It's the measurement of the percentage of sugar present in wine. I was doing it on a hydrometer yesterday when you came by. Kind of the old-fashioned way to measure. We have a refractometer, too, which is a more expensive sophisticated version of the hydrometer, but personally I like the hydrometer."

"Uh-huh." Though Nikki knew of hydrometers from her research, she had forgotten about the term *brix*. Then she suddenly remembered that Derek had already explained to her about the brix.

"I harvest at around twenty-five brix. If I let the grapes get too sweet, the alcohol content will be too high. That's okay with some grapes, if I'm looking to have a sweeter taste. That's already happened with some of the grapes, and now I'm trying to either sell them off to other vineyards that make a less-quality product or see what I can do with a dessert wine."

"Dessert wines wouldn't be where you make a profit, though."

He held up his hands and shrugged. "I may not have much of a choice."

"Why didn't you harvest your grapes already, then?" she asked.

"It didn't get done. I was in Spain on family business when it came time to sign the annual contract with the vineyard management company. I didn't think it would be a problem as we've always contracted with them, but no one alerted me from here, and as you can see, apparently it was a problem. Now we're in a bind, and I've had to do quite a bit more work, along with the guys you see out here."

"Vineyard management company? What does that mean exactly?"

Andrés palmed his hand through his dark waves of hair. Strong hands. Nice hair. "Well, at Malveaux they're large enough to have an in-house system when it's harvest time. They have the employees and things in place, and usually they have no problems with having enough employees or equipment for harvest. Here at Spaniards' Crest we aren't so commercial, and annually we sign contracts with vineyard management companies. They're the ones who find the workers to do the harvest, bring in added equipment, and many times measure the brix themselves, that kind of thing."

"Why didn't they simply honor that you deal with them each year, and upon your return home take care of the formalities?"

He clasped his hands together and cracked his knuckles. "Honestly, I had a falling out with the owner of the company, and we got into it. Needless to say," he shrugged, "I have work to do."

Hearing him tell the story, a bell went off in Nikki's head. It seemed to her that Andrés had issues with more than just Gabriel. Did this man have an anger management problem?

He climbed up onto the tractor and patted the seat next to him. "All aboard."

Nikki pulled herself up.

"You smell like a wino, girl."

"Watch it. I haven't had an easy night."

"Smelling like that, I guess not," he replied, a glint in his eye and a smile spreading across his face.

He cranked up the tractor, its throbbing engine adding to the hell going on inside her head. "So, is it kind of late to harvest?" she asked.

He looked at her. "Let's hope it's not a total loss," he replied, hesitating at his response. "I may be able to work some things out yet. The grapes that I don't feel would work for me could make a table wine for some other winery. I know you didn't come here to ask me about my harvest, Miss Sands," he yelled over the drone of the tractor.

"Nikki."

"Fine. Nikki."

She didn't respond right away, trying to straighten out the jumble of words and thoughts going on inside her head.

He kept his eyes straight ahead, stopping at a row of

vines. He jumped down off the tractor and picked a handful of grapes. He got back up onto his seat and handed her one. She bit into it. The fruit was delicate and sweet, nurtured into something so tasty it would've fooled the most discerning gourmet into thinking it was some type of confection.

Andrés popped one in his mouth. "This is what I'm looking for," he said. "All I need is enough people out here to help me pick."

He pulled the tractor back out onto the dirt road and headed for another section of vines. As he shifted the tractor his hand brushed against her leg. Nikki tried not to notice.

He paralleled the tractor over to another set of vines. This time he shut off the engine. He faced her. "Why *are* you here, Nikki?"

She straightened herself in the seat and rubbed her palms together, then clenched them into fists before asking, "Do you know Minnie Lark?"

"Malveaux's accountant. I know her."

"She was found murdered last night." Nikki watched for his reaction.

His face remained stony. Finally he bowed his head, shaking it. When he raised it to look at her there was sadness, anger and evidence of real pain in his eyes as they watered. "She was a good person. I liked her."

"You knew her well?"

"I did. We both liked art. I ran into her at the art museum over a year ago in the city during a Georgia O'Keefe exhibit. We started talking and had the art and wine in common. We became very good friends."

"Were you more than friends?" *Oops! Where had that come from?* Sure, she was sticking her nose in other folks' business hoping to help solve a murder, but when that particular question slipped from her tongue, her pulse raced.

This evoked a sort of saddened laughter from Andrés. "No. She wasn't exactly my type. A bit too bookish for me. Besides, Minnie was in love with Gabriel. Don't ask me why. She shared her feelings about him with me. They started seeing each other a few months ago. At first I thought it was strange though, because Gabriel didn't want anyone to know. It upset her, but he finally convinced her that keeping their relationship secret was fun and romantic. I knew that was bull, and my suspicions about Gabriel were right. He was only using Minnie."

Nikki raised a brow.

"He also told her he didn't want to upset Derek, knowing that Malveaux has a no-dating policy amongst his employees. It was all an excuse so he could fool around with whoever else he wanted to on the side and get away with it. Gabriel was like that."

"Why would he use Minnie? From what I've heard he had his choice of all sorts of women."

"Yes, well. I'm not much for rumors, but I had heard that Derek wasn't all that pleased with some of Gabriel's actions lately. Malveaux is fairly conservative, and I think even he had tired of Gabriel's antics." He paused. "Derek has a lot of respect and faith in Minnie. He did anyway."

"You think Gabriel was stringing Minnie along to try and help keep his job?"

Andrés shrugged. "I don't know."

"What about Gabriel and your sister?"

"Excuse me?"

"Minnie told me about the falling out you had with Gabriel over your sister."

Andrés stared at Nikki, and for a moment a hardened look crossed his eyes. "You think I murdered Gabriel because he wouldn't leave Isabel alone? Is that what you're getting at?"

"I am only curious."

He shook a finger at her. "No, you're not. You actually think maybe I did the bastard in because he bothered my sister. Trust me, the thought crossed my mind, but thinking and doing are two different acts. I did not like Gabriel at all, but I did not kill him. And, hypothetically, say I did kill him. And now with Minnie being killed, I would think that their murders would tie into each other somehow. Why would I kill my friend? Can you answer me that?"

His anger was obvious as he raised his voice and his face flushed. "Another thing, if you think that I'm a killer, then what the hell are you doing sitting next to me on a tractor?"

"You *don't* strike me as a killer," she shot back at him. "I'm only searching for answers."

"Why? What's it to you? Why do you care so much? Don't give me some trumped-up answer about trying to make a decision on if you want to take Malveaux's offer for a job."

She started fidgeting with her earring stud—a nervous habit. She honestly didn't know the answer to that.

He waved a hand at her. "Forget it. If I had to guess, I'd say that you have a thing for Malveaux, and you still haven't stepped out of your role as Detective Martini."

Nikki grimaced and shrunk back in her seat.

"I told you I caught a few episodes. Wasn't the format, Detective Martini figures out the mystery, captures the bad guys, saves the day, *and* gets her man? If I were you, I'd try to remember that this is the real world, and you might want to put the flame out on that crush of yours and be careful."

"What do you mean?" *Was that a threat?*

"There's obviously a killer out there, and I'm not it. If I were you, I'd watch my back and my heart. Malveaux got his heart crushed by that ex of his, and I wouldn't count on him to fall for *anyone*, anytime soon." Boy. Did this guy know how to deflate a girl or what?

He started up the tractor. "That answer your questions?"

"I think so."

"Good." Andrés finished collecting grapes from the various areas and headed back up the hill.

Nikki mulled over the information in her mind. She did have one more question for him.

Andrés brought the tractor to a halt at the top of the hill, gathered his various bags of grapes in one hand, and walked around to the side of the tractor, offering Nikki his free hand. She took it. "Thanks."

"What? You're looking at me kind of funny again," he

said. "Ask away, because you're obviously not finished."
He started walking up to the open patio, heading to the hydrometer to take his measurements.

She followed behind him. Here goes. "Where were you
last night?"

He stopped, turned around, and smiled. "With a group
of friends. Then, I went home with someone and stayed all
night." His smile widened. "I can give you her number if
you'd like, and you can ask her yourself."

Nikki clenched her fists, feeling the embarrassment rise
in her cheeks. He'd bested her again. "That's okay.
Thanks."

"Don't forget to come back and have that glass of wine
with me," he hollered after her.

She climbed into the truck, embarrassed and frustrated.
Andrés was not the killer. She believed him, and it
wouldn't take his last-night's lover to confirm it for her.
There were still plenty of unanswered questions and a
handful of suspects.

She remembered the smirk on Tara's face the night before when she'd found Minnie's body. Nikki got the distinct feeling looking into that vulture's face that she was
satisfied the attractive accountant was dead. There was
something vicious behind these murders, and Nikki wondered if Tara played a role in all of it. Tara *had* been seeing
Gabriel. Derek also said she had an obsessive personality.
No kidding.

Then there was the clandestine meeting between Patrice
and Meredith. Their bizarre conversation with regard to
Gabriel and him not going to work for Cal, and the need to
keep Derek in the dark didn't make any sense to Nikki. In
the dark for what? Not to mention, the two women obviously had some type of relationship going on other than
mere friends. Were they the ones behind the murders? Nor
could Nikki forget Simon and Marco, and Cal's impression
of the two of them. They, too, were an odd couple who appeared to have secrets to hide.

With Andrés out of the running, which Nikki found herself relieved about, she figured it was time to again put her amateur sleuthing skills to work and see what she might come up with on her own.

After taking a ride into town and consuming the cure-all for hangovers—French fries and a quarter pounder with cheese—she used her cell phone to get Cal Sumner's number from Information. She wanted to ask him what he knew about Meredith and Patrice. A voice-mail recording answered. Nikki decided to hold off leaving a message.

She drove back to the Malveaux Estate. All was quiet. It was early Sunday afternoon, and since Malveaux had harvested two months earlier, there were no workers out. There was plenty of time before she needed to start getting ready for dinner.

Nikki locked up the truck and set out for a walk to the Malveaux business offices on the far side of the winery. Maybe the accounting books Minnie kept would tell her something.

She felt awful about it, but she actually had to break into the main offices, using her handy dandy Swiss Army knife.

Minnie's office reminded Nikki of the young woman. She had liked beautiful things. Her walls were adorned with vineyard landscapes, but not of California wine country—Tuscany. Minnie *did* have a thing for Italy, Italian men and countryside. There was a vase of fresh daisies on the corner of her desk. Nikki couldn't help but wonder if Minnie had picked them the day before. It was so strange to think that less than twenty-four hours had passed since she'd first met a very alive Minnie Lark. Mortality was a bizarre thing.

Nikki rummaged around in Minnie's desk drawers, feeling like a criminal as she kept sneaking peeks over her shoulder, even though she knew no one was there. Everything appeared normal. The drawers were filled with to-do notes, invoices, billing statements, and of course, in the largest file cabinet, several rows of accounting books.

She pulled one out and thumbed through it. It was from a few years ago, the same year that Derek and Meredith

married, and before the bistro was opened. This particular
book only kept the accounting for grapes sold to other
vineyards. Derek wasn't kidding when he'd told her that
was where the bulk of their cash came from. She couldn't
help wondering how the murders were going to affect the
business and the Malveaux reputation.

There was an entire row of the accounting books, and
Nikki skimmed through them, losing track of time as she
got lost in the numbers. She thought about taking a few of
the books back to the cottage, but then nixed that idea, in
case someone went looking for them. Something tugged at
Nikki's conscience. She wasn't sure what it was, but she
knew it was about the books.

She glanced outside Minnie's window and then at the
clock on her desk. The time had flown by. She'd been in
there for three hours and really hadn't come up with much.
She didn't want to be trapped inside Minnie's office after
dark, plus she had to meet Derek for dinner around five,
but her gut told her to keep looking.

She pulled out three more books. One of them was for
the bistro. It appeared at first glance that there was nothing
suspicious. However, the expenses did seem kind of high.
Granted, the bistro was upscale to match the winery itself,
but the costs appeared to be quite grandiose. It didn't make
a lot of sense to be spending twenty dollars per serving
plate at wholesale cost. Why would Derek allow that? Most
folks, especially when eating at a bistro-type place, don't
come in for the fine china. Twenty bucks in these parts
wasn't that big of a deal, but when buying several dishes
and replacing them on a frequent basis, that could dig into
the profits some. The glasses, too, were expensive, even the
water glasses. Nikki made a mental note to make it over to
the bistro when she got the chance, and take a look at the
dinnerware, to see if she could determine if it was worth
the price. It didn't seem wise for a restaurant that was raising charity funds to blow through that much cash. The winery was where the money was being made.

According to the books, the flatware was purchased

from Remick Restaurant Supply. She noted that as well, and decided to get in touch with them. Was Derek not paying as close attention to the books over the last few months, but simply trusting that Minnie was doing her job?

Nikki skimmed farther down the books and noted that there were also some deposits under a category labeled Wine Club. That was another topic to research, as it appeared to garner quite a bit of income for the winery. She recalled Derek telling her that the wine club had been set up to provide charity funds for the Leukemia Foundation.

She stole a glance outside of Minnie's window. The sun was going down, and she needed to get back to the cottage and change for dinner. But first she was going to photocopy a few pages out of the accounting book and show them to Derek.

The copy room was down the hall from Minnie's office. She flipped on the light and jumped back. She laughed. How stupid that simply flipping on a light switch would startle her. Her nerves were far more on edge than she realized.

She found the switch on the copier and turned it on. The hum of the machine buzzed throughout the small room. She opened up the top cover, placing face down the first page she wanted to copy. She had run off three pages when a thought occurred to her. Maybe she should check some of the prior years' books a bit more carefully to see if there'd been a price increase with the dinnerware, or even if they'd changed supply companies at one time. She also wondered if the Wine Club entries were entered in previous years.

She turned to go back to Minnie's office to see what more she could find while the copier machine finished doing its job. She walked out the door into the now dim hall leading back to Minnie's office. A flash of movement passed by out of the corner of her eye. It all happened so fast, she didn't have time to focus on what she'd seen. The next thing she felt was something hard and heavy whacking her on the head. Nikki fell to the ground.

Chapter 14

"Miss Sands? Nikki Sands?"

Nikki blinked her eyes several times, trying to focus. The pain in the back of her head throbbed worse than any migraine she'd ever had. "Ugh," she moaned. "What happened?" she asked, sitting up and facing Manuel, the vineyard worker she'd met recently.

He bent down on one knee and held out a calloused and weathered hand to her. Gratefully, she took it as he put his other arm behind her and gently helped her to her feet.

"Everyone is out looking for you. *Señor* Malveaux is very worried."

"He is?" She rubbed the back of her head, feeling matted hair mixed with what she could only assume was dried blood. How long had she been in here? She could see that it was dark outside.

"Very worried. He was getting ready to call the police if we didn't find you soon."

The realization of what had happened to her made her dizzy, and her stomach lurched.

"Miss Sands?" Manuel asked with trepidation in his voice. He held her up.

"I'm okay, a bit dizzy is all." Someone had tried to kill her, or at least hurt her. Thank God she had such a hard head, which was always what Aunt Cara told her. It was too hard for her own good. At that moment Nikki could hear Aunt Cara's voice in the back of her aching head, screaming at her to get her ass back home and forget about vineyards, wine, hunky men, and especially, trying to solve murders.

At that moment Derek rushed through the front doors of the office building. He saw her and ran over to her. "Thank God." He touched her hand. "Are you all right?"

She nodded.

"She's got a bad bang on the *cabeza*, *Señor*," Manuel said, making a fist and lightly thumping the side of his own head.

"What in the hell happened here? Furthermore, why were you in here?"

No response. What was she to say to that? *Oh, I broke in and was snooping around, seeing if I could find out who's knocking people off around here.* No, she couldn't say that. Then a second revelation slammed her. Where were the books she'd been copying when someone decided to take her out? If they were still on the copy machine, then Derek would for certain figure out what she'd been doing. But, if they were gone, then that meant that there probably were some dirty happenings going on with the cash around here. If that was the case, Nikki knew it would all be connected to the killer.

Derek was staring at her. He shook his head. "Never mind, Nancy Drew. I've got a sneaking suspicion as to what you've been up to." He put his arm protectively around her. "More important, we need to get you over to the hospital and have that head checked out."

"I'm fine," she insisted.

"He's right, Miss Sands," Manuel said. "Someone hit

you on the head. You should go to the doctor. It could be dangerous."

Nikki thought it sweet that the man should care. He didn't even really know her.

"If you don't go," Derek said, "I'll insist you tell me what you were doing in here tonight."

Well, there was no choice there, now was there? "Fine," she replied. "I'll go. By the way what time is it?" she asked.

"It's six-thirty," Derek said.

Which meant she'd been unconscious for over two hours.

"We also need to call the police," Derek said. "Someone hurt you. I don't like any of this. I really think you should go back home until it all settles down here."

She shook her head. "No. I'm not going. Um, my purse is in the copier room, I think." That wasn't possible because she hadn't even brought a purse with her. She'd put her driver's license and a few bucks in the back pocket of her jeans before leaving that morning, but she needed an excuse to get into the copy room to see if the accounting book was still there.

"I'll get it," Manuel said.

"No. I can do it."

"He can get it for you," Derek said.

Damn! "Okay. I have to use the rest room."

"I'll take you," Derek insisted.

"I think that's something I can do on my own," she replied.

"I know that. I'm just going to go inside the stalls first and make sure nobody is hiding out."

"Oh."

They slowly walked to the bathroom, his strong arm a comfort around her. Luckily they passed by the copy room, and Nikki was able to get a peek inside. She didn't see the accounting book. She also knew that she'd left a couple of them sitting out on Minnie's desk. She realized she wouldn't be able to get back in there, but she had the sneaking suspicion that they were probably missing, too.

"Miss Sands?" Manuel said coming out of the copy room, as Derek went inside the rest room. "There's no purse in there."

"Really? I could've sworn that that's where I left it."

Derek came out and told her it was okay to go on in.

"I'll look around for it," Manuel told her.

Once inside the stall, Nikki sat down on the toilet. She really didn't have to pee, but it made for a good excuse to get past the copy room. Her head feeling like it was trapped in a vise, she sighed. What to do here? Nikki knew that if there wasn't a Derek Malveaux standing outside the bathroom door waiting for her, she'd have been out of this place the second she'd found the dead winemaker.

She gave herself ample time, and then left the rest room. Manuel explained that he still hadn't found her purse but that he would look a little while longer and then lock up for Derek. Derek thanked him and took Nikki outside. A cold chill enveloped her, and she wrapped her arms tightly around herself. A heavy mist settled on the vineyard. The spookiness of it sent shivers throughout Nikki, along with the thought that she'd been unconscious inside that building by herself for so long.

Derek's Range Rover was outside the business office, even though he wasn't that far from the house. She saw two figures approaching.

"Thank goodness you found her," Simon said, Marco at his side. "We were beside ourselves thinking maybe the killer had gotten to you, too."

"You poor thing," Marco said. "What happened to you? You don't look so good. Your hair, I am so sorry, but it is such a mess."

Derek shot him a nasty look.

"Oh. My apology please. Accept it. No?" Marco said.

"Thanks for your help," Derek said to them. He opened the door for Nikki and helped her into the SUV. They left his brother and Marco in the dust.

"They were helping you look for me?" Nikki asked.

"Believe it or not, they were."

Nikki was sure that both Simon and Marco had their motives. She wasn't buying into their concern whatsoever. "What made you start looking in the first place?" she asked.

"When I came to the cottage about five to take you to dinner and you weren't there, I thought maybe you'd gone out for a run and were late. After a half hour of waiting on the cottage porch and you still weren't back, I started to worry. The farther the sun went down, the more my gut told me that you weren't out for a jog. I also knew you hadn't gone into town, because the truck was here. It bugged me, too, that Oliver wasn't with you. He was waiting at my place earlier before I left to meet you. I put him inside my house, then went over to the cottage."

"Ah."

"I walked the entire vineyard and then up to the main house thinking you might have gone there for some reason. Simon and Marco were sipping their nightly cocktails, and I guess they could see the worry on my face and asked if they could help me out. At that point I was willing to get any help I could, because I was about ready to call the cops. I gave Manuel a ring at his place, and he joined in the search. Who could have known you would be inside the offices?" He raised his eyebrow and gave her a look from the corner of his eye. "Okay, no questions about that—yet, anyway."

Whew. Nikki found it interesting that Simon and Marco volunteered to help Derek look for her. She hadn't gotten any indication the other night when she met them at the party that they cared any more for her than a fly. What were they after?

Derek made a call on his cell phone. From the sound of it, Nikki could tell that it was the police. He ended the call a few minutes later. "Jeanine Wiley is going to meet us at the hospital to take a statement, and I think afterward we should talk some more about new accommodations for you. I'm not comfortable with you alone in the guest cottage any longer. But I also am not too sure about how well

you would fare up at the main house. Even I've grown suspicious of my family members."

Could it be? Could this mean that Derek would have her
stay with him? Nikki was in one sticky mess, and part of it
was a real good kind of sticky, like taffy from a carnival,
that is if Derek did invite her to stay with him. The bad
sticky part was like bubble gum on the bottom of her only
pair of high-heeled Via Spigas. It was the fact that she was
going to have to come up with a convincing story about
why she'd been inside the Malveaux Estate business offices, and fast. She knew that she wasn't ready to tell him
the real reason, or her suspicions, because she didn't really
trust the local police to get the job done. Nikki thought she
was getting closer than they were to figuring out the murders at Malveaux Estate, because someone had tried to
stop her only hours earlier. Chances were that the someone
who'd whacked her on the head was also the murderer.

Chapter 15

Derek didn't know what to make of anything, while he waited outside Nikki's hospital room. Angrily, he paced back and forth. She'd taken to sleuthing on her own, that was clear. He stopped and sighed, shoving his hands into his pockets, staring out a window onto the valley below. Nikki had good theories and thoughts, but they were leading her into dangerous territory. That was obvious. He was as upset with himself for encouraging her by asking her opinion, prompting her to get involved. He should've stuck to business with her, and when it turned to something else like *murder*, then he should've done the right thing and insisted she go home. He chastised himself, wondering if any of it with Nikki had ever truly been about business. A question he did not want to answer, even in his own mind.

He left the window and sat down in a waiting room chair. Somehow he could've convinced the police to allow her to leave, but his own selfishness had caused him to do what wasn't in her best interest. He shook his head at all of this nonsense. He really cared for Nikki, and he knew *that* was in no one's best interest, his included. He didn't want to lead her astray, knowing that he wasn't ready for any type of relationship containing the word commitment in it. He was sure after only knowing Nikki for a few days that she wasn't a fly-by-night kind of girl. She deserved better than that. He stood up and started pacing again. Thankfully, his cell phone rang, jarring him from his thoughts.

"Mr. Malveaux, sorry I haven't been able to get down there yet and see Miss Sands, but we may have a lead on the murders, and it's taking up some time."

"Really? That's great, Jeanine. What's the lead?"

"I can't discuss it with you right now."

"You can't even give me an indication?" Jeanine Wiley paused on the other end of the phone. "Jeanine?" Derek implored impatiently.

"No. I can't. I'll be out to the vineyard later to take a statement from Miss Sands. We have a policeman over at your offices right now doing some dusting for fingerprints."

"Tell me this, does your 'lead' have anything to do with any of my relatives?"

"No."

"In your opinion, since someone tried to harm Miss Sands tonight, would she be safe up in the estate mansion? Considering this strong lead?"

"I'd say she'd be safe there, yes. I can't tell you anything else. It is an ongoing investigation, sir, and I have to be discreet about the information that the police force has obtained," Jeanine replied. "I have to go."

Derek turned off his phone after the short conversation with Jeanine. His head was starting to pound when Nikki came out of the hospital room. The sight of her almost took away the oncoming headache.

He put his arm around her. At first she tensed up, but a moment passed, and she finally relaxed. Twenty minutes later they pulled up in front of the main house after retrieving Ollie from Derek's place.

Before getting out of the truck, he placed a hand over hers, which was resting in her lap. "I know I told you that I was hesitant about your staying here. I'd initially made

some arrangements for you to stay in a B-and-B down-
town, but thankfully that's changed. You won't have to
leave the vineyard after all. You are safe here at the main
house."

She frowned and nodded her head, looking away from
him. Dammit. Should he just take her to his place? Maybe
she would be safer there. Derek didn't have any correct answers anymore. No. She'd be safer in the mansion. Jeanine
Wiley had eased his mind about that. He'd never really believed that anyone in his family could commit murder.
Derek also knew that if he invited Nikki to stay, things
might rapidly travel in a direction one or both of them
could regret later on, and he didn't want any further regrets
in his life. More than that, he didn't want Nikki to have any.

"How do you know that the killer isn't in there?" she
asked, pointing at the house.

"I know they're all a bit kooky, but I don't think any one
of them is capable of murder," he chuckled, trying to make
light of a situation that wasn't even remotely funny.

She didn't laugh. "Maybe they're not capable of the actual act, but have you ever thought that one of them could
be paying someone else?" she remarked.

He didn't know how to respond to that. He finally shook
his head. "I find it hard to imagine."

"Derek, I have to be blunt with you. You find a lot hard
to imagine. You can't imagine that your family members
who hate you for what you've inherited and worked for,
might actually scheme against you to take over. You can't
fathom that your trampy ex-wife could sleep with your best
friend and partner. You can't imagine that employees might
back stab you and steal from you. People can be horrid
some times, and all of these scenarios are *real* possibilities.
You might want to rethink your naïve viewpoints and consider exactly what the patrons in that insane asylum might
actually *be* capable of," she again pointed to the house,
"like *murder* or paying someone to do the deed."

He raised his eyebrows at this.

She turned away from him for a moment and then faced

him again, this time her face drawn. "Tell me why you'd let me sleep in that house with the possibility that a killer could be living in there?"

He heaved a deep sigh and closed his eyes, resting his head against the headrest. "I'm going to shoot straight with you."

"I wish you would."

"That can go both ways, Nikki. You haven't been exactly up front with me tonight, have you?" She didn't answer. "I didn't think so. You will come clean with me, but I'll go first. I wouldn't let you get close to this place if I thought Patrice, Simon, Marco, or Meredith were capable of murder. A few days ago, I made the suggestion you stay here, and then after Minnie was murdered, I rethought that idea because I, too, wasn't so certain about my family. But something has changed tonight."

"What's that?" She crossed her arms in front of her chest.

"I received a call from Jeanine Wiley while you were in the hospital being checked out. She said that they had a good lead, and it was solid."

"Really? Who? What is this solid lead?" Nikki asked.

"I asked her what it was, and she said that she couldn't divulge any of it. I also questioned her on whether or not she felt it was safe for you to stay in the main house. She said that what they'd discovered didn't involve any of the family members."

"Are you serious?"

He nodded. "I think until the police do make an actual arrest, you are safer here than alone."

"Fine." She shrugged and got out of the car. He escorted her into the house. All was quiet except for Simon and Marco seated in front of the fireplace sipping Grand Marnier.

"What do we have here?" Simon cooed.

"Nikki is going to be staying in one of the spare rooms until the police wrap up this murder case."

Marco clapped his hands lightly together. "Fun, fun, fun.

What a delight to have you here. Come." He patted the sofa next to him. "Sit. I tell stories. We have vino together. No?"

Both Derek and Nikki answered simultaneously with a resounding, "No."

Marco cocked his head to the side and frowned. "Ah." He clucked his tongue. "*Buena notte.*"

"Yes, good night, Goldilocks," Simon chimed in. "Glad to see that you're all right."

"Nikki muttered, "Good night," back to them.

"Where is everyone else?" Derek asked them.

"My mother and Meredith have toddled out for the evening. Apparently there's a cocktail thingy down at Domaine Chandon," Simon replied.

"I'll deal with them in the morning, then." Ollie walked up next to Derek and nudged his hand, coming in from the entryway, sniffing the new surroundings.

"Wait a minute, what is he doing in here?" Simon asked, raising his voice by at least an octave.

"He's protection for Nikki from all of you."

"Oh, my, aren't you man enough to protect her?" Simon asked.

Derek shot him a dirty look. "You are a very disturbed individual." He took Nikki's hand, leading her up the staircase. The entire time they climbed the stairs Simon bellowed about his pet allergies and Derek's insensitivity. He glanced at Nikki, and both of them couldn't help but laugh quietly, easing the tension between them somewhat.

He took her to the spare room that had been his when he was a little boy. Not much had changed. No one ever used this room any longer.

"I feel like a ten-year-old boy," she said.

"That would be accurate." He sat down on the end of his old twin bed, covered with a checkered plaid print, and patted it. She sat down next to him, and they were silent for a long time. The room held a lot of memories for him—some good, some bad; it all depended on if they were memories prior to his mother's death.

"I'm not going to pry about why you were in the offices

tonight. We can talk about it tomorrow. You need some rest, and for that matter, so do I. I have a feeling after speaking with Jeanine tonight that tomorrow will be quite a day if an arrest is made."

"Who do you think it is?"

"I don't know." Derek shrugged and gave her a kiss on the forehead. "I don't care right now. All I care about is your safety, and that this nightmare will be over and done with soon. Then, we can all move on with our lives and repair the damage that has been done here at the winery."

She nodded and smiled at him, but it was a sad smile, and it tore at his heart.

"What is it, Nikki?"

"I don't know if I'm the right person for the job here."

At first he didn't know what to say. What he did know was that he didn't want to see Nikki leave. "Why don't we talk about that tomorrow, too? It's late. It's been a long day, and sometimes our emotions at night do more of the talking, if you know what I mean. And by the way, I know you can do the job here." He meant that, but the question was, did he want her to stay for the job or for him? "Do you need me to go down to the cottage and bring you back some clothes?"

"Do you have a T-shirt here, or something?"

He got off the bed and rummaged through his old dresser. He found a shirt and a pair of boxers that he thought might fit her. "How about these? They're not exactly fashionable, but . . ."

"They'll do." She took them from him and said, "Good night."

"I'll come by first thing in the morning, so we can talk, and you can go down to the cottage for your clothes."

He stroked his hand lightly across her face.

She turned away from him, and when she faced him again, he thought maybe she was fighting back tears.

"I'll see you in the morning."

"Okay," she replied.

He told Ollie to lie down on the rug next to the bed. The

dog obeyed. He wanted to say something more to Nikki, but he didn't know what, and even if he had the right words, he wouldn't know how to say them. By the way she looked at him with confusion in her eyes, she obviously didn't want him hanging around. He told her good night and closed the door to his childhood room, hoping Nikki would be able to sleep tonight, because he knew he wouldn't be able to.

Chapter 16

Nikki tossed and turned half the night, until finally right before dawn she fell into a deep sleep, only to be woken up by the sound of sirens. She got out of bed and peered out the window of Derek's old bedroom, which held a faint scent of gym socks. Something was happening on the vineyard, but she couldn't tell exactly what. She could see a faint red-and-blue light flashing up into the sky. Emergency vehicles of some sort were out there.

She pulled on her jeans and called to Ollie, who reluctantly woke up and followed her down and out of the house. The place was quiet, signifying to her that the disturbance down the road hadn't woken anyone else.

After shutting the front door quietly behind her, she broke into a jog, heading down to where the lights were coming from. They were farther down past Derek's and the cottage. She knew that some of the workers lived on the vineyard in smaller homes that Derek had hired contractors to build for them. He'd shown them to her the other day on their tour, and she was impressed by the idea that he would do that for his employees.

"Basically they pay me rent. I keep it at a low cost for them, so they can get ahead somewhat. Most of the men and women working in the vines are migrants and don't have a lot to their name. I try hard to give back to the ones who have been here for some time and shown their dedication. This is one of the ways I can do that," he'd explained to her.

Nikki found Derek's generosity endearing. As she increased her pace, a gust of chilly wind hit her, causing her bones to ache further from stress and lack of sleep. The thought crossed her mind that the police were on the property because of the murders, then a more frightening thought filled her head. *What if someone else had been murdered?*

She stopped, stiffening at the sight of three police vehicles parked in front of Manuel's house. At least she thought it was his house, if she remembered correctly from one of the tours Derek had taken her on. Could someone have hurt that gentle, sweet man?

She made it up to the front of the house seconds later, only to witness Manuel being dragged out of his home in handcuffs by the brute cop, Mark Anderson, whom she'd met during the investigation. Jeanine Wiley was behind them. Nikki recognized shock on Manuel's face. His eyes widened in what could only be fear. He kept trying to look back behind him, but the bully of a cop continued to shove him forward, pushing him into the backseat of the police car.

Nikki's arms rippled with goose bumps as the chill of the early morning went through her, combined with the wails of a child. Now she knew why Manuel had been glancing back. Nikki remembered Derek referring to Manuel's children the other day. She rubbed her hands up and down her arms and searched around for Derek. He had to be there. The child's cries grew louder, and an instinct Nikki didn't quite recognize kicked in, almost like a punch in the stomach. This punch traveled straight to the heart. She hated hearing that child cry out in such desperation. Adrenaline flowing through her, Nikki went to the house, stopping before reaching the porch to ask Jeanine Wiley what was going on.

"We got our murderer. You know he's being coined the Wine Lovers' Killer?"

"That's ridiculous. Manuel is no more a killer than you are." Nikki stepped back from Jeanine.

"We've got the evidence."

"What kind of evidence? I've met this man, and there is no way he killed anyone."

"All I can say is we got a good tip from a trustworthy source, and that's that. Read the paper tonight, and you'll get your information. I've got to take my suspect down and book him."

Nikki rolled her eyes at her and lowered her voice. "Use your head, Jeanine. This man was set up. I'd put money on it. Your murders aren't over, and even if they are, you let the killer get off scot-free by arresting an innocent man."

Jeanine shoved her hands into her uniform pants pockets and swayed back and forth from one foot to the other. "Really? Do you know something that you haven't told us, Miss Sands?"

"Of course not." *Maybe a few things, but . . .* Nikki heard the child in the house cry out again. She turned toward the house. "It's a gut feeling."

"I can appreciate that, and believe me, I understand where you're coming from. You had a great cop show there for a while. I am really sorry it was canceled, like I told you. But the facts are, Miss Sands, you are not a bona fide police officer. That's my job."

"You didn't do your job, then."

Jeanine Wiley turned red in the face. "If you'll excuse me, I have to take Mr. Sanchez down to the station. A word of advice. Leave the police work to the *real* police. And, I lied, your show wasn't that good. I was being nice." Jeanine walked away.

Nikki called out after her. "What about Manuel's children?"

"CPS will be here soon. Mr. Malveaux is in there with them now."

Child Protective Services. A rush of memory filled her

mind, of her childhood best friend—the one she'd shared the best-friends' charm with—being taken away by them, and for Nikki never to see her again. "Oh, no," she muttered as she walked into Manuel's house, spotting Derek sitting on the couch with Manuel's children.

The little girl was sitting prim and proper, her hands in her lap—very stoic. Nikki recognized that behavior, and her heart hurt even worse for this child, even more so than for her little brother who was huddled in the corner of the sofa crying and wailing in obvious pain and confusion. At least for him, he was in touch with his feelings and could let them out. His sister, on the other hand, had probably taken over the mothering role in the house after her mother's death and was now trying to remain strong for her baby brother. Nikki shook her head, tears welling in her eyes as she tried desperately to hold them back. Her crying would not help these children.

Derek's face was drawn and as pained as her heart felt.

"It can't be true," she whispered.

He shrugged and shook his head. Nikki could see that something needed to be done here and fast.

"Hi, kids," she said in a soft voice. The boy buried his face deeper into the pillow, muffling his cries. The girl looked at her suspiciously. "I'm Nikki, and I'm a friend of your daddy's."

"You're here to take us away," the little girl said dully. "Like they took my daddy away. Like God took my mommy away."

Nikki knelt down next to the sofa and took the girl's icy cold hands from her lap, holding them in her own. "Oh, no. No, I'm not going to take you away, and I promise your daddy will come home, too."

Derek gave her a sharp look.

"I'm here to make you and your brother pancakes. You like pancakes, don't you?"

The boy peeked out from the pillow, his sobs becoming whimpers. He nodded his head.

"They're his favorite," his sister replied.

"They are? Hmmm, I thought so. Have you ever had chocolate chip pancakes?"

This even got a smile out of the girl. "No. I don't think so."

"You don't think so, huh? Well, if you don't think so, then you've never had them, because I guarantee that you would remember chocolate chip pancakes."

"All we have here is cereal, and it's kind of stale."

"I can solve that," Derek chimed in. "I happen to have chocolate chips and all the necessary ingredients to make pancakes over at my place."

"Why, Mr. Malveaux, that would be so kind of you. You don't by chance have any bacon or sausage? I bet two beautiful, smart, growing children like these two, would love some bacon or sausage with their chocolate chip pancakes."

"You know what? I do have some bacon at home. I'll be right back with it." Derek stood up, mouthing the words "thank you," to her. She smiled back.

While Derek was gone, she sat down on the couch in between the two children. "You know what? You both know my name, but I don't know yours. Don't tell me." She pointed to the girl. "You must be Snow White?" The girl shook her head, a slight smile spreading on her lips. "Cinderella?"

"Nope."

"Aurora from *Sleeping Beauty*."

"Nah, her name is Catalina," the little boy said, looking up from the pillows.

"That was my next guess," Nikki replied, elated that he'd spoken to her.

"Mateo," Catalina cried out.

"Ha. Now I know both of your names. Okay, let's get ready to make some chocolate chip pancakes." She jumped off the couch and took both of the children by the hand.

"When is my daddy coming home?" Mateo asked.

Nikki lifted the small boy up onto the kitchen counter. She looked him straight in his large brown eyes. "That's a good question, and I wish I knew the answer." Mateo started to tear up. Nikki rubbed his arms through his pajamas. "But I know that your daddy loves you very much, and he *will* be back."

Mateo's lower lip trembled as he stifled his sobs. "What if he never comes back? Like my mama. What if he's gone forever, like Mama?"

Nikki pulled the child close to her, hugging him. "I promise, he'll be back. I don't make promises that I can't keep, okay?"

"Okay."

Thankfully at that moment Derek walked through the door with the goodies in hand, and for an hour the four of them cooked and ate, and even laughed some. The time wound into the eight o'clock hour. Nikki heard a car pull up in front of Manuel's house. She gave Derek a knowing look; he returned it. This was not going to be easy.

Catalina looked up from the picture she was drawing with Nikki. "Who's that?" she said, her voice laced with fear.

Nikki swallowed hard. "Listen, Catalina, you are going to have to go and spend some time with some very nice people for a little while."

Nikki hugged Catalina. She raised her eyebrows at Derek.

He pulled Mateo up into his lap. A car door outside the house slammed shut.

A moment later a knock at the door caused all four of them to turn and look. Derek set Mateo on the chair next to him and got up to answer it. Nikki noticed that Catalina had gone back to the same stance she'd taken when Nikki first walked through the door—the ever-so-courageous child. Once again, Nikki wanted to cry.

Mateo ran over to her and held onto her leg.

The woman at the door was tall, thin and middle-aged, with cropped dark hair, and blue eyes accentuated by tiny lines, which made her appear friendly and caring. She wore a sincere smile and in a calming voice said, "Hello, I'm Mrs. Stein. You must be Mateo and Catalina."

Neither child said a word. Mateo held Nikki's leg tighter.

Finally, Catalina said, "We don't want to go with you. We want to stay right here."

Mrs. Stein sat down at the table across from Catalina and Nikki. "I know you don't, but I'm sorry, you have to." Catalina looked at Nikki with imploring eyes.

Derek picked her up. "Catalina, it's only for a little while." Catalina shook her head. "No. I want to stay here and wait for my daddy." With the mention of their father, Mateo started crying again.

"I'm really, really sorry. It's best if we do this quickly," Mrs. Stein said, directing her words at Nikki and Derek.

Nikki wanted so badly to keep the children here. She didn't know the protocol, but she couldn't let them go without saying something. "Can't they stay with me, or with us?" Her eyes pleaded back and forth between Derek and Mrs. Stein. The word *us* slipped out, but it didn't matter. Nikki was willing to say anything to spare the children any further pain.

"I'm afraid not. At least not until the paperwork is processed, and then you'll have to contact their social worker and see what kind of arrangements you can work out with him." She pulled two cards from her purse. "This is my card and Mr. Martin's, who will be their social worker. We really should be going. Can you help?"

The last thing Nikki wanted to do was help put either one of these children in the back of Mrs. Stein's car. She froze on the chair. Derek set Catalina down, taking her by the hand. He lifted Mateo up and began to walk out. Catalina followed obediently, but first she turned and looked at Nikki, an unmistakable sadness in her eyes. Nikki got up and came over to her. "Wait. Can I have a hug?" she asked.

Catalina put her small arms around Nikki's neck. "You promised to bring my daddy home, remember?"

Nikki nodded, fighting back the tears. "I remember. I cross my heart." She walked out with them and stood outside the car door as Mrs. Stein started the engine, watching the children, tears in everyone's eyes. As they drove away, Nikki held her breath, knowing that the promise she made had to be kept. She would find the *real* killer and see to it that Manuel Sanchez came home to his precious children.

Chapter 17

Hours after Manuel's arrest, Nikki dressed in black pants and silk blouse, ready for Gabriel's funeral. She and Derek hadn't spoken much after Manuel had been carted away, and his children put in the backseat of Mrs. Stein's car. There wasn't much either of them could say. She could see that he was visibly shaken and as distressed as she was. He did, however, ask her to dinner again for the evening— some where quiet where they could talk. She said she was game, even though she was sure that what he wanted to talk to her about had to do with her snoop session in the business office. She'd have to come clean. She didn't want to keep lying to Derek.

She didn't know if she should be going to the funeral or not, but her instincts told her it was advisable. She wanted to watch the faces of the mourners, see if she could pick out anything strange among them. Who knew? A gesture or an overheard remark could lead her down the right path.

Derek left early for the ceremony, wanting to go over the details with the pastor. Nikki could've driven the truck, but opted to ask Simon and Marco for a ride, hoping to discover if they were harboring a secret.

At twenty minutes before one o'clock Nikki found herself scrunched up in the backseat of Simon's Mercedes convertible with Marco driving.

"It is not believable about that worker," Marco said.

"Manuel?" Nikki replied.

"You knew his name?" Simon butted in.

"Yes. I met him the other day. Derek introduced us."

Marco turned around and faced Nikki. "He did? Why would he do that? Fashion designers would not mix with the backstage helpers. Why would the *datore di lavoro* associate with the commoner?"

"He means the boss man, and I can tell you why my brother would do that, because that's Derek. Always trying to be a do-gooder. Whatever floats your boat. Marco, watch the road and quit looking at me," Simon scolded, then glanced over at his lover. "We know what floats your boat, now don't we?"

"You have such a . . . how do you say? Silly bone?"

"Funny bone," Nikki corrected Marco.

"So what is he like? The killer?" Simon asked.

"I don't know him that well. I'd only met him a couple of times. He seems like a nice man." Nikki was not about to let on to these two knuckleheads her theory that the police had the wrong man behind bars. Hell, for all she knew *they* were the real killers.

"I heard he had a diary and wrote some dreadful things about the industry and Malveaux Estate, and how he blamed the industry for his wife's death," Simon said.

"Please. Where did you hear such a foolish thing? The man probably could not read or spell. How could he write in a journal?" Marco asked.

Nikki clenched her hands together. She agreed with Marco that it was unlikely Manuel kept a journal, but not for the reasons he so ignorantly touted. Fact is, most men don't keep diaries. "Where *did* you hear that?" Nikki said in the nicest voice she could muster, pouring on the Southern charm that still existed deep down.

"I have my ways," Simon grumbled, obviously not happy that his lover had chastised him. "We do know people who run in the media circles."

Tara Beckenroe's face flashed across Nikki's mind.

"No, it was not a journal. I have heard it was some paintings, some very violent and dark artwork that the man did that was the cause for the *polizia* to look onto him. You know what I hear? I hear that he has a *past* in Mexico. Yes. It is true. I hear that he killed someone there," Marco said.

"Where did you guys hear all of this?" Nikki could barely contain herself, listening to this rubbish slip off their tongues.

"Darling, one doesn't live in Napa Valley for as long as I have without having friends in high places. We would be fools to reveal our connections to you. But, I can say that they're *reliable*," Simon replied. "I do have to add, though, that I am a bit shocked by the turn of events. I was terribly suspicious of Derek, even though he's my brother and all."

"Half brother," Marco chimed in.

"Right. Half brother, but really I did think he did it. Everyone knows that Meredith and Gabriel were fooling around, and Derek can be a bit jealous at times. I was confused, though, as to why he'd knock off his accountant."

"No need to worry about it any longer," Marco said, grabbing Simon's hand and winking at him. "Our *reliable* sources say the right man is in the jail."

"I'm sure," Nikki said, deciding that the only way to get some info out of these two was to join their lowly ranks. She put on her most syrupy voice. "So, what do you two know about Meredith?"

"Tut, tut. Not a wee bit jealous, are you?" Simon asked.

"Should I be?"

"Maybe, maybe not. But she's not the only one who's left her heart in Derek's bedroom, if you know what I mean," Simon said. "He's broken many hearts in his day."

"I'm not concerned with any hearts other than Meredith's."

"Meredith is still pining for Derek, it's obvious. She
mopes around the house like a lovesick teenager. Too bad
for her. If she'd only stayed home and eaten bonbons while
my brother traveled on business, she might still be doing
the hanky-panky with him. But nope, she had to flaunt herself all over town. She's a trampy one. At least she could've
been discreet about her infidelity. *C'est la vie.* And, that
thing with Cal Sumner is a fraud. He might not think so,
but it's so obvious. She's recently mentioned to me how
she wanted to get back together with Derek."

Nikki tightened the scarf around her head as Marco
sped up, remembering the conversation she'd overheard
between Meredith and Patrice. Were the two women in fact
lovers? What was their plan concerning Derek all about?
She wished Marco would put the top up, but she was just
along for the ride—and a bit of a fact-, or at the very least,
a rumor-finding session.

"Anyway, Meredith messed up real bad with my
brother. He's not the forgiving kind. But, she was smart because she grabbed onto my mother like a bee on honey, and
they've been close pals now for a few years. No one can
figure that one out, certainly not me."

"Where did she come from?"

"Meredith? You know, I don't really know. I think I remember something about her being from a small town in
Nebraska or Kansas, or one of those out-of-the-way, no-
life-type places."

"She is not so elegant, I think, as she pretends to be. I do
not see the class in her to be married to a Malveaux,"
Marco interrupted, reaching over to take Simon's hand.

"My mother adores her, though, and pushed hard for
Derek and Meredith to become an item. I think that her
beauty blinded Derek, and the fact that our dad had died
only a year earlier, caused him to seek out love in all the
wrong places. It was hard on all of us when Daddy died,

and Derek fell for Meredith's wiles. I could never understand it. Anyone could see she was a small-town, poor girl from the time she came here. She's since tried desperately to earn her stripes among the rich and famous."

Nikki wondered if they were digging at her. So what if they were? Let them get their jollies. This was the most she'd been able to collect on Meredith, and she was going with it. She only hoped they were telling her the truth and not playing her. Nikki shifted in her seat, trying to get comfortable. "What about her parents? They didn't come to the wedding?"

"Parents? I don't think she has any. I don't ever remember her talking about them," Simon replied.

Great. Nikki was starting to think that she and Meredith had more in common than just their taste in men. The last thing she wanted was to have anything in common with Meredith Malveaux. "Everyone has parents," Nikki commented.

"I suppose, but she's never mentioned them. Maybe my mother would know. Frankly, I don't care. I wish she'd go away. She's a real pain. Why all the questions about her?"

"Let's say it's always good to know one's enemy."

"True, true," Marco said with a snicker, holding up a finger. They pulled into the church parking lot. It was packed with cars.

The three of them got out. Simon whispered into Nikki's ear. "I wouldn't worry so much about his ex. There are other enemies lurking around, if you know what I mean."

Nikki wasn't *exactly* sure what he meant, but before she could ask, the church bells started ringing. Simon and Marco walked in front of her. She lingered behind for a moment, and they didn't notice. She didn't want to sit with them. She didn't want to sit with anyone. Nikki wanted an easy escape route, for she was planning on leaving before the funeral was over. She had some research to do on Meredith Malveaux.

Chapter 18

After watching the last of the mourners straggle into the church, Nikki scanned the rows for recognizable faces, wanting to gauge reactions to Gabriel's memorial. There was Meredith seated next to Patrice. It struck Nikki as funny to see Cal Sumner seated a few rows away. Maybe Meredith chased him off the other night after the murder. Cal did mention possibly wanting to distance himself from her. Nikki still needed to talk to him about what she'd heard Patrice and Meredith say about trying to get Gabriel to go to work for Sumner Winery.

Meredith brought a tissue up to her face and dabbed at her eyes. Was it an act? Hard to tell. Patrice didn't appear particularly unhappy or upset. What she looked like was downright bored. If Nikki hadn't known better, she'd have sworn that Patrice was about ready to take out her emery board and start filing those tiger-lady fingernails of hers.

Cal Sumner, on the other hand, appeared genuinely upset. Nikki noticed him at one point wipe his face with the palm of his hand. Maybe Gabriel was more to him than a

possible business associate. Could it be that he and the late
great winemaker were indeed good friends?

Then, there were Simon and Marco. They looked as un-
interested as Patrice. They did however, appear to be very
much in love as they occasionally gazed into each other's
eyes. It was all very, very interesting. Nikki found herself
clucking her tongue at one point, and immediately stopped,
taking note of Tara Beckenroe, who looked as if she were
studying the crowd in the same manner that Nikki was. Actually, Tara Beckenroe looked to be studying her. They
stared at each other for a good few seconds, which to Nikki
seemed a horribly long time. She leaned uneasily against
the back wall of the church, then, finally looked away, being the first to break the standoff the woman had posed.
When Nikki looked back, Tara was nowhere in sight.

Nikki also noticed Andrés Fernandez in one of the back
pews. He turned his head and spotted her. He gave her a
slight wave, and she smiled back. He may not have liked
Gabriel, but he was apparently compelled to pay his re-
spects. He, too, appeared shaken, as his face was bathed in
sorrow, if not for the man, at least for the loss of life.

The last person Nikki noticed was Derek. She watched
him wipe his eyes. She felt herself begin to choke up. It
was a good time to make her exit. She wasn't going to find
any answers here. There was plenty of body language going on, which she could probably assimilate later, while
alone and in bed, running the theories through her mind.
The first thing she was going to do upon leaving the church
was stop at a drugstore and buy a spiral notepad to jot down
her thoughts and ideas. It was time to start connecting the
dots, and right now everything was so jumbled she couldn't
even think about all the different angles. She had to start
with one man or woman at a time and break them down until she uncovered who the *real* murderer was, because she
wasn't buying it that Manuel Sanchez had murdered anyone. She was starting with Meredith, because she did seem
like a good place to start.

She left the church, grabbed a cab, and had the driver

stop at a drugstore to get the necessary notebook. She thought about heading back to the vineyard to get the truck, but since she was already in town and her mind was working at a rapid clip, she didn't want to take the time to do so. After she left the drugstore, she had the driver drop her at the public records office.

Behind the desk stood a plump gray-haired woman with a pleasant smile and the scent of lilacs drifting around her.

"Something smells wonderful." Nikki knew a little sugar always helped pave the way.

"Oh, maybe it's me. My granddaughter bought it for my birthday. It's Crabtree and Evelyn."

"It's wonderful." Nikki leaned on the old wooden counter separating the two of them.

The elderly lady smiled and clasped her hands in front of her on the counter. "What can I do for you, dear?"

"I'm looking for some public records." Nikki didn't quite know what she wanted to know about Meredith, but her past was as good a place to start as any. "First I'd like to see a marriage certificate for Derek Malveaux and Meredith Malveaux."

"Alrighty then, I'll simply need the day, month, and year they were married. It would also be helpful to have the bride's maiden name."

"That's kind of a problem for me. I don't have any of those answers, other than the year."

The woman frowned. "Yes, uh-huh. I see. Well, what we can do is type in their names and see what shows up."

"Great."

Doris, which was the name pinned on the woman's floral printed dress, found the answer in mere seconds. "Oh, here we go, dear. I have something. I'll print this out for you." She went into a back room behind some file cabinets and came out a minute later with a copy of the marriage certificate.

They were married in June almost five years earlier, and divorced a few years later. The bride's maiden name was Fletcher. Nikki looked up from the certificate. "Can I see a birth certificate for the bride?"

Doris typed in what information she had. "Sorry, dear, she wasn't born in this county in the last thirty years. Do you know where she was born?"

"Either Nebraska or Kansas."

"Then I can't help you any further. You may want to try the Internet. It's the best way to hunt down information on folks." She raised her eyebrows. "Malveaux is quite a name in this county, you know."

"I was under the impression that you didn't know them," Nikki replied.

"I am a civil servant," Doris said lowering her voice. "One messy divorce between those two. You aren't the only one who has come around recently looking for some information on them."

Nikki leaned across the counter. "Really? Who else?"

Doris looked from side to side, as if what she was about to reveal was top secret. "I don't know the gal myself, but she works for *Winemaker Magazine*. She gave me her card."

"Thank you, Doris." Nikki paid her the pittance for the copy of the marriage certificate and walked over to the library, seeking an online hookup. *Winemaker Magazine, huh? Wonder what Tara's motive is to go snooping?* Most likely it had to do with her obvious desire to be the new Mrs. Malveaux. Maybe it was as simple as the need to be sure Derek was actually divorced. Doubt it. Nothing was so simple with this crew. Nikki opened her notebook and jotted down Tara's name and next to it in capital letters she scribbled "snoop." Now if that wasn't the pot calling the kettle black.

Three hours and a hundred dollars on her Visa card later, Nikki had quite a bit of information on Meredith Fletcher Malveaux. She knew it was easy enough to get public records off the Internet, but it came at a steep price. She hoped somehow all of it would be useful. She wondered how much of what she'd learned, Derek had been privy to. She would have to broach the subject tonight over dinner.

She put stopping off at Tara Beckenroe's office on the back burner and set out for Minnie's house, hoping to find a clue as to why Minnie was in Derek's mother's room the night she was murdered. It was a long shot, but anything was possible. And, even though she figured the cops had done a thorough job searching Minnie's house, something nagged her at the gut level. It made her think that maybe the answer to the murders was tucked away at Minnie's place.

Nikki fished out her Swiss Army knife, and for the second time that week, committed the felony of breaking and entering. She sighed as the lock turned. Aunt Cara would not be proud of her for this.

The ranch-style exterior of Minnie's place didn't go with the ultra-modern interior of the place, with its cold white walls and sparse contemporary furniture that really should've been in a high-rise in Manhattan. The one thing that toned it down, which paralleled Minnie's office, was her choice in art. The woman obviously had a thing for Tuscan landscapes, which Nikki could appreciate, and it did soften the stark interior of Minnie's home. Nikki had the distinct feeling that Minnie Lark was a far more complicated woman than anyone suspected. Andrés was certainly a complicated man, so it would go hand in hand that the two of them would've been friends.

Where to look? Kitchen? Doubtful, but one never knew. It didn't turn up anything other than the finest in cookware and cutlery. An office? A single woman living in a three-bedroom place had to have a home office. Sure enough she did. Nada, nothing, nil, void and barren, all but for a few personal files and bills.

There was one more place to look, and by the time she was completely through scavenging Minnie's bedroom, she was glad she'd done it. She'd found something very interesting in Minnie's entertainment/bookcase unit. When Nikki entered Minnie's room, she'd searched high and low through her nightstands, her dresser drawers, and her closet. All of it to no avail, other than to confirm to Nikki that the woman had good taste. Her lingerie came from La Perla. Delicately beautiful. Gabriel would have had to appreciate that. No wonder he didn't want to let her go. But he still couldn't control his extracurricular activities. Minnie's skincare, which totally explained that flawless complexion, was that miracle of the sea, La Mer. And her shoes, well, damn if those weren't to die for, from Manolos to comfortable Cole Hahn flats. Minnie had some fine accessories indeed. But all of that aside what drew Nikki like a guy in a light blue tuxedo to a girl in a taffeta dress was that entertainment unit and the entertainment it contained. Her mind spun as her eyes caught the sight of the *Under the Tuscan Sun* DVD. She picked it up and read the back. She opened it. Nothing but a DVD. Something about it though . . . Minnie's near obsession with it. It was her dream to go to Tuscany. She'd mentioned she loved the movie, loved the book. *The book.* Nikki *knew* she had to find the book. It didn't take long as she rummaged through the unit. And, when she opened it, her eyes widened. For a second she thought about Aunt Cara, who loved the classic book *Wuthering Heights*, so much so that she had a couple of copies. One of them she used for safekeeping extra cash in case of an emergency. She'd cut out several pages to store the cash and showed it to Nikki one evening after having a couple of glasses of wine. They'd laughed about it at the time—Aunt Cara calling herself a paranoid broad. Nikki clucked her tongue. Ah, thank God Aunt Cara was a paranoid broad.

Nikki hadn't found any cash inside the book, but she did believe she was looking at account passwords on the inside and back jacket of the book. That's exactly what they had to be. And, even more of a find, was a handful of love letters written from Minnie to Gabriel—letters she'd obviously never given him. Maybe she had some kind of intuition that her feelings were better kept inside a book versus opening her heart completely to Gabriel. Minnie had been far from the bookish exterior she put out, and Nikki felt her face warm at reading the letters, almost ashamed—*almost*.

She had to keep reading, for goodness sakes, what if there was a clue in the letters? Much to her dismay she couldn't find any, but she hoped that what was written down on the inside of the jacket would reveal something.

She took the book with her and headed to Minnie's home office. After turning on the computer she saw that Minnie's Internet server was Netscape and that under Minnie's user I.D. she had e-mail. In the book jacket written next to the word "N. Scape" was the word "vineyard." Nikki went into Minnie's e-mail and typed in "vineyard." It opened right up. Certainly the police had found her e-mail address and were able to get a hold of the password. Nikki browsed through it to find nothing of consequence. Most of the e-mails were sent from Minnie to Derek in regards to orders, the books, etc. There were a couple there from Gabriel but nothing that remotely suggested they were carrying on with each other. The latest e-mails were of course the typical spam. Other than that, nothing.

Nikki then looked at the inside of the book again, and read "B of A"—Bank of America. Next to it was a six-numbered password. Nikki decided to use the same user ID to get online with the bank. It worked, too. Once again, nothing of consequence. Minnie had automatic payroll deposits and an automatic bill pay service. Her debit charges were within reason. So, how in the hell was she buying La Perla et al? Unless as Nikki assumed, they were gifts from her lover.

Nothing else was written on the inside flap, but that nagging feeling that urged her to come to Minnie's house still remained. She started thumbing through the book, and found what she hoped was an answer on page seventy-seven. On the side of the page, in Minnie's handwriting, was the word "y.hoo," then "Chiantigirl," then "Gabriel." Nikki went to Yahoo's site and hit mail, then typed in "Chiantigirl" for the user and "Gabriel" for the password. She got lucky, because there was e-mail after e-mail from Gabriel denying his love for anyone else and Minnie's responses of jealousy, anger, and hurt. Poor woman. If only

Dr. Phil could've gotten a hold of her. It was the last two e-mails between them that she read over a few times: Minnie telling Gabriel that she had the money to purchase the tickets to Tuscany and start the vineyard they both wanted so badly. Gabriel kept asking her how she'd gotten the money, and she told him that it didn't matter, that they could go whenever they wanted and start their life in Italy. Gabriel told her they needed to talk, that he had to know where she got the money. They'd agreed to meet the day that Gabriel was murdered. That meeting apparently never took place.

How was Minnie getting the cash? Obviously the woman had an obsession for Gabriel and Tuscany and she liked the finer things in life. Nikki knew she made decent money working for Derek, but not the kind that could get her a vineyard in Tuscany.

Nikki sighed, stood up, and stretched. Sleuthing was hard and tiring and she knew she had to be getting back. She felt like she'd found some answers but not all of them. She put Frances Mayes' book back in the case and picked out the DVD again. There was Diane Lane with that satisfied look on her face. Yeah, satisfied all the way to the bank. Nikki shook her head. There was no time for resentment. Fact was, Diane Lane was a kick-ass actress and Nikki was, well, simply not meant to act. Life seemed to be leading her in other directions.

Since she was a couple of years over her hissy fit of not wanting to watch someone else play a role that she coveted, out of curiosity Nikki popped the DVD into Minnie's player. She wouldn't have time to watch the movie, and she figured she should get out of there, but she also didn't want to take it. She'd committed enough crimes as of late. She thought she'd just check out the interview that Diane Lane did for the DVD. After a few minutes nothing came on the screen. So she took it to Minnie's computer. Maybe the DVD player didn't work, but the computer should play it. Looking closer at the DVD, it appeared that it could have been pirated or burned—she could see that the title of the movie was simply written in neat handwriting. Maybe she should look into getting glasses. She should have noticed that the first time she opened the case. She slid the movie into the computer pocket and hit open, soon discovering why it hadn't worked in the player. It wasn't a movie after all, but a spreadsheet. And what a spreadsheet it was.

It told a tale of exactly who, how, what, and when the bistro cash was being skimmed, and crazily enough, it had nothing to do with Meredith Malveaux, but everything to do with Minnie, as far as Nikki could see. Pleased with herself for taking a computer course last year, Nikki did some more searching. The profits were coming from the Wine of the Month Club, and a lot of profit it was. The books Nikki had seen in the offices showed that the club brought in fifteen thousand dollars a month, and a second entry showed a check in that amount had been sent to the Leukemia Foundation. The reality, from what Nikki was seeing on the screen in front of her now, was that the Wine of the Month Club was bringing in thirty thousand dollars a month. Minnie then, was taking the other fifteen thousand and depositing it monthly into a Grand Cayman account. And Derek was none the wiser.

Minnie then padded the pricing on the dishware from Remick, to make it look like it was Meredith doing all the stealing. Now, all that had to be done was to prove it. Derek hired Nikki to help Minnie prove Meredith was the one stealing from him and, thus, the charity. Minnie had been the *real* thief. She was smart enough to know how to glide under the radar and stash away $180,000 in a year's time.

Nikki quickly went back to the Internet and browsed through a couple of Tuscan real estate sites. Yes. One hundred eighty thousand would be a decent down payment for a plot in the countryside. Not a big plot, but still one where grapes could be grown. Minnie's obsession with Gabriel and her need to make her dream to be with him come true had caused her to steal from her own boss. Nikki couldn't help but feel sick to her stomach. Love, lust, whatever one called it could make even nice people desperate, as it had with Minnie.

"But who and why did someone murder them?" Nikki asked out loud, as she indicated "print" on the computer screen and turned on Minnie's printer. Someone else had to be involved. She took the printed copies and tucked them into her notebook. She only theorized that Minnie had set up Meredith with the Remick dinnerware.

Nikki thought about calling Jeanine Wiley. *And say what? I broke into Minnie Lark's house, and this is what I found out?* She didn't like keeping this information to herself one bit, but it proved nothing, other than that Minnie was a thief. Nikki did not want to be the one to tell anyone about this. She thought about Derek, and the saying about being the bearer of bad news. What a mess.

There was a lot more Nikki wanted to do, but she wouldn't have any more time today. According to her watch, it was almost six o'clock. She was supposed to meet Derek at his place in an hour. She took her cell phone from her purse and saw that the battery was dead. She had no choice but to call the cab company from Minnie's home phone. She waited for almost an hour before the taxi arrived.

The driver dropped her at the front of the main house, where some of the mourners were still at the get-together following the memorial. She went in the house, looked around for Derek, but didn't find him. It appeared that instead of mourners remaining, they were mostly caterers cleaning up.

"Hey you."

Nikki turned around to see Cal Sumner behind her. "Oh, hi. You startled me. I was looking for Derek. Have you seen him?"

Cal pulled a note from inside his coat pocket. "Sorry I frightened you. Actually, I did see Derek, and he wanted me to give you this."

Nikki took the note and read:

*I have to cancel tonight. I'm exhausted. It's been a trying
day. I hope you understand. Also, if you want to go back to
the cottage in the morning, we can arrange that. I tried to
call you on your cell, but it went to voice mail. I'd like to
have dinner tomorrow, but I'm supposed to have dinner
with Cal. I'm thinking about selling off my premier grapes
to him. I'm expecting fallout and some very bad publicity
from all of this. We'll talk about it tomorrow. I missed you
today. Where did you go? I needed a friend. Derek.*

She cringed reading his note. He'd needed her. Well,
anyway, he'd needed a friend, and she hadn't been there for
him. Instead, she was off playing amateur sleuth and making further discoveries about people Derek genuinely
cared for—people who'd stabbed him in the back.

She hadn't even thought about where she was to stay tonight. It was getting late, so she figured she would have to
settle into the nuthouse again. Who knew? Maybe her
sleuthing for the evening wasn't over after all. She looked
up from the note and noticed Cal studying her.

"He had to cancel on you tonight, huh?"

She nodded. "He told you?"

"Yeah. He was pretty shook up today. It's been a long
one. He thought of Gabriel like a brother."

"Yeah, one who steals," Nikki muttered.

"What?" Cal asked.

"Nothing, never mind."

"Since your date canceled, would you like to have dinner with me tonight?"

It was a nice thought, and if she were truly a savvy
woman she could juggle two men at once, especially one
who looked like Johnny Depp, and one who looked like a
young Robert Redford. It was time to face it, Nikki was far
from savvy, and there was no way she could juggle more
than one man at a time, no matter how gorgeous they were.
It did matter, however, that her heart raced faster each time
Derek Malveaux spoke to her, looked at her, and especially
when he touched her. "That's a lovely invitation, but I'm

pretty tired myself. However, I have an idea. It says in the note that you two are scheduled to have dinner tomorrow night."

"True, true."

"Why don't I make dinner? I miss cooking, and I'm decent at it. It might be nice."

"I'd say it would be very nice."

"Great. We'll do it at the guest cottage. I'm here for another night, but then I'll be moving back there tomorrow. Derek doesn't seem to think I'm in danger anymore."

"Do you?"

"Think I'm in danger? No, not really. But I don't think Manuel Sanchez is a murderer."

"Then you should read the evening newspaper. You might change your mind. You sure you won't have dinner with me?" The twinkle in his eyes and the dimples on his cheeks when he smiled almost made her reconsider.

"I'm sure. But, can I ask you something real quick?"

"Of course."

"I know you said that there was an ongoing joke between you and Derek about trying to get Gabriel to come to work for you at Sumner."

"Not that again. Why the curiosity?" He put his arm around her.

"Well, I know you said that it was all folly, but do you know anything about Patrice or Meredith talking to Gabriel about going to work for you?"

He removed his arm from around her shoulders. His face contorted into confusion. "No. I don't know anything about that. Though I might understand why Meredith would do such a thing. She's been trying to get me to deepen my commitment to her, so maybe if she did speak to Gabriel about switching wineries, then my guess would be so she could get on my good side. But for the record, I wouldn't have taken Gabriel from Derek. He belonged here. Patrice doing something like that makes absolutely no sense at all. I can't see any reasoning in that. She may not own the winery outright, but her portion alone makes more than my winery, and Gabriel played a large part in producing the profits. Where did you hear something like this anyway?"

"You know, it might have been Simon or Marco, or maybe even Tara Beckenroe. I've met so many people who appear to live for spreading gossip and rumors." She hoped she'd covered her bases.

"Right. Don't believe everything you hear."

"Of course not." She smiled at him.

Cal kissed her good-bye on the cheek, and she went in search of the newspaper.

Chapter 19

The news story was shocking, and the evidence reported to have been levied against Manuel pretty compelling.

A tip from an anonymous source led police to search the home of Manuel Sanchez early Monday morning, where they later made an arrest. They found evidence suggesting that Mr. Sanchez is the Wine Lovers' Killer, including the other half of the grapevine that was used to murder Gabriel Asanti.

Mr. Sanchez was also seen at the charity event given by Derek Malveaux on Saturday evening. A source reports he was seen walking up the back steps leading to an outside veranda, outside the room Minnie Lark was killed in. Mr. Sanchez claims he was at the event helping the caterers load and unload food items, and that he went up the back stairs to set up some decorative lights. No one has confirmed this statement.

It *has* been confirmed that Manuel Sanchez did kill an American man in Mexico, in what he claims was an act of self-defense in 1997. He and his wife left Mexico shortly after that incident, whereupon they came to the United States, where he found work at the Malveaux Estate. He is a naturalized U.S. citizen.

Another source has said that disturbing pencil drawings Mr. Sanchez sketched depict violent slayings of both men and women. In the background there is always a bushel of grapes.

Nikki shook her head. The story went on to relay the tragic deaths of Manuel's wife and baby son the year before, and how many thought it was possible that the man, in his grief, had turned against the industry that supported him and his family.

She put the paper down on the ottoman in front of her. She was seated in the living room by the fireplace. Her "housemates" were MIA.

No matter what the newspaper story relayed, she still refused to believe that Manuel Sanchez was guilty. The memory of Catalina and Mateo's faces when they drove away from the vineyard the other day were etched in her mind and haunted her, along with the promise she'd made to them.

"My, my, you know how to make yourself at home, don't you? I wouldn't get too cozy," Patrice Malveaux said, entering the front room.

"You people are good at sneaking around," Nikki replied, startled.

Draped in sparkling jewels, holding a beaded clutch purse in one hand, and carrying a martini in the other, Patrice cleared her throat. "What do you want, Miss Sands?"

"What do you mean?" Nikki stood, crossing her arms in front of her.

Patrice Malveaux set her purse on the mantelpiece and twirled her olive around in her martini glass. "Why are you here? You aren't a career-type of a woman. Are you after Derek's money? If that's it, you're wasting your time."

"You have no idea what type of a woman I am." This was unexpected. She knew both Patrice and Meredith to be catty and secretive, but confrontational? She considered confronting her in turn about what she'd overheard Meredith and her talking about out at the shed the other night. However, she had her wits about her and couldn't help wondering if the woman might not have a gun in her purse. Nikki had not ruled out the matriarch of this clan as the killer. Mum was the word for the moment.

"I'm pretty sure I do. I recognize poor white trash when I see it, and you, darling, are it."

The back of Nikki's neck grew warm, starting to itch. "You don't know me at all."

Patrice Malveaux set the martini on the mantel and took down the small purse. Opening it, she pulled out a pen and checkbook. "How much?"

"How much what?"

Patrice sighed. "How much do you want so that you'll leave the Malveaux Estate and our family alone?"

"I don't want your money," Nikki scoffed. "And, why would I leave?"

"Because I want you to. It's too bad for you that I have friends all over this community who care a great deal about me and mine. A little bird whispered in my ear earlier today that you're as curious as a cat. Now, my guess is that you've found out something you shouldn't have. Meredith is very dear to me, and she's had a rough couple of years. I don't want her hurt any further." She wrote out something on the check, ripped it off, and handed it to Nikki. "Make this easy on all of us, especially yourself. You wouldn't want to get tangled up in something you couldn't get out of. You may be white trash, but I think you're fairly smart white trash. I trust you'll do the right thing. Take this, leave here, and go crawl back under the rock you came from. I'd like you gone by tomorrow. I also think it best that you stay in the cottage tonight, instead of here in *my* house. Frankly, you're not welcome. I would expect that this amount would keep your trap shut, and your scrawny rear out of the Malveaux family and business matters." With that, the woman turned on her heels and left Nikki standing there, mouth agape, holding a check made out to her in the sum of two hundred fifty thousand dollars.

"Talk about raining on the parade," Nikki muttered. The phony-baloney bitch had done just that. That sweet grand-motherly Doris at public records had been a spy for Patrice, or else someone looking over her shoulder at the library had been, but Nikki doubted that. She would've no-ticed lurkers among the literati.

Patrice was certainly wound up. Nikki had found out a bit about Meredith, but nothing that would matter to any-one. She was only waiting to speak to Derek to see if he knew about his ex-wife's past, which she was pretty sure he did. Most married people knew each other's family history. But then again, maybe not. Would Nikki ever want to re-veal her family history to Derek, even if they were mar-ried? She wouldn't *want* to, but she knew that she would have to.

Maybe what she'd found out about Meredith mattered because Derek didn't know, and Meredith and Patrice were definitely in cahoots on something they were cooking up that Nikki knew involved Derek. Did it all have to do with murder? What was their big secret? And why was Patrice two-hundred-and-fifty-thousand-dollars-worth interested in Meredith's welfare? Unless they were lovers as Nikki sus-pected, or . . .

Nikki grabbed her purse and headed out the door to the truck. She was going back to the library. She hoped it stayed open late, because she had a hunch, and Aunt Cara always professed that trusting hunches was a wise thing.

Chapter 20

It was almost eight o'clock by the time Nikki arrived at the library. It would only be open for another hour, which was probably not enough time for her to find what she wanted, but it would be a start.

She started with Patrice this time and worked her way back. Chandler Malveaux died the same year Derek and Meredith were married. Nikki found all sorts of photos from various charity events and wine tastings in the *Napa Valley Register*. Nikki could see where Derek got his good looks. There was that same reflected sadness that shone in Derek's eyes. The first Mrs. Malveaux had obviously been very well loved by the men in her life, and she'd left her mark upon them.

Nikki went back several years and found articles about Derek's mother, Shandon Malveaux, and her support of various charities, and then, sadly Nikki read her obituary. It included a long list of accomplishments, including being a teacher for special-needs children. There was a lot about the late Mrs. Malveaux that Nikki would like to discover, but right now she needed to learn as much as she could about Patrice Malveaux.

Chandler Malveaux and Patrice Spanos were married on the island of Crete in Greece. Sort of interesting. But, going back further, she found nothing more of interest. Patrice was from Greece. Her family's wealth came from publishing books on mythology. That was interesting, too, but not important. Nikki was digging for something more, and she wasn't finding it here.

She rubbed her eyes and leaned back in her chair for a minute. The library's fluorescent lights, along with the stress and length of the day were making her tired and weary. Where would she find what she was looking for?

The librarian came over the p.a. system announcing closing time. Nikki got up, stretched, and walked out into the crisp night air. She needed coffee if she was going to even attempt to work on this convoluted puzzle anymore tonight. She walked a couple of blocks, and to her joy found a Starbucks. A hazelnut mocha with whipped cream was exactly the fix she needed. Standing in line, she tried to clear her mind. It was a challenge, considering everything, but as she stepped up to order, her mind went into overdrive.

"Can I take your order?" asked a young man with a barely-there goatee, mussed blond hair, stark green eyes, and wearing a half of a "best friend" charm around his neck.

The best-friend charm. What luck. "Nice charm," she said. "They used to be really popular when I was a kid. You look a lot younger than me, though." Nikki never remembered any guys exchanging those charms.

"I can still have a best friend," he replied in a surly voice.

"Of course you can."

"So, is your best friend a girl or a boy?" Nikki asked coyly.

"Can I take your order?" he replied, blushing.

Nikki gave him the order and waited for her coffee. She decided to stay at the Starbuck's for a bit, and see what she could get out of "Skippy."

She wound up ordering another mocha and feeling quite full before the Starbucks' line slowed down for the evening. Skippy kept glancing her way. She smiled at him a few times, tried to make small talk again with him when she ordered the second mocha, but he was having none of it.

She'd wait it out and see if a bit of Southern charm worked. She kept her fingers crossed that she would be able to get him to reveal how he'd gotten the token treasure around his neck. It had to have come from a bosom buddy, and one she suspected was one of the arrogant gay men living at the Malveaux Estate. Which one of them was keeping the boy toy? Or were both of them involved with him?

It appeared that Skippy was going to be tonight's Starbucks' closer. Lady Luck strikes again.

"Can I get one last mocha, only make this one nonfat minus the whipped cream?" Nikki asked, walking up to the counter one last time. She'd more than exceeded her calorie count for the day.

"Sure," Skippy muttered.

She almost laughed while thinking of the young man as a Skippy, but for some reason, that was the name that came to mind. He was young, would've had a great sailor look minus the goatee and long hair, and he seemed so innocent. "Skippy" fit.

"I don't mean to be a pest. I'm sorry if I offended you earlier. It's just that when I was a kid I had a best friend, and we saved our money for a long time to buy a charm that looked exactly like yours. Not long after I gave it to her, she moved away. I never saw her again."

He went behind the counter. "I'm sorry," he said. He sounded like he meant it.

"I'm new around here. Everyone seems so nice."

Skippy shrugged. "Where are you from?"

"L.A."

He peeked around the barrista. "L.A.? I'd love to move there. This place is *totally* stifling." He handed her coffee to her.

She sipped the warm brew. No sleep tonight. "Really? I like it here. It's very quaint."

"Ha. Grow up here, be a bit different, and you'd change your mind," he said, looking over his shoulder. He was the only employee left. "No one likes you much around here if you're different. They're all pretty set in their ways. They're mostly rich pompous jerks."

"You must have one friend," Nikki replied.

"I guess." He fingered the charm.

"Your friend leave, too? Like mine did, when I was a kid."

"Something like that."

"Make a coffee, sit down with me. I've got nowhere to go. I'm lonely here, and as sad as it might be, I wouldn't mind having someone to talk to," Nikki said, hoping he would open up.

He paused for a moment, ran his fingers through his hair, and finally said, "Why not? I don't have anywhere to go, either. But the minute I get my cash, I'm out of here."

"Your cash?"

"I'm due to score some decent money. Then, I'm headed down to L.A. I want to be an actor."

"Don't we all, kid."

He gave her a confused look and sat down across from her with a cup of hot brew. "No, really. That's the plan."

Nikki didn't respond. Spoiling the kid's dreams wasn't in her. And who knew, maybe he had a real shot at it. "Acting is your thing, then?"

He nodded and took a sip from his coffee cup. "My parents hate the idea. They're not the typical Napa Valley socialites. They have a small place with a bit of farmland, but my dad can't seem to cultivate much of anything. He doesn't have a green thumb, and my mom is her own worst enemy, trying hard to fit into a place that turns its nose up at her."

"What do they want you to do?"

"Computer stuff, or farm like them, or I don't know. I don't care, either, because in a week I'm out of here."

"When your cash comes in?" Nikki crossed her legs, leaning back in her chair. She wanted to make him comfortable, get him to open up.

"Yep."

"What did you do, win some type of settlement, or inherit some money? You don't mind me asking, do you?"

He shook his head. "No one asks me much of anything, so, no, I don't mind. Besides you said you didn't know anyone here, and I haven't seen you around. I'll be gone in a few days. What can it hurt?" He fingered the charm again. "My friend used to tell me that sometimes strangers make the best confidants. That's how we became friends in the first place."

"He's right." She was taking a chance here assuming the friend was a man. "I'm a good one for keeping secrets."

"I hope so. My friend is very rich, and people know him around here. We've had to be careful."

"So I take it, you had more than a friendship?"

He nodded and bit his lower lip. "But no one could know. That's why he gave me the charm. It was silly, but one day I told him I saw it in the window at the jewelers, and the next thing I knew, he bought it, and he has the other half."

"I take it that you two haven't worked it all out?"

"Not exactly. Simon has a lover, and he didn't want anyone to know because he was afraid his partner would leave him."

Simon.

"Kind of a jerk though, to be cheating like that, isn't he?" Nikki finally replied after taking a long sip of her coffee, trying hard to digest what the young man told her.

"I suppose, but we were only having fun. We got carried away. Someone found out about us, and Simon said that we couldn't see each other anymore. He said that he'd give me the money I needed to get started in L.A., and that this was the best for everyone. He was supposed to give me the money last week, but he had some family trouble and couldn't see me. We're going to meet in a few days. I kind of don't want to see him because it hurts so bad. He was my first love, you know. He's the reason I've been able to accept being gay. But, I need the money. I don't know if it's right for me to take it, but I have to get out of here, and there's no other way."

"Someone found out about you? Who?"

"I don't know. He wouldn't tell me, all he'd say is that the person had some pictures of us and was blackmailing him. I guess he really loves his boyfriend, and he said that he didn't want to cause me any pain. He said that the person with the photos had the kind of power to see the pictures published in the local paper, which could cause him and his family a lot of grief.

"Personally, I think my parents are uptight jerks, but they're still my parents, and when it comes down to it, I love them. I don't want anyone hurting them, and pictures like what this person supposedly has could destroy simple people like my folks."

"I understand." Nikki feigned a yawn. She'd gathered enough information in one evening to write a gossip column worth its weight in gold. "I can't believe I'm so tired, especially after so much caffeine."

"What are you up here for?"

"Some business in the wine industry. I'm thinking about doing sales for one of the wineries."

"Which one?"

"Whoever is looking to hire." Not a lie really, maybe an outside-the-lines response, but technically not a lie. She didn't want to upset the young man by telling him that it was for Malveaux. He'd totally trusted her, and he'd figure out that she was being a mere snoop rather than a pal. She did want to help him, though. If there were pictures of him and Simon floating around, and that person was blackmailing Simon, then Nikki wanted to find the blackmailer and the photos.

"Cool. It's been great talking with you, but I better close

this place down. I've still got a lot of plans to make."

"Good luck."

"Same to you."

"Hey, I didn't catch your name," Nikki said.

"Sammy. Samuel Eades."

Not Skippy, but close. Nikki stuck out her hand. "Nice to meet you Sammy. I'm Nikki Sands."

At the front door, Nikki turned around. Sammy was wiping the barrista down. "Hey, Sam?"

"Yeah?" He looked up at her.

"Don't feel bad about taking the money." Nikki walked out of the Starbucks, leaving Sammy Eades behind. She had a lot more to think about than before she'd entered the coffeehouse. Could Simon have murdered Gabriel and Minnie for blackmailing him? Had one of them had the photos? Did Simon know about Gabriel and Minnie's relationship, and then figure the two were sharing information, and so he killed them both? Is that why Simon hadn't coughed up the money for Sammy yet, because he'd felt he'd gotten rid of the threat? Nikki didn't have any answers, but she knew she was tangled up in a web filled with deceit. It scared the hell out of her because the closer she got to figuring this all out, the closer she might get to being snared by the predator spinning the web.

Chapter 21

Nikki made her way back to the cottage, using the key Derek had given her. "Screw you, Patrice," she said aloud as she walked into the house and took the check Patrice had written from her purse. She tore it up. "I can't be bought, and I'm *not* white trash." Her time spent here at the vineyard, and her dealings with these people reaffirmed her belief that class cannot be bought.

She propped herself up on the bed, missing Ollie. She opened the notebook she'd bought at the drugstore and began to write her notes and thoughts, from the moment she'd met Derek to the present. By the time she was done, it was close to two in the morning and her mind was more boggled than ever.

Two people were dead—murdered. Manuel Sanchez was behind bars, his kids in some foster home. Simon had a boy toy he was paying to get out of town because someone was blackmailing him. Did Simon murder Minnie and Gabriel?

Patrice held a vested interest in her former stepdaughter-in-law. Minnie, and possibly Gabriel, the victims, had been stealing a chunk of change from Derek. Cal Sumner wanted to buy the premier grapes, and Tara Beckenroe had the hots badly for Derek and was apparently conducting her own investigation into the family. She also had once been obsessed with Gabriel. Could she have been so obsessed as to take out Gabriel and Minnie? Did she know that Minnie and Gabriel had a relationship, and maybe her whole act to get her claws into Derek was just that—a façade in order to take any limelight off of her?

Someone had made a veiled attempt on Nikki's life, and now Patrice was trying to pay her to get out of town. The whole thing stunk to high heaven, and the question still remained as to who murdered Gabriel and Minnie.

She got out of bed and walked over to her travel bag, thinking about the pack of cigarettes she'd found in the shed. They had to belong to Patrice, and the charm she figured to be Simon's. They both had something to gain if Derek were behind bars. A vineyard. But it hadn't gone that way. Someone had set Manuel up to take the fall.

The conversation she'd overheard between Patrice and Meredith confused Nikki. They wanted to keep Derek out of the know, but they also said that he had a purpose to serve. What were all these people up to?

The caffeine finally wore off, and Nikki couldn't keep her eyes open any longer. Tomorrow she would get the rest of her answers, or at least hoped she would.

When morning came, Nikki dressed early, walking over to see Derek. She needed to confirm their dinner for that evening. There was a lot she wanted to accomplish in a short amount of time.

Derek came to the door in a black robe, his hair ruffled. Immediately, her hands were clammy, and she found it hard to speak. "Hi."

"Hi," he replied. "I was just getting up. I had a restless night. I missed you yesterday."

"I'm sorry. I didn't feel like I belonged. I decided to go into town and check out the sights."

"I understand. It wasn't a great deal of fun. Want some coffee? It's brewing," he said.

"I'd love to, but there are some things I want to do in town this morning."

His eyes narrowed into slits. "What kind of things, Nikki? You're not still trying to be one of Charlie's Angels, are you? Because, if that's what you're up to, you don't need to. I didn't want to believe it, but after talking to Chief Horn, I think that Manuel is responsible for the murders. They've brought in a psychiatrist, and the chief says he has some of the traits of a serial killer."

"I read the paper. I want to go into town because I've offered to make you and Cal dinner tonight, instead of us going out to a restaurant. Maybe after Cal leaves we can have dessert together. I thought this could work out as a win/win, and we can finally talk some more about the job."

He leaned against the doorjamb. "Sounds good to me. I'll call Cal." She could tell by the inflection in his voice that Derek was still suspicious about what her plans were for the day. Nikki couldn't blame him.

"When he gave me your note last night, I invited him. He said it worked for him, too. I hope you don't mind."

"Not at all. And, I'll take you up on having dessert together." He smiled. It almost took her breath away. "You can take my car if you want, instead of the clunker. I'll be here all day. I've got a lot to catch up on. I want to try and put the chaos behind me. I also want to make a few phone calls and see what I can find out about Catalina and Mateo. I'm wondering if it would be possible for me to become their foster parent."

"Derek, that's very kind of you."

"Here you go." He took the Range Rover keys from the key holder hanging by the front door. "Be careful."

"Always. Thanks."

Nikki hit the highway. Her first destination was the library again. While she drove she couldn't help thinking about Manuel. She'd looked into his eyes as he was cuffed and shoved into the backseat of the patrol car by that rude cop, Mark Anderson. They were not the eyes of a killer. And, as for his motive, that seemed almost ridiculous to her. Yes, people sought revenge all the time, but Manuel was not a dumb man as far as she could tell. He had two children to raise, and he seemed to genuinely love his work. He definitely loved those kids.

Nikki also didn't buy Chief Horn's theory that Manuel could be a serial killer. She knew enough from her Aunt Cara that serial killers didn't just *happen*. They were people who had certain characteristics and backgrounds. Granted, Nikki didn't know what Miguel's upbringing was like, but this was a man with a family, and he was a hard worker. He didn't seem to fit the profiles Aunt Cara had talked to her about.

She would visit him today, if the cops let her. She wanted to hear his side of things, especially the story about him killing a man in Mexico. She still believed that the evidence they'd found in his home had been planted.

Nikki spent a good part of her morning in the library and finally found what she was looking for. A phone number in Wichita, Kansas. She crossed her fingers as she punched in the number on her cell phone, that the man or woman on the other end would confirm her suspicions.

A sweet-sounding voice like that of an older woman answered the phone.

"Mrs. Fletcher?" Nikki asked.

"Yes. Who is this?"

"My name is Nikki Sands, and I'm the coordinator for an adoptee and adoptive family rights organization." She hoped that came out right. She couldn't stop now that she had the ball rolling. "We're organizing a reunion with children and parents, both the adoptee and their biological families from the past thirty years, and your name appeared on our list, showing that you adopted a daughter thirty years ago."

Nikki thought she heard the woman gasp on the other end.

"I know this is a very sensitive matter, and please forgive me, but there are quite a few families who have wanted to make these connections for various reasons.

We've already put on two of these types of functions, and they've been very successful and healing for many people."

"I believe that my daughter has already made a connection with her biological mother."

"Oh, well, that's great, but as I said we're doing a party in the Los Angeles area in March, and we would love to have all family members present. Is this something you and your daughter would be interested in?"

Nikki heard a definite sob. "I would be very interested in seeing my daughter again, but she wants nothing to do with us. She married some bigwig in California, and rumor has it that she did find her birth mother. I don't know for sure."

"Would you like me to see if I could use my resources here to track her down? Sometimes these things can be a simple matter of miscommunication."

"Meredith wants no part of us," Mrs. Fletcher replied.

Nikki's heart skipped a beat, but she calmly said, "Maybe I could at least give it a try. I could contact her or her biological mother."

"Go ahead. But I'm telling you, she's moved on to bigger and better things. We're simple folk, and the one thing Meredith has never been is simple."

"I'm sorry to have bothered you. Can I ask one more question? My résumé here on Meredith is incomplete. I don't seem to have her biological parents' names."

"Her mother's name was Patrice Spanos. Her father is unknown. My husband and I did our own search after Meredith left us and never found Meredith's biological father. We assume he lives in Greece. Meredith's mother was very young. We learned that her family was fairly affluent in Greece and embarrassed by their daughter's pregnancy. They sent her to the United States to have the children and place them for adoption. She must've remained here after they were born, because, as I said, we've heard Meredith is in close contact with her now."

"You said children?"

"There were two babies born."

"Twins?" Now Nikki's heart was racing.

"Why, yes. We didn't know that when we adopted her, but it must say that in your information. Meredith has a twin brother."

Nikki's hunch had paid off. The two women were not lovers, but mother and daughter. And now this new revelation of a fraternal twin totally shocked her.

"You know, whoever filled this out wasn't on top of it. That bit of information is missing, too. Do you know her brother's name, or where he might be?"

"No. I've told you all I know."

Nikki tried to say thank you, but the poor woman hung up the phone before she got a chance. "I earned some bad karma there, now didn't I?" she mumbled. She didn't like deceiving people, but it had confirmed her hunch. Patrice was willing to pay big bucks to keep the fact that she was Meredith's biological mother under wraps. And now there was a brother.

She got back in Derek's Range Rover and sped down the road. She had another stop to make before finally getting to the grocery store and back in time to prepare dinner.

Manuel Sanchez had aged in a matter of two days. He was thinner, haggard, and sad looking. His eyes were red rimmed, the creases on his face tugged at the weathered skin.

"Why are you here?" he asked, talking to Nikki through a thick Plexiglass window, using the provided phone.

"Because I believe you're innocent, and I'm trying to prove it."

"You won't prove it. I'm a poor Mexican migrant worker. What does anyone care if I sit here and rot?"

"I do, and I know your children do. They need you."

His face brightened some. "Have you seen Catalina and Mateo?"

"I was with them right after you were arrested. They're wonderful kids, Manuel, and I'm certain they miss you, so you have to fight this thing. You need to tell me a few things. How did you know to look for me in the business office the other night?"

"Easy. I was walking the vineyard and saw a light on. I thought maybe you'd gone in there."

She could accept that. "What about the drawings?"

"I drew those because of the pain in my heart. I would never kill anyone. People say they are scary and violent, but they are of me and my wife, and how I die every time I think of her. The grapes in the pictures that the newspaper talked about, is only because I see the grapes as a part of our life. Sometimes the grapes seem evil, and sometimes they are good. There are days I blame the grapes for killing her, and other days I know that is not right. I want to blame someone or something."

"Of course you do. You say you wouldn't kill anyone but what about—"

"The man in Mexico? He tried to rape my little sister and to kill me. What was I to do? I had a knife, and I fought until he was dead. Another American man saw it happen and told the police it wasn't my fault. They let me go. There's nothing more to talk about. I'm not proud of what I did, but I will always protect my family."

"Do you know who killed Gabriel and Minnie? And why they would set you up?"

"I don't know who did it. They set me up for the reasons I told you. I'm here in jail, and no one around here cares much. I don't know why you care, and maybe Mr. Malveaux. But my lawyer, he says it looks bad for me."

"Don't give up hope, not yet. I've been making promises I aim to keep, and buddy, you're a part of those promises."

He looked at her oddly, not understanding what she was talking about.

"I'll be back." She hung up the phone and waved at him. He stared at her as she left, the palm of his hand against the Plexiglass window.

Manuel Sanchez did not possess the eyes of a deranged killer, and the words from his mouth were heartfelt and sincere. Nikki had heard enough bull in her day, and she had made up enough of her own bull to know the truth when she heard it.

She made a quick stop at the grocery store and headed back to the vineyard, her mind not on the evening's dinner but on all of the events that had taken place since she'd arrived in Napa.

Hearing UB40 playing on the 'eighties station, she turned it up and sang along. " 'Red, red wine goes to my head.' "

After unloading the groceries, she went to work on the evening's meal, which she really wanted to go all out on. She'd planned on making pork tenderloin in salsa verde along with a candied walnut salad and a fruit compote. Her only specialty was the tenderloin, which was a recipe she'd learned from Aunt Cara, who'd picked it up on a trip down in Guadalajara a couple of years ago, and was one of her all-time favorites. Everything else was coming straight from a cookbook that she'd checked out from the library during her investigative session that morning. Glancing down at her watch, she knew she'd better get her butt in the kitchen and open up the cookbook.

Forty-five minutes later, marinated tenderloin in the oven, and walnuts candied, she opened a bottle of Red Meritage, which was a good match for the spicy fare they were going to have that evening, and poured herself a glass.

Nikki rested for a minute at the kitchen counter and polished off her wine. She set the glass down to go in search of a lighter for the candles she'd bought. When she didn't find one in the kitchen or front room, she remembered seeing a lighter in the drawer of the bedroom nightstand. While in the bedroom rummaging through the drawer, she heard the front door shut. "Derek?"

"No, it's me, Cal. Sorry, I'm a bit early."

"Only five minutes. I'll be right there." She came out of the room a few minutes later, after sprucing up her makeup and pinning back her hair. "Hey," she said.

Cal handed Nikki a new glass of wine. "I didn't think you'd mind if I took it upon myself to pour you one."

She nodded and took a couple of sips. "Thanks. Derek should be here soon. Maybe I should give him a call."

"Let's give him a few more minutes. He's a busy man.

Drink some more of the wine. Tell me what you think. It's one of my latest creations, and I think it could be a big seller."

Nikki didn't really want to drink any more wine until Derek arrived. She didn't need to be loaded before he showed up.

"What do you think of it? It's a pretty bold cab, isn't it?" he asked.

She took a few sips, not wanting to offend him. "Very bold. Nice. I like it." It was a decent wine, but not a Malveaux creation.

She drank about half a glass of the wine as the two of them made small talk. After about ten minutes, Nikki decided that it would be a good idea to phone Derek. She went over to the phone, suddenly feeling a little woozy. "Wow. I've only had one glass of wine, and a few sips of this, but I'm feeling it."

"Would you like some water?"

"Sure." She sat down on the sofa. "I guess I really didn't eat that much today."

Cal brought her the water. "Your dinner smells and looks delicious," he said as he came out of the kitchen.

"Thanks." She tried to remember what she'd eaten earlier, realizing it hadn't been much.

She took a few sips of the water. Cal got up. "I brought another new wine from my winery I'd like us to try."

"No more wine for me." Nikki shook her head emphatically.

"You can't say no. This is going to be a great bottle of wine. Better than the last."

"I haven't even finished the other wine yet."

"That's fine. It'll be sort of like our own wine tasting." Cal took off his jacket and laid it across the back of the sofa where Nikki sat, trying hard to stay sober.

She turned to watch him as he went back into the kitchen and took a bottle of Chardonnay out of the fridge. "You and Derek will love this. In fact, your boyfriend will want to buy grapes from me once he tastes this."

"Derek isn't my boyfriend," she said.

He uncorked the wine. She knew she shouldn't have any more. She couldn't understand how she'd gotten drunk so easily. Sure, she was no drink-you-under-the-table kind of girl, but she could hold her own. One and a half glasses, even on an empty stomach shouldn't have had her slurring her words and making a total ass of herself, which she was pretty certain she was doing.

The wine bottle Cal was opening fascinated her, as drops like tears flowed down the glass when he held it up to the light. He poured the wine, brought it to his nose, and sniffed as if it were a bouquet of roses. He then looked down at the wine again, held it up to the light, and swirled it one more time before bringing it to his lips.

As if knowing she was watching him and on the verge of laughing, he looked back at her and smiled. "It's very good."

He slowly walked over to Nikki who couldn't help feeling nervous. This was all wrong—Cal being in the cottage alone with her, and acting different. She reached for the phone on the table to call Derek and instead knocked it off. Man, that wine was making her far more off-kilter than she imagined. The room spun like one of those carnival rides that go round and round, causing the kind of dizziness that usually leads to a date with the porcelain god. *What the hell?* A wave of nausea rushed over her, and she tried to stand up, wanting to head toward the bathroom. She attempted to speak, but all that came out was a garbled mess. What was happening to her?

"You okay, love?" Cal asked. His voice sounded like he was speaking in slow motion.

He caught her as she started to fall. Strong hands wrapped around her neck. His grip grew tighter, and in a flash she realized who the murderer was. Manuel was definitely in jail for something he didn't do, and Nikki wouldn't ever be able to tell the authorities. Where in the world was Derek? A cold wave of fear traveled through her, a horrid thought coming to mind—Derek might be late, because Derek might be dead. Cal may have gone to Derek's and killed him before coming over for dinner. She prayed that wasn't the case, and that he would come bursting through the door, because she knew that she was going to die at the hands of Cal Sumner, right here, right now.

Pork Tenderloin with Salsa Verde

Too bad no one even got a taste of Nikki's gourmet dinner; however you can and should, especially the pan-roasted pork tenderloin with salsa verde. The wine to pair with this recipe is St. Supéry's Red Meritage. It is made with fruit from St. Supéry's estate vineyards in Napa Valley, and is a blend of Cabernet Sauvignon, Merlot, Cabernet Franc, and Petit Verdot. It exhibits deep red and purple hues. The aromas are bright, ripe, and forward with a strong concentration of ripe blackberry and anise, with vanilla and oak integration. The generous palate is dominated by ripe, sweet berry and cedar-oak qualities, credited to the extended period spent in barrel. The flavors are long and round, finishing with firm yet elegant tannins.

    2 pork tenderloins
    1 8-ounce jar of salsa verde (Herdez is a good one.)
    1 package of Lawry's taco seasoning
    3 large cloves of garlic
    2 seeded, drained, and chopped canned chipotle peppers (these are spicy—so be careful if you don't care for spicy)
    2 tablespoons minced red onion
    2 tablespoons brown sugar
    4 tablespoons fresh lime juice
    ½ cup of red wine
    salt to taste
    ¼ cup low-sodium soy sauce
    2 cup orange juice
    2 tablespoons extra virgin olive oil
    2 tablespoons canola oil

Mix together all of the ingredients except for garlic, onion, and 1 cup of orange juice, half of the salsa verde jar, and pork, in a large Ziploc bag. Place the pork in the bag and marinate overnight. When ready to cook, preheat oven to 425°. Remove pork. Season pork with salt and pepper. Heat oil very hot and sear pork in a large, ovenproof, sauté pan until browned on all sides. Sauté onion and garlic with roast. Place pan in the preheated oven with the other cup of orange juice poured over the meat and into the pan, along with the rest of the salsa jar, and roast for approximately 45 minutes to an hour, basting and turning the roast halfway through. Be careful not to overcook. It's also important to keep basting with the juices. Remove from oven and let rest for ten minutes to distribute juices and complete cooking. Serves 8.

Chapter 22

The room swirled, and the lights grew dimmer. Fear coursed through Nikki's every nerve ending, and she settled her mind into an acceptance that she was going to die at the hands of a murderer. Her eyes fluttered shut while twinkling lights shot through her pupils, like sparklers on the Fourth of July.

The lights were followed by darkness as oxygen escaped from her lungs. Before completely fading away, she thought she heard a door close and then a voice—a woman's voice. The grip on her neck loosened, and the sparklers came back as her lungs filled again with air. There was intense pain where Cal's hands had squeezed her neck. She slid to the floor and could hear heated words exchanged. Everything was still foggy, and she knew, even in the state she was in, that her drunkenness was from more than a couple of glasses of wine. Cal Sumner had drugged her.

Nikki couldn't make out whose voice it was she was hearing, but she knew that it was someone she'd heard before.

"This is fascinating, Cal. I would've never thought it of

you. But, you know a girl like me knows how to do her research, and I've been able to put a thing or two together."

"Put that thing down. If I kill her, it only works in your best interest as well," Cal said.

"Maybe, maybe not. You're a killer, Cal, and frankly, that scares me quite a bit. You're also a bit freaky. Your own sister—yuck, and a twin at that. You look surprised. Everyone thinks I'm only concerned with wines, but I'm also a damned good researcher, and there are all sorts of conspiracies and weird things going on around here. And, you know what I smell behind all of it? Cash. Lots and lots of cash."

Oh, my god, the twin. Cal was Meredith's brother. It had to be Patrice he was talking to. No. That didn't make sense, not if she was truly his mother. Who was he talking to? Nikki had to open her eyes to see. They were so heavy. Prying them open was the hardest thing she ever had to do.

"I do see your point about you killing Goldilocks here being a good thing for me."

"I don't know what you think you know, but we can work something out," Cal said.

"I know we can."

"Put the gun down, and let's make a deal," Cal replied.

Nikki opened her eyes slightly. The room was still a blur, but those spiked heels could only belong to one woman—Tara Beckenroe. Nikki figured her troubles were far from over. She didn't think Tara was here to rescue her from the madman. She needed to think clearly, but it was almost impossible. Where was Ollie? If he knew that she was in trouble, he'd have come running. He had to be with Derek, and that thought turned her blood cold, because she had no clue where Derek was, and she didn't want her mind dwelling on dark thoughts about where he might be.

"Don't be hasty, Tara. Let's work this out. I can give you Malveaux on a silver platter."

Nikki heard a tremor in his voice. Tara clucked her tongue. Nikki stayed still, her mind beginning to think a bit more clearly.

"Let's cut a deal. I've always liked you, and I know you've had some satisfaction where I'm concerned."

"I'm a good actress, and one helluva liar."

"Yeah, you are a liar, because I made you scream, and that was no lie," he scoffed.

What a typical man. Here a woman was holding a gun on him, and he could still think about his prowess in the bedroom.

"Now, come on, Tara, be reasonable. We can work this out. Why not leave Manuel in jail? He's the perfect fall guy. You get the man you want, and I'll get what I want. Let's get rid of Nikki, and everything is status quo. She can simply disappear."

Tara cackled. "Don't insult me. The only way you'll get what you want is if Derek tells you what you want to know, and then winds up dead. I can't let that happen. I suppose I could hook up with you after you're rich and in hiding, but that doesn't appeal to me. Besides, darling, your family jewels simply don't do it for me. I want Derek. I always have. I can finally have him, because I'm going to save the day." She let out an aggrieved sigh.

"No," he yelled. "You can't do this."

Nikki opened her eyes to watch as Tara came over to Cal, continuing to point her gun at him. "Get on your knees," she ordered. He didn't respond. Tara cocked the trigger. "I won't hesitate to use this, you know. It wouldn't be too difficult to prove self-defense, once a jury finds out your sordid tale."

Cal did as she told him to. Nikki continued to watch as, once Cal knelt on the floor, Tara brought her arm back, and with a force Nikki didn't believe the woman had, swung her arm and connected right onto the side of Cal's head. He slumped to the ground.

Nikki needed to think fast, even if her brain was only working at fifty percent, because who knew what this nutcase had in mind for her.

"Okay, Goldilocks, I'll do you a favor and tie this lunatic up so he won't hurt you, but then I've got to go and save my man."

Nikki heard Tara fishing around inside what she assumed was a bag. Nikki moaned and rolled on to her side.

"Hey," Tara said. "I knocked the bad guy out cold, there. Wanna help me tie him up?"

Nikki found her voice. "You're not going to hurt me?"

"Why would I do that? Here drink this." She handed Nikki a travel coffee mug from off of the table next to her. "Bad habit, but looks like you need it worse than I do."

Nikki took it from her and sipped. Yuck. No sugar or cream. She drank it down anyway. "Thanks."

"You're a thorn in my side with your golden hair and bright smile, and too flipping chipper for your own good, but I'm not a killer. Besides, I want Derek, and this will look good on my résumé. How can you not love a heroine? I get the bad guy here, save you, then save him. I'm like Lara Croft. But you, Goldilocks, you gotta get on the road and head on home. There's no room for you here. The way I figure it, there's only room for one woman in Derek's life. And know what else? You owe me. I just saved your skinny ass."

"Right." Nikki shook her head and took another big gulp from the coffee, trying hard to clear the cobwebs. "Look, I think you've got the wrong idea about me and Derek. I'm only looking for a job." She sat up, her head throbbing.

"Oh, please, who are you trying to fool? Me or yourself? You got it bad, girl. But you're way out of your league. Listen, I don't have any more time for this chatter. Let's get him tied up." She pointed to the knocked out Cal.

"Why don't we call the police?"

"Go ahead, but I don't have time to wait for them. I've got a man to rescue."

"Once again, shouldn't we let the police do that?"

Tara sighed. "You don't get it, do you? It bodes well for me if I ride in on my white horse. I happen to know where my knight is being held captive. I'm good with electronic devices and just so happened to have a bug in Cal's phone. Once I found out about him and Meredith's DNA, I figured the two were up to no good and eventually, whatever that no good was, I could use it to my advantage. Granted, I never caught any whiff of them murdering Gabriel or Minnie, because I didn't sneak my little bug into Cal's phone line until the day of Gabriel's funeral. Remember when you caught my eye across the way at the church? I left you high and dry wondering where I'd run off to, didn't I? I had to plant my bug. What I did catch wind of this afternoon was that Cal had taken Derek to the caves at Sumner Winery."

"That's great, but since you know that, aren't you in some way guilty of accessory to kidnapping? You have to be guilty of something other than wearing trashy clothes that look better on Britney Spears than you."

"Ouch. Watch yourself. I lost my cell phone, and I don't have a landline at my place. I got the info only a little while ago. I knew Cal was coming here to *take care* of you, so instead of wasting time going to the cops, I drove straight out here to save you. I'm thoughtful like that. And lucky for you I had already poured myself the java right before I got the tip. You really should be a bit more grateful."

"Right. Again, thanks." She held up the cup of coffee. "But I do think we need to call the police. We can use the landline here." Nikki struggled to stand up. Getting to her feet, she wobbled a bit. "I'd hate for you to be a part of this lunacy, too, and wind up in jail."

"Fine. I'll call myself." Tara picked up the phone, bringing the receiver to her ear and then replaced it. "Back to plan A. The line is dead. Cal must've cut it."

Nikki grabbed the phone from her hand. She was right. No dial tone. "Where's my cell?" Nikki muttered to herself, still trying to connect the dots.

"I don't have time for this." Tara bent over Cal with the roll of duct tape she'd fished from her purse, and pulled his hands behind his back. She wrapped the tape around his wrists. "Done." Tara rubbed her hands together. "Gotta go, Goldilocks. Why don't you hike up to the mansion and call the cops for me."

"The hell with that. I'm going with you."

"That's not a part of the plan, and as I explained a minute ago to your simple mind, you *owe* me. Ta-tah." Tara picked up her gun, put it back in her purse, and headed out the front door.

Nikki glanced over at the unconscious Cal, now taped up. He wasn't going anywhere, that was for sure, and Nikki would be damned if she'd let the vulturous Tara go after Derek.

She picked up the Range Rover keys off the kitchen counter and followed Tara. Nikki knew she shouldn't drive, but hanging around here wasn't an option, and the drug Cal had given her must've been a short-working one because she was seeing and feeling pretty clearly. He used a drug that lasted just long enough to relax her so he could kill her. *Yikes!* The coffee and adrenaline were also doing the job.

Tara got into her older-model Mercedes. She rolled down the window. "Now don't get any foolish ideas of ruining my show. You'll never beat me to Cal's. I know a shortcut." Tara revved the engine, a trail of dust billowing up behind as she sped off.

Nikki made it to the Range Rover still parked in front of the cottage and hopped inside. There in the front passenger seat sat Ollie, as if he'd been waiting for her. She now realized as she slammed the car door shut, that Cal must've put Ollie in the car to keep him from trying to protect her, which Nikki knew he would have, given the chance. She figured that because the dog knew Cal, he was able to get Ollie into the car.

"What'd Cal do, offer you a Scooby snack?" Nikki asked, as she turned over the engine. She blazed down the dirt road and onto the paved drive. "Am I glad to see you. Now where is your master?" Caves. They had to be the same caves on the Sumner vineyard that Cal mentioned the other night. She'd have to find them before Tara did. She noticed her cell phone in the center console and picked it up to phone Jeanine Wiley at the station. Her battery was blinking on low. One bar left. Damn. She took a chance anyway and called Jeanine's direct line, which she'd given to Nikki the other night after Minnie's murder.

"Officer Wiley," Jeanine's high-pitched voice came through the phone.

"Jeanine, it's me, Nikki Sands. Listen, there's no time to explain, but you and Chief Horn need to get out to Sum—" The phone died. "Damn, damn, damn." Nikki tossed the phone onto the backseat. Ollie cowered at her angry voice and throwing motion. She reached over and gave him a quick pat on the top of his head. "It's not you, boy. You're a good dog."

Nikki pressed down on the gas pedal and crossed her fingers in hope that she wouldn't be too late for Derek. She focused on the drive to Sumner Winery, remembering that she'd passed it on one of her rides into town.

Five minutes later she pulled off the highway and into Sumner Winery, which was far smaller than the Malveaux Estate, and headed to the back of the property. The entire place was dark, not a soul around as far as Nikki could tell, and she didn't have a flashlight, but she did have man's, or in this case, woman's best friend with her, and lucky for her, Nikki was aware that Ridgebacks are renowned hunters. They were originally bred to hunt lions in Africa.

Nikki scanned the darkened property, not spotting Tara's car, either. Still quite dazed, but more determined than ever, she got out of the car, and Ollie followed behind her. "Okay, boy, put your nose to the ground and do your thing. I've got a feeling you've got yourself a decent smeller. Lead the way."

Ollie tilted his head from one side to the other.

Nikki found a sweatshirt of Derek's on the backseat and took it out of the car, bringing it up to Ollie's nose. "Go. Find Derek." Ollie charged off, and Nikki tried to keep up with him.

"Hey, wait up." They were on a dirt path, and she hoped it led down to the caves Tara had mentioned. She trusted her gut and the dog, and the light of the moon to get her there.

After about ten minutes, they were at the entrance to the

caves. Nikki went in behind Ollie, who balked. C'mon," she whispered. "This is no time to chicken out." She knew she was saying it more for herself than the dog, who caught a whiff of a jackrabbit that went speeding by. Ollie followed suit. "Some best friend you are." With trepidation she ventured into the cave.

Not able to see, Nikki felt her way with her hands out in front of her. The smell inside the cave was dank. She jumped back as her forehead came in contact with something slick and wet from overhead. She hoped and prayed it was just moss.

She started to yell, but stopped suddenly as a dim glow of light shone up ahead, and she could hear a woman's voice. Meredith.

"You've basically ruined my life."

"Ruined your life? You're the one who thought it would be fun to play 'screw the men of Napa Valley' behind my back."

"Please. A little transgression, and you couldn't forgive me? All I needed was one thing from you, and you couldn't accomplish it. I was trying to get knocked up, you idiot. It was all my mother's plan. Get pregnant, have a kid, divorce you, hold the kid over your head in an ugly custody battle, and knowing what a *good* guy you are, trade you the kid for the vineyard. But I'm not exactly patient. I wanted my share sooner rather than wait for all that, plus ruining my body is not all that exciting to me."

"You're delusional, Meredith. Now untie me, and let me go before Cal gets back to finish me off. You can get out of town. No one has to know anything about your involvement in this. Let Cal take the fall. I know you, Meredith. You're a good person."

It was Derek. Now it clicked for Nikki. The conversation she'd overheard between the Botox buddies made a helluva lot more sense now. Their deceitful plan was to lure Derek back into Meredith's bed, thus making "his purpose" one of getting Meredith pregnant. Waiting to implement their plan at the right time, they had to continue to keep their true relationship under wraps, because if Derek ever found out, he would've never fallen into Meredith's trap from the get-go.

"You expect me to believe that's what you think? Am I talking to the same man who has called me every name in the book? I don't recall 'good person' being in that book. Call me stupid, but how can your opinion change so rapidly and drastically? The funny thing is, Derek, Cal didn't murder Gabriel or Minnie. Wrong. I killed them. Cal protected me. He is my brother, and blood is thicker than water. However, Cal is as capable of murder as I am. He's at the vineyard right now, taking care of Miss Busybody. Your hopefully new *employee*. If she'd minded her own business, I may not have gotten quite this impatient. She's a problem. And, my brother and I know how to deal with problems."

"What have you done, Meredith? What is Cal going to do to Nikki?"

"Exactly what I'm going to do to you. I want it all, and that imbecile *mother* of mine is going to get it all when you're gone, and well, need I say more? I know all about your father's provisions for the vineyard. What he left you, and what he left Patrice and Simon. Simon is easy to deal with. I know that if you're dead, the vineyard, according to your father's wishes, falls back into the hands of Simon and Patrice."

"This is crazy. Leave Nikki out of it. She doesn't know any of this."

"She's smarter than she looks."

What the hell was that supposed to mean? Nikki inched her way closer to the flickering light only a few feet ahead of her.

"I believe she knows about Cal's and my DNA, and that's enough to ruin all of this for us," Meredith added.

"Okay, since you know so much and have this all figured out, why didn't you kill me in the first place? Why murder Gabriel and Minnie?"

"Those, lover, were unfortunate events. My temper got the worst of me. It all had to do with that four-letter word."

"Excuse me?" Derek asked.

"Love. Yes. True love. I killed them because I fell in love with Gabriel."

Aha! Nikki's initial theory about Meredith being the killer and her reasons for doing so was right after all. Go figure.

"Gabriel and I did have a thing. The rumors were true about us. It may have been only a few nights, but it was love. Guaranteed. The kind of love that lasts forever. But then Miss Lark had to seduce him, and he didn't want anything to do with me after that."

"Sounds like true love to me all right," Derek angrily remarked. "True love doesn't usually walk out on you when the next pair of legs go cruising by."

"What do you know about true love? Not a lot, or you would've paid more attention to me. Gabriel had his reasons for walking out on me. He said it was all wrong for us to be together. He felt guilty about *you*. Not so guilty he couldn't steal money from you, mind you. What you don't know is that your trusted Minnie was ripping you off. I know you were suspicious of me. But I never planned to *steal* your money. I was going to get it legitimately, by killing you and extorting it from my mother."

"Real upstanding of you."

"Thanks. Anyhow, I wasn't pleased that they were trying to make it look like I was the thief. It pissed me off. The bitch takes my lover away, and then she wants to frame *me* for her crimes. I didn't think that was very nice. On the day I killed Gabriel, it was out of rage because he'd ended things with me and had partnered in more ways than one with the conniving numbers broad. I snapped."

"What happened exactly? Don't you think I'm at least entitled to know, since you're going to kill me?"

"Sure, why not? You are after all a nice guy, and you do have some assets that I continue to think fondly of, even now, and probably will after you're gone. Gabriel and I were in the barreling room. He broke it off. I started to leave, but instead grabbed a bottle of wine, came up behind him, and smacked him on the back of his head with it. I knocked him out cold and called Cal to tell him what I'd done. He came to the rescue and finished the job for me with the grape vines. He's a smart one, my brother. The next afternoon when it seemed like all was quiet on the vineyard, Cal placed his body by the pond. That was what your gal pal, Nikki, saw.

"After she found the body, we had to think fast. Cal came up with the idea to set up the poor Mexican worker because it was easy to do. Apparently, Cal had seen him one afternoon a few weeks ago, drunk and sketching his pitiful drawings at a café in town. At the time he didn't think much of it, but it became of use to us. All I ever wanted was true love. Cal tried to steer Nikki in a different direction because she was asking all sorts of questions. He thought he had her believing that Simon may have done the evil deeds. But after tailing her around town, he realized she was still snooping. That's when I plunked her on the head inside the offices the other night. We were trying to scare her off. I didn't need the bodies adding up.

"Minnie was easy to knock off. The woman steals my man and tries to frame me for stealing your cash. I called her before the party and told her I knew she was cooking the books and trying to frame me. She said that she'd meet me at the party. I told her to meet me in your mother's old room. I thought it would work nicely and make it look like the killer was some psycho nut."

"You *are* a psycho nut," Derek said.

"You need help. Let me ask you, do you give it up to every man who asks?"

Nikki now had a view of both Derek and Meredith. Derek was tied up, his back against the wall of the cave. Meredith held a gun on him. She watched as Meredith slapped Derek hard across the face with her open hand.

Nikki's blood boiled, and without thinking, she charged Meredith, low and fast. She took the surprised larger woman down, the gun flying out of Meredith's hand.

"You really are a bitch," Nikki said, pinning Meredith to

the floor of the cave with every ounce of strength she could muster.

Meredith brought her knees up, and in a rocking motion, swung Nikki off of her and back to the ground. Uh-oh. The tables were turned as Meredith pounced on Nikki's smaller frame, pushing her arms down. "And you really are as trashy as white trash comes. My mother is an idiot, but she was right on that account. You were stupid not to take her check and run. No one would've ever bothered you after that."

"Sure," Nikki groaned.

Meredith released her grip on one of Nikki's wrists, leaning to the side to grab the gun, which was now within her reach.

With her left arm free, Nikki gathered all her strength and smashed Meredith on the side of the face, just as Meredith picked up the gun. Nikki used her body weight to roll onto her side before Meredith could aim and fire the gun at her. She squirmed forward just enough to be able to kick Meredith in the stomach. Meredith fell to the ground beside Nikki, giving Nikki enough time to stand up. She didn't think, the adrenaline was pumping through her, and the rigorous physical training she'd taken when doing her TV show paid off as she brought her foot down onto Meredith's arm, pinning it to the ground. With her other foot she kicked the gun to the side.

A bark echoed through the cave as Ollie bounded in and landed on top of Meredith, laying his tremendous body across hers, further pinning her to the cave floor. Sirens could be heard in the distance.

Out of breath, Nikki turned to Ollie. "You're a little late, Scooby, but thanks." Nikki picked up the gun and held it on Meredith, in case she tried to get out from underneath Ollie.

Derek laughed. Nikki went over to him and bent down. Blood trickled down the side of his lips. She reached out and wiped it with the palm of her free hand. "Turn around."

Nikki set the gun down for a minute, keeping an eye on Meredith and Ollie while working Derek's hands free from the ropes.

He shook out his hands. "Thanks." He brought both hands to the side of her face.

His touch was warm and brought tears to her eyes. She wiped them away, as Jeanine Wiley and Mark Anderson rushed into the back of the cave, guns drawn.

"You found us," Nikki exclaimed.

"Tara Beckenroe phoned us from a tow truck up the road. Seems she was on her way to get us at the station, when her car broke down," Jeanine replied.

Sure.

"She told us everything that happened. Chief Horn is on his way now to the Malveaux Estate to arrest Cal."

"Interesting," Nikki said.

Derek looked at her quizzically.

"Tell you later. Right now we need to get you checked out at the hospital."

"There's an ambulance on the way," Jeanine said.

"I don't need an ambulance."

"Let's play by the rules," Nikki said, as an EMT technician arrived on the scene.

Derek grumbled. Jeanine asked him to tell Ollie to get off of Meredith, who was in a whimpering heap on the cave floor. A few minutes later, Derek was put into the back of the ambulance. Nikki told him that she'd meet him at the hospital.

"There's a shortcut to the main highway," he said, then explained to her how to get there.

On her way to the hospital, Nikki passed by Tara's car being hooked up to a tow truck. As she sped by, Tara glared at the tow truck driver, hands on hips, looking more disheveled than a whirling dervish. She caught sight of Nikki driving by, who thought about stopping and giving Tara a lift. Payback for the coffee? *Nah.* Nikki smiled to herself and sped toward the hospital, cranking up the stereo to an old Eagles tune—"Witchy Woman."

Chapter 23

Nikki and Derek drove back to the estate after he was treated at the hospital for some minor scrapes and bruises.

"Why don't you stay at my cottage tonight? After all that's happened, I'd like some company," Derek said.

"Okay," Nikki replied hesitantly.

They stopped by her cottage first. Nikki turned off the stove, horrified at the black, shriveled pork roast. "I don't know about you, but I'm starved, and I think the dinner I'd planned is ruined." She laughed, pulling the roast off the pan with a turning fork. "I'm sure I can whip up something for you in your kitchen."

She was right. He had all the ingredients to make what she coined "Simply Pasta Salad." Seeing that it was approaching midnight, she renamed it "After Hours Pasta." It's amazing what a savvy woman can do with some Italian dressing, a few veggies, and some pasta, and only in a matter of minutes. And, at that moment Nikki felt damn savvy.

"What are you fixing in there?" Derek called from his chaise longue.

"Nothing much."

"I have to ask, after all that's happened, do you still plan on coming on board here at the winery?"

She came around in front of the kitchen counter. "Do you still want me to take the job?"

He laughed. "Of course. I have to tell you, though, that I have a secret."

"Oh, no. Not you, too. What is it?"

"When I *interviewed* you over dinner in L.A. about wines, my initial thoughts weren't so much about the job. You knew a lot, I'll give you that, but honestly, I found you interesting."

She gave him a look. "Interesting."

"Yes. And sweet. And pretty."

"Ah, you had ulterior motives, then."

"Maybe."

She went back into the kitchen to find a bottle of an assertive, floral red wine to pour. She decided not to partake in the vino, as her head still pounded loudly. She took a sip, though, to make sure she'd made the right choice. It did go very nicely with the garlicky pasta. She brought the food over to him and set it down on the coffee table. She couldn't help but wonder about that dating policy among employees and decided that it was best not to ask.

"Usually, I'd serve this salad chilled, but I figured you're starving, so . . ."

"No, it's perfect. This is delicious," he commented after taking several bites. "I *was* starving."

"Hey, I've been wondering, how did they get you into that cave?"

He set his plate down. "Cal came by and said he wanted to show me some of his new vines. He claimed that they could be the best he'd cultivated yet, and wanted my opinion. I'd finished my business for the day around here, so I told him I'd go with him. Back at his place, we shared a cup of coffee, and I got real woozy."

"He drugged you, too."

"Yep. Once I was down, he dragged me into the cave. They said that they wanted to know where I kept my wine collection and my mother's diamond, claiming they weren't going to hurt me. They said that they only wanted the collection and the diamond, and once they were far away and had sold off everything for their asking price, then they'd let someone know where I was."

"You obviously didn't believe them."

"No way."

"Can I ask what the collection is worth?"

"Two million dollars," he replied.

"Wow."

"My mother's diamond is worth half a million."

"But land here is worth at least that. He could've sold his vineyard."

"A year ago, maybe. But Cal wasn't the best business-man, and he had too much ego. What came out in the few hours of the hell I spent in the cave with him, and then Meredith, was that he was about to lose the place. I think they were looking to cash in, but I don't think they planned to let me live. I think their ultimate hope was they would murder you and me, and hopefully cover it up so they could take Patrice for all she would be worth."

"Stupid."

"Yes, it was. It's too bad that both Gabriel and Minnie had to die," Derek said, a tone of sadness creeping into his voice as he uttered their names. "All out of jealousy and greed. But I wonder if things might not have gone so hay-wire for them if Meredith hadn't murdered Gabriel and Minnie. I think that's when they panicked. Their initial plan never involved murder, and Patrice was in on it."

"I thought for a bit that Patrice could possibly be the murderer, especially after what I found out about her be-ing Meredith's mother. I was wrong. Obviously. She was simply another victim of two greedy children who proba-bly had bad feelings toward her for giving them up so many years ago. She turned out not to be a killer, but Patrice is no brain surgeon, letting those two get their fangs in her."

"She also isn't exactly the most upstanding of women,

not with the plans she made with the two of them. But as I've said before, I've never thought highly of my stepmother."

"Did you know she'd asked Gabriel to go to work for Cal?"

"Patrice? Gabriel never said anything to me about that," Derek replied. "I knew Cal wanted to lure him, but Patrice? Why?"

"He might not have told you because he took it as a joke, or maybe he never got the chance."

"You found this out when you were playing Nancy Drew?"

"Hey. I wasn't playing." She smiled at him, but she was serious. Nikki knew she'd conducted a better investigation than Jeanine Wiley and Chief Horn. "I think I know why Patrice asked Gabriel to move over to Sumner's."

"Let's hear it."

"Those two murdering lunatics are her children, and she wanted what's best for them, like all mothers. My guess is that she thought Gabriel could make Sumner a better winery and increase his profits, and be successful. I'm sure if she ever got her hands on all that you have, Patrice would've used the money to promote her son's vineyard."

"I'd say you're probably right. Love is blind," Derek replied. "I'm sure the love for a child is even more blinding. It's crazy to think I was married to my *stepsister*, and that she planned it all from the beginning to get into this family. Then I find out that the vintner down the road is my *stepbrother* who thinks he deserves a share of what my father built. I owe Simon an apology, because for a moment there I thought he was behind it all."

"I thought so, too," Nikki said. "Trust me though, he's no angel. Simon and Marco would love to see you give up the goods here and hand it all over."

"Fat chance." Derek sipped his wine. Nikki sat down on the chaise next to him. "I still can't believe Minnie would steal from me," he said suddenly. "I didn't want to believe Meredith when she said it, but it makes sense."

"Sadly, it's true. I found the proof." Nikki proceeded to

tell him about what she'd found at Minnie's place. "Greed is a funny thing. Money changes people. The thought of having it so close at hand, thinking you'd never suspect her, was too tempting."

He shook his head and took her hand. "I suppose you never really know people completely. Look at Minnie, Gabriel, Meredith, Cal. They all had secrets. What about you? Is there anything more I should know about you?"

"Nope. What you see is what you get."

"Funny thing is, even after all this and finding out that people I trusted weren't exactly what they seemed, I believe you." He gently squeezed her hand. His voice softened. "By the way, thank you for coming to my rescue."

She squeezed his hand back, looked into those baby blues of his, and replied, "Any time."

After Hours Pasta

If you find yourself hungry late at night or just want a quick and easy meal to prepare, you won't have to look much further than your cupboard and fridge to whip up After Hours Pasta. As a bonus to it being an easy meal to make, it will also impress your loved one. Many would say that the wine should be a white, but a good Red Zinfandel will work well with this recipe. One to try would be Bonny Doon's Cardinal Zin. It has a rich, chocolate-cherry flavor that is smooth and satisfying. Absolutely yummy.

> 1 pound penne pasta
> 6 ounces fat-free Italian dressing
> 1 large ripe, but firm tomato
> 1 medium green pepper
> 2 ribs celery
> 1 medium carrot
> 5 small green onions
> 3 ounces thinly sliced pancetta or bacon

Cook pasta according to package instructions, drain, and while still hot, pour Italian dressing over, toss lightly and set aside for the pasta to absorb dressing. Chop vegetables and bacon and toss with pasta. Chill and serve.